D0680069

Brooklyn GIRLS

30131 05374841 1
LONDON BOROUGH OF BARNET

Also by Gemma Burgess

Brooklyn Girls: Pia
Brooklyn Girls: Angie

GEMMA BURGESS

Brooklyn GIRLS

Quercus

First published in the US in 2015 by St. Martin's Press,
175 Fifth Avenue, New York, N.Y. 10010

First published in Great Britain in 2015 by

Quercus Publishing Ltd
Carmelite House
50 Victoria Embankment
London EC4Y 0DZ

An Hachette UK company

Copyright © Gemma Burgess 2015
Excerpt from Love and Chaos copyright © Gemma Burgess 2014

The moral right of Gemma Burgess to be
identified as the author of this work has been
asserted in accordance with the Copyright,
Designs and Patents Act, 1988.

All rights reserved. No part of this publication
may be reproduced or transmitted in any form
or by any means, electronic or mechanical,
including photocopy, recording, or any
information storage and retrieval system,
without permission in writing from the publisher.

A CIP catalogue record for this book is available
from the British Library

PB 978 1 78206 738 2
EBOOK 978 1 78206 739 9

This book is a work of fiction. Names, characters,
businesses, organizations, places and events are
either the product of the author's imagination
or used fictitiously. Any resemblance to
actual persons, living or dead, events or
locales is entirely coincidental.

10 9 8 7 6 5 4 3 2 1

Printed and bound in Great Britain by Clays Ltd, St Ives plc

FOR EVERYONE

CHAPTER 1

"Snort the salt, slam the tequila, squeeze the lime in your eye!" screams Pia over the music.

"Snort! Snort!" Angie pounds the bar with her fist.

Two guys lean over, snort a line of salt through a straw, take a shot of Patrón, and—howling in pain—squeeze limes into their eyes.

"SUICIDE TEQUILA!" they yell in unison.

Pia and Angie fall against one another, laughing so hard they gasp for air. But I can't bring myself to laugh with them.

I'm kind of stressed out.

I haven't seen my boyfriend, Ethan, in ages, and I really wanted my friends to get to know him better tonight. Instead, I'm standing at the bar with two random dudes who haven't said a word to me. Being the least hot girl in group sucks. Hard.

"That hurts so much! Let's do it again!"

"Fuck yeah!"

Two random, *stupid* dudes.

We're at a dark nightclub—well, the lobby of the Jane Hotel in the West Village, all velvet sofas and giant ferns, but at midnight on a Saturday, it's throbbing chaotically with music and people and drinks. And that makes it a nightclub, right?

It's certainly not like any club I've been to before. But I'm not exactly New York's craziest party girl, so how would I know what's normal? I still get nervous when I come to a place like this, as though someone's going to look at me and tell me I don't belong. And that makes me babble in my head—

"This is the shit, huh, Coco?" shouts Angie, breaking into my thoughts.

"It's the poop, all right!"

"The poop. You're adorable," says Pia, pinching my cheek.

"We're on a mission to get Coco to swear with confidence," explains Pia to one of the dudes. I think his name is Nick. Or Patrick. "But she's too much of a good girl."

Nick/Patrick glances at me and nods briefly, then looks back at Pia. "I bet you do *everything* with confidence," he says to her, winking. Pia's eyes flicker to Angie's. "Where are you from? Venezuela? I met a girl from Venezuela once. She was hot like you."

Pia and Angie look at each other again, and crack up. Pia is half Indian and half Swiss, and beautiful, but people never know where she's from. Angie has been her best friend since birth, and she's equally stunning, albeit in a platinum punk princess kind of way. The two of them have a kind of friendship shorthand that means they're always laughing at private jokes. It's fun to be around, but inevitably, you can feel a little left out.

We all got here about two hours ago. By "we all" I mean Pia,

Angie, me, my boyfriend, Ethan, and our other roommates: Madeleine and my older sister, Julia.

The evening started well. We all had a couple of drinks, and Ethan told everyone about his childhood summering in Oregon ("you use 'summer' as a verb?" asked Julia, before I gave her a look and she shut up). Then the club/lobby/whatever it is became really crowded, and Maddy disappeared and Jules went to find her, and then these guys started hitting on Angie and Pia. And now, somehow, I've lost Ethan.

I want to know where he is, but I stay put. I'm trying not to seem needy. Guys hate that, right?

Anyway, he's probably just hanging out with my sister, right?

"Your turn!" Nick/Patrick holds the salt straw out for Angie.

"Oh, no." Angie laughs. "Snorting salt is, like, totally dangerous."

"Yeah," Pia adds somberly. "Did you know that your nasal passages have a direct route to your brain?"

"Don't you mean my dick?" says Nick/Patrick, suddenly serious.

Angie arches an eyebrow. "Your nasal passages have a direct route to your dick?"

"No. My dick has a direct route to my brain."

Angie and Pia look at each other and dissolve into shrieks of laughter again.

"Oh, my God! My song! My song!" Pia and Angie are climbing up on the coffee table behind us. If there is anything that can be used as a platform for dancing, Angie and Pia will find it. In the past year I've seen them dance on dining tables, chairs, benches, stoops, and even Pia's food truck, Toto.

"Coco!" Pia holds out a hand. "Get up here!"

I climb up obediently next to Pia. Dancing on tables isn't really my thing. A few months ago, I was dancing on a chair and kind of fell off it and ended up in the hospital. Of course, that had less to do with the dancing and more to do with the cocktail of prescription meds and booze and hash I'd accidentally-sort-of-on-purpose-but-no-mostly-accidentally taken.

But let's not talk about that right now.

Angie leans over to shout in my ear. "You okay, sugarnuts?"

"I'm fine. Totally awesome."

"Good girl!"

From up here, I can finally see my boyfriend. That's Ethan, with his downy pale brown hair that he seems determined to brush up rather than brush down . . .

Wait.

Ethan isn't talking to Julia or Madeleine. He's with some girl I don't know. She's short and thin and pretty and smiling at him in the way that I smile at him and flicking her hair and—

OhmyGod.

I feel my heart miss a beat as I see my boyfriend, *my* boyfriend, lean in to her, grinning, trace his finger slowly down her cheek, and—

Oh, my gosh, he's kissing her. Ethan is kissing *her,* not *me. HER.*

My stomach flips over so fast that I lose my balance, falling face-first to the floor.

Please tell me I didn't just fall off a coffee table in a crowded night-club. Pleasepleasepleasepleaseplease . . .

I just want to hide right here and not get up, ever. Maybe I could roll under the coffee table and live there. It would be so nice and quiet.

But before I can settle in for life, Angie and Pia pull me up.

Pia is laughing. "Coco! Killer moves."

I scan the crowd, trying to see Ethan, but the place is too busy.

"Are you on something again?" Angie peers into my pupils.

"No! No, no, no," I say quickly. "I'd never—I mean, not again, you know, I wouldn't—"

Pia narrows her eyes at me. "Are you sure?"

"Totally sure." I smile as brightly as I can. "I just lost my balance. Um, and I have to pee."

"Do you want us to come with you, ladybitch?" asks Angie.

"No, no. I know how to pee. I've been doing it for, like, years . . ."

I feel sick.

The bathroom is full of girls, all gossiping and preening and laughing. I push my way in to the only empty stall, locking the door behind me, and sit down on the toilet, my breath coming in stops and starts.

I lean on my knees, staring at my feet, trying to calm down. I hate these shoes. They're my work shoes. I only wore them because I hate all my other shoes more.

My boyfriend is cheating on me.

My chest hurts. I can't breathe.

How do I deal with this? What do I do now? Like, seriously, what am I supposed to *do*? One of the other assistants at the preschool where I work introduced us a few months ago. And Ethan seemed, you know, really great.

I didn't, like, *fall* for him immediately or anything. But he has a good job and he seemed nice and all that. And he asked *me* out. Me. And my family—I mean, Julia and my father—said he sounded great.

So I went out with him.

But then I started caring about him, because that's the kind of person I am.

Plus, it's way easier to be twenty-one and living in New York City if you have a boyfriend. I don't know why, it just is. Ethan is someone I can hang out with when my friends are busy, you know? If I'm feeling lonely, I can text him. We go to the movies together. He just makes me feel secure.

Or he did.

Who the hell is that girl, anyway? How dare she kiss another girl's boyfriend as though it's a totally okay thing to do?

But maybe, oh, gosh, maybe he didn't tell her he had a girlfriend. And it looked like *he* was kissing *her* first, not the other way around . . .

Breathe, Coco. Breathe.

The last time I felt like this was at prom. When I found out Eric—the guy I'd been crushing on, lusting after, pining for, seriously, just pick a verb, you know what I mean—had just slept with my (now former) best friend. I'd liked him for so long, it was like being punched. And then—no, actually, I can't talk about Eric right now, I can't even think about him. I'll get even more upset.

And now Ethan is cheating on me. My first real boyfriend ever. I'm such a loser.

If I was like Pia or Angie or any of the other girls, I would unlock the toilet door, walk back out there, right up to Ethan, and slap him, yelling, "How dare you cheat on me?" Or, "It's over, motherfucker, yippee-kay-yay!"

But I can't. I'm not like them. I'm too scared of doing something I can't undo.

Anyway, all I really want to say is: "How can you treat me like this when I'm always so nice to you?"

No, really. Why couldn't he just be *nice* to me? I'm so nice to him! I iron his shirts whenever he sleeps over, and I read the books he suggests. And when I make him dinner, I send the leftovers home with him in a Tupperware container for work the next day. Tonight I even got him to come out with my friends by offering to pay for everything, which was fine, really—

No, it's not. It's not fine.

Great, now I'm hearing things. Maybe I really am crazy.

No you're not. You're perfect. And you're better than this.

My eyes narrow as a tiny fire sparks deep inside me.

I *am* better than this. I don't deserve this—this kind of *bullshit*. I'm going to kick his ass.

But as I walk out of the toilet cubicle ready to get back out there and confront Ethan, Madeleine bursts into the bathroom. She's half carrying, half dragging my big sister, Julia, who has puke running down the side of her face. She's hammered.

With a high-pitched chorus of "ewwwwws," the other girls in the bathroom part, scattering like a lip-glossed red sea.

"Coco!" says Madeleine, her long hair swishing behind her. "Thank God. Jules just barfed on a sofa."

"I am allergic to vodka and cranberry juice," Julia enunciates slowly.

"Everyone is allergic to vodka and cranberry juice if they drink nine of them." Madeleine splashes water on Julia's face. "Coco, paper towels?"

This is unusual. Julia is probably the most sensible one at Rookhaven. She's not the one who gets out-of-control drunk. She just works long hours in her entry-level position in an investment bank and saves twenty-five percent of her salary (seriously, who *does* that?) and talks about "M&As" and "AUMs" and "DDMs" and other confusing aconyms. That's it.

Madeleine is the quiet, skinny accountant, Chinese American, obsessive about two things: working out and Spektor, the band she sings with.

Angie is naughty and sarcastic, always. She works in fashion.

Pia is a party-hard drama queen. She runs a small food truck empire.

Me? I'm . . . I don't know.

I work as an assistant in a Brooklyn preschool. I like to read and bake.

The good one. I'm the good one.

"Coco," Maddy snaps. "Towels."

I grab a huge fistful of paper towels from the dispenser just as Jules flops forward and starts vomiting in the sink. Ugh. I don't think it's actually the vodka and cranberry that's the problem, it's the pre-dinner wine and flask of schnapps that Angie passed around on the subway from Brooklyn to Manhattan, but whatever.

"That is, like, totally gross," says one of the glossy-lipped girls, looking at Julia's shiny brown ponytail flopping over the sink.

"Shut up," I snap. "You don't like it, find another damn bathroom."

Madeleine glances at me in surprise.

Julia squints at her vomit. "Carrots!" she exclaims. "Always carrots. I'm going to stop eating carrots, you know, as an experiment, and next time I puke, we can—" She pauses to throw up again.

"Great idea," says Madeleine. "Conduct a science experiment with your binge drinking."

Angie and Pia burst in. "What is going on?"

Julia stands up. "I'm a lil' drunk! Fivies!"

Pia and Angie automatically reach to high-five Julia. Somehow my sister manages to miss both of their hands.

"I'm taking her home." Madeleine tucks her dark hair behind her ears. "Julia! Stand up!"

"I'll come with you," I say, putting Julia's arm over my shoulders so I can help her walk.

"We'll come too," says Pia. "It's not like we're here to score anyway."

Pia and Angie are both in long-distance relationships while Julia and Madeleine are single. And I have a boyfriend . . . who is cheating on me. And now we'll break up and I'll be single again, with no more texts and no more Saturday-night movie dates and no more . . . anything. I'll be single again. No one will ever ask me out. And my life will be empty. I will be alone. Forever.

I can't bear it.

I stare into space for a moment, holding up my swaying sister.

Maybe I can pretend it didn't happen.

Should I find Ethan before we go? Tell him I'm leaving, at least? No. Staying with Julia is the right thing to do. She needs me. I'm good at looking after people, I always have been. Besides, that strange, fiery anger I felt is gone now.

I just want to go home with my friends. And for everything to go back to normal as soon as possible.

"Turn the radio up, Mr. Taxi Driver!" shouts Julia.

Maybe it didn't happen.

Maybe I imagined it.

Maybe everything will be fine.

Or maybe it won't.

CHAPTER 2

I hate my job, by the way.

I'm a preschool assistant. I really love the *idea* of it—reading and singing and playing with adorable children. But the reality is very different. It's hard and tiring and kind of lonely. Boring, even. It's just . . . not what I expected.

All day I'm exhausted, yet at night I can't seem to fall asleep. I feel all twitchy and unfulfilled, you know? And I'm hungry, all day, every day. This morning I had a really big breakfast—oatmeal, a buttered bagel, fruit. But now I'm starving and it's only ten in the morning. *Starving.*

"Class?" Miss Audrey claps her bony hands together. "Cleanup time!" She shoots me a look and hisses. "Wake *up*, Coco."

Ah, yes. That's the other reason I hate my job. Miss Audrey.

Miss Audrey is kind of, um, a bitch. Apparently she's gone through three assistants in five years. She's skinny and dried-out-looking and brown around the edges, like an apple core that was left outside for a month.

I know what you're thinking. Why don't I just quit if I hate it so much?

This is my first job, and quitting would look bad, you know? Plus it's the only thing I'm qualified to do, and the preschool is only a five-minute walk from home. Besides, I was so nervous at this job interview, I'd do anything to avoid having another one ever again.

Maybe I'm just not one of those shiny, golden people who get to have a job they love. In the past year I've seen Pia and Angie both go after exactly what they want—their dream careers—and get them. And Julia and Madeleine work so hard sometimes that I think they're going to make themselves sick.

I don't have the same drive.

Or maybe I do, but I haven't figured out what to drive toward yet.

I don't know. I'm just so tired of everything.

I wait for Miss Audrey to become busy on the other side of the room before sneaking over to the storage cubbies. I keep candy in my purse at all times, for sugar attacks on the go.

I snack way too much, but lately I can't help it. I've always been a little bigger than I want to be . . . but at least I'm not as big as I was in high school. At the time I was on these antidepressants that I don't think helped. Luckily, I went off of them and managed to lose some weight. Not that it mattered, it's not like it did any good when it came to guys.

Ethan.

My stomach flips as the memory of Saturday night pops back into my head, as it has with annoying regularity for the last forty-eight hours. Ethan went to Philadelphia for work yesterday. We haven't spoken. He called last night, but I couldn't bring myself to pick up. I can't confront him. I know! I know. It's so pathetic. I haven't told the girls either. I just can't do it. Not yet. Acknowledging it out loud would make it real.

Eventually, the day is over. The children all run to the open arms of their mommy or daddy or nanny. Finally I can go home and be alone.

"Coco, a word?"

A chill goes down my spine.

I walk over to Miss Audrey. She flashes her apple-core smile at me.

"Mrs. James and I would like to have a talk with you."

My stomach clenches. I'm going to the principal's office. I never got called to the principal's office in high school. Never.

I follow Miss Audrey through the halls toward Mrs. James's office. My mind is a blank on the way there. I stare at floors a lot. I am *so* over floors.

"Coco!" Mrs. James smiles warmly. "Come on in. Take a seat."

Mrs. James is the opposite of Miss Audrey. She's cozy like a grandmother—mono-boob, twinsets, pearls.

"Miss Audrey and I wanted to have a little talk," she says.

I try to smile back, but my heart hammers so loudly I actually want to put my hand over my chest to calm it.

"We're concerned that you're not enjoying your role to the fullest extent possible."

"And it's reflecting in your job performance," interjects Miss Audrey.

"Little Gardens is a magical place," says Mrs. James, smiling so widely that I can see her molars. "We want everyone here to be happy, including you, Coco."

Happy?

"Are you happy?" asks Mrs. James.

"Um," I mumble, my voice barely audible. Do you ever find it difficult to speak loudly? I do. My voice gets lost somewhere deep down inside me. "I—um, I'm happy." I pause, choking over the word. *I'm not happy.*

"Are you sure?" asks Mrs. James. "Sometimes you seem a little—"

"Look, you're not doing your job properly," interrupts Miss Audrey. "You spend half the damn time daydreaming!"

"Maybe it's time you took a leave of absence to think about whether or not Little Gardens is the right place for you," says Mrs. James.

"You're expelling me?" I whisper.

"You're not a student. You can't be expelled," snaps Miss Audrey. She looks over at the principal. "See? She's a child."

"I'm not, I'm twenty-one . . ." My voice squeaks. *Oh, God, shut up, Coco.*

"We're putting you on probation." Mrs. James sounds excited, like she's telling me about a promotion. "Between now and the end of the school year, we want to see what you can make of each and every day at Little Gardens! We want you"—she lowers her voice, as if telling me a secret—"to be happy!"

She claps her hands and stands up, smiling cheerfully.

Meeting over.

"Thanks, um, thank you, thanks, Mrs. James, thanks, Miss Audrey, thank you," I stammer. Why am I thanking them for putting me on probation? Why don't I just thank Ethan for cheating on me, while I'm at it? "Um, totally great to see you. Thank you so much for your time, as always, I—"

Shut up, Coco. Just shut up and get out.

CHAPTER 3

I'm not fired. I'm not fired. I'm not fired.

Yet.

I know I'm not fired, but I still can't shake that jumpy, panicky feeling. Food. I need food. If I am chewing and swallowing, I can't think about what just happened, and when my body is full and buzzing from sugar, everything will feel better. Right?

That's what I always think, anyway. So when I get home I practically inhale the last slice of the pecan pie I made yesterday in a hey-my-boyfriend-cheated-on-me baking fit and a glass of nice cold milk. Why does dairy soothe my nerves? I don't know, but it always does. Then, because I don't know what else to do, I make some mac and cheese for everyone to have for dinner. Madeleine won't eat it, and Pia might not either, but Julia and Angie will.

The secret to a good mac and cheese, by the way, is three kinds of cheese. I like the stuff from the box as much as the next gal, but that's not real food. That's what my mom always said, and I agree.

Then I go upstairs to my little attic bedroom, the same one my mom had growing up. The décor hasn't changed in about forty years. Flowery wallpaper and faded glow-in-the-dark stars on the ceiling, a pale pink curtain over the crooked little window. It still doesn't quite feel like home—we only moved in last summer, after all. But it feels safe, and familiar. We spent vacations and weekends here all the time when I was growing up. The only thing I changed about my bedroom was the full-length mirror. I put it in Julia's room. I hate mirrors. I never look at myself if I can help it.

Sighing, I sit down on the bed, taking in all my stuff. My books. My photos. My life.

Then I call my dad. He's very reassuring in the same way that Julia is: he always takes charge. When I talk to him I always feel like I don't need to worry about anything, because he's got it all figured out.

But today he doesn't pick up. This isn't unusual: he works about fourteen hours a day.

I leave a message.

"Hi, Daddy! Just me . . . um . . . love you. Call me! Bye."

I hang up and *boom*, the big thought that I've been avoiding all afternoon comes back.

What am I going to do with my life?

Then I hear the front door bang. Someone is home. Thank goodness! I run downstairs and into the living room, where Pia is sitting on the sofa, going through our mail. She starts work super early, but she's often the first home after me.

"What up, sugarnuts?" she says as I come into the living room. "Isn't it nuts that junk mail still exists? Like, don't you think they should just use the damn Internet? The Internet doesn't cut down trees."

"Um . . . totally," I say.

I suddenly don't want to tell anyone about what happened at work today. Just like I don't want to tell them about Ethan. It's too . . . I don't know. It's too personal.

So I just grab an old copy of *Daddy-Long-Legs* from the bookshelf and sit on the sofa next to Pia. I love this book. I remember reading it, lying on a picnic rug, one summer when we went to Martha's Vineyard. I love how, with books, you are connected to the past—and to everyone else who ever read and loved them too. It's so comforting.

Gradually, everyone gets home from work and assumes her usual position and activity on the living room sofas. Julia settles in with a bowl of my mac and cheese, watching some crappy cop show. Madeleine's on her laptop. Angie is sewing a little green clutch bag—she's been working on a collection for the last few weeks, for a fashion brand called Serafina that apparently likes to develop young "up-and-coming" designers. ("They get my genius and talent. In exchange I get exposure. And basically no money at all," Angie likes to point out.)

It would be pretty obvious to anyone who knows me really well—you know, anyone who paid a lot of attention to me—that something isn't right with me. That I'm upset, or stressed, or whatever. My mom would have known, and she would have charmed and cajoled the truth by now. But here in Rookhaven, no one even looks at me.

"What are you doing, Maddy?" says Julia, when her show cuts to a commercial break.

"Working. I didn't finish something for my boss today."

"You know you don't get extra credit for that, right?" says Pia.

Madeleine gives her the finger. Pia grins, just as her phone beeps.

"A text from your lovah?" asks Julia. "Is he coming this weekend?"

Pia reads the text, and suddenly her mood plummets. "Mother-fucker. He canceled, *again*. He has to work all weekend."

"I bet he'll come the following wee—"

"Screw that," says Pia, her eyes filling with tears. "I'm sick of be-ing in a long-distance relationship. It's not fun. No sex, no dinners out, no hangover snuggles. All I do is plan what to wear on our next Skype call. And try to figure out good lighting tricks to make my gigantic nose look smaller. It's just not enough. He lives on the other side of the country now! What's the point?"

"Pia, there is nothing wrong with your nose," says Julia.

"That's not the point." Pia stares blankly at the ceiling. "I just can't see how our relationship is ever going to work like this. It's doomed. *Doomed.*"

Angie glances up from her sewing. "At least you get to see Aidan once every few weeks and have sex. Sam and I literally kissed and then, sayonara."

"Angie! He might have a *teeny* penis!" exclaims Julia in mock horror.

"Please. The man is hung like an elephant. I can tell these things."

"You can?" I say. "How?"

Everyone looks at me and cracks up. Goddamnit. I hate it when I say dumb stuff.

"So, um, I was wondering," I say, changing the subject, "what makes you guys happy? Is that a stupid question?"

"There are no stupid questions," says Angie. "That's a quote from *Heathers.* Anyone? No? My God, you people are philistines."

"My career makes me happy," says Julia, flicking through the TV channels. "I used to feel like I didn't fit in, you know? But I've been there almost a year now, you know? I *belong.* And the walk from the subway through the crowds to my office every morning is the hap-piest part of my day. I don't know . . . I feel like I'm really part of something."

"I *hate* midtown rush hour," says Madeleine. "And my job."

"You hate your job? You never told me that," says Julia. "So what makes you happy? Singing?"

"I guess so. Maybe." Madeleine shrugs. We all wait for her to continue, but she goes back to her laptop. She is seriously the most reserved person ever.

"Creating makes me happy," says Angie. "You know. Sketching, cutting, sewing, making something where nothing existed before with just my imagination and my hands. And Sam, of course. Sam makes me very happy."

"Aidan doesn't make me happy right now," Pia looks like she's about to cry again. Then she glances over at the TV and brightens. "Is that *NCIS*? I love that show!"

Angie is stunned. "Seriously?"

"Don't be a snob, Angie. We already know how cool you are," says Pia in a singsong voice, her Aidan misery forgotten.

Thank God no one even asked me what makes me happy. I mean, what would I answer? Books and baking? How lame is that? And do they really make me happy? They can't, right? Because I'm not happy. I'm just . . . I'm not happy.

I will never be happy.

Suddenly, I feel like I'm suffocating. I'm going to cry, or scream. I have to get out of here.

I quietly stand up and hurry out of the living room. No one even notices. Then I open the front door and step outside onto the stoop, closing the door quickly behind me.

I can't breathe. I can't get enough air into my body, I'm choking, gasping for oxygen . . . *One breath in. One breath out. In. Out. In. Out.* Slowly my breathing calms as I stand on our stoop, looking out over Union Street.

It's a beautiful sunny evening, the kind that makes you feel like you should be out enjoying every second or else you're a failure.

Forcing myself to breathe slowly and evenly, I look out at the classic brownstones. The usual weekday afternoon suspects abound:

local stay-at-home dads wearing babies in slings, competitive moms in Spandex with strollers, bored iPhone-clicking nannies, shuffling nanny-grandmas, the actors/dog walkers, the sophisti-kids skateboarding home from school with more cool than I'll ever fake. There are a hundred ways of belonging in Brooklyn, and everyone has one.

Except me.

It's times like this that make me really miss my mom. My dad is good at telling me what to do, but my mom was good at just making me feel like everything was going to be okay.

I don't want to think about her too much; I'll get upset. Today is one of those days when I can feel my grief is closer to the surface. I slump down on the stoop and put my arms over my knees, resting my forehead on them.

I will never be happy.

"Why, if it isn't little Coco," says a familiar voice.

I look over the other side of the stoop. It's Vic, our eighty-something downstairs neighbor. He's lived at Rookhaven since forever, since my mom was a baby and long before that. You can always find him outside his basement apartment door watching the world go by.

"How's life?"

"My life sucks so hard," I say.

Vic grins. His face is like a cartoon of an ancient oak tree, all gnarly crevices. "And why's that?"

"Um." I take a deep breath, and suddenly everything just spills out. "My boyfriend cheated on me. And I think I'm about to get fired because apparently I don't believe in myself."

"Okay . . ." Vic says slowly, inclining his head toward mine. I swear his ears are, like, the size of my hand. "Go on."

"I can't tell the girls, because they'd just hate him. And I don't need to hear that right now, and I don't have anyone else to tell." The words tumble out of me. "I saw him kissing another girl on Saturday night and I haven't said anything to him, like at all, I just really don't want to break up—"

"Why?"

"Because then I'll be single!" It comes out louder than I mean it to. Then I realize I don't want to talk about my relationship with an eighty-something-year-old guy. "And, um, more important, I just got put on probation, my boss thinks I'm really bad at my job . . ."

"You're an assistant at a primary school?"

"Preschool," I say.

"Sounds fun," he says.

"It's not. At least, not for me. I mean, the kids are cute, but there's a lot more to it than just kids." Like Miss Audrey.

"So why'd ya choose it?"

"My dad and Julia said it was a good idea, you know, because I liked babysitting, and I'm not very good at being, um, aggressive? Both of them work in finance, and I guess they didn't think I'd thrive in that particular, um"—I search for the right word—"environment." I'm talking too much. Shut up.

"Coco, there's a whole load of jobs that aren't finance or teaching," says Vic. "Maybe your destiny is somewhere else."

"Maybe . . ."

But what I can't say is the real reason my dad and Julia told me what to do with my life.

They think I'm stupid.

They'd never say it, but I know it's true. Did you know I have an inheritance from my mom? Julia used her inheritance for college, but my preschool qualifications didn't cost anywhere near as much as Brown. After I was certified, I heard Dad and Julia talking about it once. The rest of my money is locked away until I'm old enough to trust with it. They'll probably give it to my husband if I ever get married, like a dowry. They never tell me anything.

I guess it's because I wasn't a great student in high school. I just found it really hard to concentrate, and I felt sad a lot of the time, and so I sort of got locked up inside myself. If that makes any sense. It felt like my teachers had already decided who the brainy kids were, and I wasn't one of them. I really only did well in my Advanced Placement English class . . . but it's only because I love reading. *Love* it. Books are like friends. They make you feel understood.

My dad always said that reading was nothing more than a hobby, that you can't make a career out of books. I'm not sure that's true now—I mean, what about book editors and stuff?—but at the time it made sense.

"You've always been the smart one," says Vic, interrupting my reverie.

"I am not!" I say, with such venom I surprise myself. "I'm just . . . I'm not. My dad once said that some people are school smart and some people are people smart and I'm people smart."

"People smart, my ass. You were sitting out here reading *Little Women* when you were six. You read more than any kid I've ever known, except my niece Samantha, and she's got a PhD in sociology. She's a smart one too. You're school smart. Trust me. You don't give yourself enough credit, Coco."

My eyes suddenly fill with tears. I love Vic. He always tries to make us feel better. He's like our guardian angel or something.

"But I don't know what I'll do if I get fired," I say. "It's so scary."

"You'll figure it out," he says. "That's the only thing I can promise you."

"What if I can't? I feel . . ." I pause, trying to keep my voice steady, willing my tears away before he notices. "Lost. Like my life is empty."

"Empty? You live in the best city in the world, with your sister, your best friends . . ."

"I know, I know," I say quickly. "But they're more Julia's friends, really. Julia went to college with Pia and Madeleine, and Pia and Angie have known each other since they were babies. They only live with me because Julia and I inherited the house and they couldn't afford to live here any other way."

"Doesn't mean you're not important to them."

I nod, using my sleeve to mop up the tears sneaking down my cheeks, hoping he doesn't notice. Vic's being nice, but it's totally not true. Everyone else in Rookhaven is special and beautiful and funny. I am (d) none of the above. I don't belong.

"And I don't usually get involved in the, uh, the love stuff," Vic says. "But any man who cheats is not a man. Full stop, end of paragraph, end of story. So don't waste any more tears on him."

"Okay," I say.

Suddenly I realize that I haven't really cried about Ethan that much. I'm not heartbroken, and I don't feel sad, exactly . . . I just feel scared. Why does everything make me feel scared? And if I don't even like him enough to be heartbroken about him, why was I even dating him in the first place?

I just want to be happy.

And I don't know how.

"What makes you happy, Vic?"

"Me?" Vic pauses. "Being me. No one else gets to be me except me. No one else gets my life, no one else gets my memories. I like being me."

I don't like being me.

Vic thinks for a moment. "There's something else too. While I could, I made the love of my life happy . . . Making the people you love happy. That's the real secret."

I don't have a love of my life. I can't even imagine feeling that way. I can't even imagine *saying* it.

"But how am I ever going to figure out what to do with my life?"

"Just think about what you truly love. What makes you smile. After that, everything will be easy." I nod, gulping. Nothing makes me smile.

"So, listen. You wanna help me join up this Facebook thing?" says Vic finally.

"Sure!" I hurry down the stoop, delighted to have a distraction. "Do you have a computer, Vic?"

"I do. It's got a piece of fruit on it."

I sign Vic up to Facebook pretty quickly, and within twenty minutes, he's requested about fifty friends, and messages keep popping up. Jeez. He's eighty-something years old but has more Facebook fun than I do.

"You're so popular," I say.

He shrugs. "You live this long, you meet a lot of people," he says. "Imagine if half my friends weren't dead."

I laugh despite myself. It does not seem appropriate.

Vic stares at the screen for a few moments, then frowns. "So, what does it do now?"

"Um, nothing, you have to, you know, find people you know, or find things you like."

"And then what do you do when you find things you like?"

"You press the Like button."

"Why?"

I pause. *Why?* "So everyone knows what you like?"

"Who cares what I like? I don't care what everyone else likes."

"Oh," I say. I do. I really care what everyone else likes. It's how I learn what's important.

Vic stands up. "Well, this has been great, but I gotta get down to Esposito's before they sell out of my lasagne. Want to join?"

"No . . . I think I'll stay here and try to think about what would make me truly happy."

Impossible things would make me happy.

That my mother was still alive.

That I'd never slept with Eric . . . I shake my head quickly, before I can think about the termination and everything that happened that day and after. I'd be happy if I'd never dated Ethan, especially when I didn't really like him at first, I just liked that he liked me. If Ethan never cheated on me.

If I had a body like a Victoria's Secret Angel, and I could magically erase every piece of junk food from my eating history.

If my former best friend who slept with Eric on prom night gets alopecia so all her hair falls out.

If I never have to work at Little Gardens again.

But, gradually, I whittle it down.

This is a secret list—I'll never show anyone—and it's the bare essentials.

These are the three things missing from my life, the things that I need in order to truly be happy.

My Happy List
1. Be thin
2. Fall in love
3. Figure out what to do with the rest of my life

If that's my happy life . . . no wonder I'm so unhappy now. I am so far from all of those things.

Thinking this, I lie on my bed, staring at the ceiling, at the tiny glow-in-the-dark stars my mom put there when she was a little girl. A few of them were traced around in colored pencil and then removed, leaving little star stencils all across the ceiling. My mom was very naughty when she was little, apparently. I never would have done that. You know how all families have roles that everyone plays? Julia was the spirited one, always pushing boundaries and having tantrums and time-outs, and I was the opposite. I was quiet and shy and never got in trouble. I was the good one.

That's it.

The good one.

I've always been the good one. I've always done everything right, everything careful and obedient and considerate. And look where it's got me.

Guys treat me like crap, my boss thinks I'm an idiot, no one expects me to achieve or be able to handle anything.

I lie to myself, telling myself things are okay when they're not. I told myself that my job was fine and my relationship was good enough when they weren't. I never have the confidence to say what I'm thinking, I second-guess myself at every turn. I spend all my time in my head, or in the kitchen. Or both.

The only way I can be happy is by being the exact opposite of the person I've always been.

So from now on, I don't want to be the good one.

I'll be the wild one.

CHAPTER 4

I can't start being wild while I'm dating a douche bag and hate my job, right? So I have to quit working at Little Gardens and break up with Ethan. When you think about it like that, these are the next, the *only*, logical steps.

So the following Friday afternoon, after all the kids have gone home and I've finished all my cleanup jobs, I walk over to Miss Audrey and clear my throat.

"I'd like to talk to you. And Mrs. James," I say. "Now. Please."

Her little dried-apple mouth flickers in surprise. I haven't spoken without her addressing me first in . . . ever.

Once we're sitting in front of Mrs. James, her smiling warmly at me in that well-rehearsed grandma way, I take charge. It feels strange. And amazing.

"I'd like to give notice," I say. "Effective immediately."

Their mouths drop open.

"I am allowed do that," I add. "I read over my contract. It says that once I'm on probation, I can be fired with no notice period, and I can also resign without the standard notice period."

"That's correct, but"—Mrs. James looks at Miss Audrey—"we really thought—"

"I am sorry. I've enjoyed working here, but this isn't the job for me." Wow, the more I say exactly how I feel, the better I get at it.

"You picked a fine time to decide," snaps Miss Audrey. "With just weeks to go until the end of the school year."

"You picked it, actually, when you put me on probation," I meet her gaze steadily.

Her eyebrows shoot up in surprise. That would normally be enough to scare me into mute submission. But instead my voice is strong; I'm maintaining eye contact . . . That fire bursts to life in my stomach again, the spark that started whispering to me the other night at the Jane Hotel.

Suddenly I know what that voice is. It's me. The me that has never dared to speak up for herself before.

Where the hell has she been?

I stand up, feeling stronger than I think I ever have before. "Look, Mrs. James, you said you wanted me to be happy. Well, I can never be happy while I'm working here with—that woman."

Mrs. James glances at Miss Audrey, who looks like she might throw up.

"Thank you for your time," I say. "Good-bye."

Then I turn and walk out of Mrs. James's office and straight out of Little Gardens. Forever.

CHAPTER 5

Of course, by the time I get back to Rookhaven, I'm completely freaking out.

What do I do now?

How can I survive without a job? My rent is taken care of because Julia and I inherited Rookhaven—the other girls pay rent directly to our dad and he uses it to take care of maintenance and stuff, like fixing the place up after the storm earlier this year. But what about bills? What about food? What about Metrocards and tampons and toothpaste? It's not like I'm a big spender, but simply being *alive* costs money. What if I can never get a job again? Will I have to move home to Rochester and live with Dad? Would Dad just give me my inheritance? I doubt it, but even if he did, it wouldn't last forever, I'd still need a plan . . .

Seriously. *What do I do now?*

I walk into the kitchen and find Angie, dressed like some kind of albino Hells Angel in a white leather dress.

"What up, ladybitch?"

"Nothing," I say. "What up, uh, I mean, what's up with you?"

"I just got a present from Sam!" Angie squeals uncharacteristically, pulling two martini glasses out of a cardboard delivery box in front of her. Sam is her absolutely gorgeous, totally nice boyfriend. He's currently working on a boat in the Greek islands or something.

"He sent you a present?"

"Yup. Martini glasses and a shaker, and vodka and vermouth too! Isn't that so thoughtful?" A dreamy look comes across her face.

"He just ordered you a present for no reason?"

"Well, you know . . . I guess just to let me know he's thinking of me. Anyway," she continues, opening the bottle of vodka, "work finished early since it's Memorial Day weekend and everyone in the studio wanted to get the fuck out and get drunk, so I figured I'd go ahead and christen them. Besides, we should pregame before Maddy's gig."

"Oh. Um . . . cool. Nice dress, by the way."

Angie looks down at herself. "You like? White leather? I don't look like I belong in a Whitesnake music video? I was working on it all day, so I figured I could borrow it for the weekend."

I sigh. I could never fit into that dress. Angie is extremely slim. And she eats whatever she wants. It's totally unfair.

I watch her shaking the martini. Her arms are so toned, they don't even jiggle. My arms are one of my least favorite parts of myself.

"Are you okay?" asks Angie, concerned. "You look stressed out."

I take a deep breath. "I just quit my job. And I am going to break up with Ethan."

Angie's face lights up. "That is fucking outstanding news."

I wince slightly. I'm getting used to how much my friends swear, and I get it, that's just how they talk . . . but sometimes it still shocks me.

Angie checks herself. "Sorry. I just meant, I knew you didn't like that job, and he's a nice guy but, um, you are way out of his league."

"Like I'm out of anyone's league," I say.

"Coco, don't be silly! Now, and this may be the most important question I ever ask you"—she turns deadly serious—"how do you like your martinis?"

"Um . . ." I have no idea. "Strong?"

"I like them icy-cold, dry, and dirty. I'll make you one like mine, and if you hate it, we'll try another approach. Now, go change your outfit to cleanse your sartorial karma, and come back." She glances at me. "Scoot!"

Ten minutes later I'm showered and dressed in my favorite jeans and comfy old black top, and I walk out to the stoop. Angie assesses me.

"No."

"No?"

"Go to my room. There's a top resting on the chair next to my sewing machine."

"I'm not skinny enough to wear your clothes, Angie."

"Just do as I say, ladybitch." Angie has been experimenting with her eyeliner lately, replacing her usual thick rings of black with thicker rings of navy, and the result is somehow even edgier. And more intimidating. It's hard to say no to her.

So I head up to Angie's room and on the chair is a silky blue top. I'm positive it's not going to fit me, but put it on, trying not to breathe in case I split it in two.

It fits.

I am stunned. I quickly glance in the mirror to confirm I haven't somehow made a mistake and not put it on properly, but it's really me. I take a second to look. Big boobs, round face, blond bob . . . Same old me. No. *New* me.

"I can't believe I fit into your top!" I exclaim, running back out to the stoop. "That is insane!"

Angie drops her cigarette in delight. "I knew that would look amazing on you! I bought that top at AuH$_2$O in the East Village, and my tits are too small. Yours are magnificent."

"Um, thanks."

"Ladybitch, your clothes are too big and droopy. And I say that with love. Wearing clothes that oversize doesn't do anyone any favors." Angie lights another cigarette. "When was the last time you went funderwear shopping? My boss says that when she learned how to dress for her boobs, everyone thought she'd lost, like, eighty fucking pounds."

"Oh," I say. "Gosh."

"The right structure means the twins reach out to the future, not down to your knees. Dig?"

Angie has such a ballsy way of talking sometimes; I'm never sure what to say in response.

"I wish I was skinny up and down like you," I say.

"Well, I wish I had perfect boobs like you, and an ass that didn't droop like a sad balloon. Everyone is different."

She hands me my martini, clinks her glass to mine, and we both take a sip.

It's strong.

"That's pretty good," she says thoughtfully. "I went to a bunch of Web sites to figure out how to make a perfect martini. How did people learn anything before the Internet? Like, seriously."

"I don't know."

"Tell me about work and Ethan. No! Wait! Screw work. You hated it, you quit. Just tell me about Ethan."

I take a big sip of my martini. "He kind of cheated on me last Saturday . . ."

Angie chokes on her drink. "He fucking what? Why didn't you tell us? And what do you mean 'sort of'?"

"I just . . ."

I stare at my martini for a second.

I hate talking about myself. Particularly about why I do the dumb shit I do. Then I remember. I need to be the exact opposite of the person I've always been. That doesn't just mean being wild instead of always good, it also means being open and honest, even about things I'm embarrassed about, things I think no one else could ever understand.

I clear my throat. "I was scared."

Angie frowns. I bet she's never been scared in her life. "Scared of what?"

"Of being single, of being alone," I say. "If you're single, then you just sit at home all the time waiting to meet someone, but you never do *because* you're at home all the time! And let's say you do meet someone, and against all odds, he actually likes you . . . He still might hurt you, you know? He might lie to you or dump you, or, um, cheat on you, though I guess that happened anyway since Ethan lied and cheated . . . And you know, guys with whom you might make the mistake that I . . . I made with Eric . . ." I pause briefly, before the sweet rush of confession spurs me onward. "I never slept with Ethan."

"Say what?"

"We tried once and I freaked out and made him stop," I say. "You know. Because my only other time was Eric."

Angie nods. She knows about my horrible Eric story. Okay, I haven't told you the whole thing yet . . . So. Imagine having a crush on a guy for years, all through high school, even after he slept with your best friend at prom. Like a massive, heart-stopping crush of adoration and lust. Imagine finally hooking up with him, years later, and losing your virginity to him. Imagine getting pregnant, because he wouldn't wear a condom. Imagine that afterward, he won't even return your calls or texts. Imagine getting an abortion. That's the Eric story.

See? It was horrible, absolutely the worst.

Angie was so good to me during that time. She and Pia really looked after me. It amazes me, when I look back, how understanding and supportive and nonjudgmental they were. I would never have expected them to be so nice to me. I don't think Julia and Madeleine would be like that. I guess that's why I haven't told them about it.

"Do you want to talk about it?" Angie asks.

I think for a moment. "No. Not really."

Sometimes there's nothing to say. I feel sad and sick and tiny inside when I think about that day. I don't regret it—I totally do not regret it—but I still wish it hadn't happened. I think that's how everyone who has to have an abortion probably feels. All of us millions of women, feeling sad and sick and tiny inside when we think about the memory that will never go away.

"Who'd be a chick, huh?" I murmur.

Angie cracks up. "It's better than being a dude. Can you imagine? Having a dick jangling around all the time? Ew."

"Do you think I'll ever want to sleep with someone again?" I ask Angie. "I will, right? Ethan just wasn't right, you know? He's a really bad kisser, and his mouth tastes wrong, somehow. I don't know how, just wrong."

"Well, sugarnuts, if his mouth tastes wrong, you can sure as shit bet his dick wouldn't taste right." Angie swallows another gulp of martini. "Of course you'll sleep with someone again. And it'll be fucking great. Now. Tell me all of Ethan's dirty little secrets."

An hour later, we have a plan.

"Text Ethan now! Now!" says Angie. "Invite him to Maddy's gig tonight. We'll nail his balls to the fucking wall."

"He's not in New York. He's on a train back from Philly. He was there all week for work."

"Ew. Trains." Angie wrinkles her nose. "Send the text."

I tap out the pre-agreed text. Then there's a beeping on the street, and Pia rolls up in Toto, her original Skinny Wheels food truck. She has a small fleet of food trucks now, but Toto is still special to her.

"You're not supposed to park that on the street," calls Angie. We've had some complaints from the neighbors.

Pia shrugs, walking toward the stoop. "Fuck it. I've had a *merde* day. Is that vodka?"

Pia bounds up the stoop, takes a huge slug of Angie's drink, and then plucks the cigarette out of her mouth and takes a drag.

"Are we having a party?" a voice calls.

Julia and Madeleine are walking up Union Street toward home, still in their work clothes. Julia is wearing her huge gym backpack that would, I swear to God, take out an old lady if she turned too quickly on a crowded subway.

"Coco quit her job and is going to dump Ethan!" calls Angie.

I feel embarrassed to have all the attention on me. "Angie, stop it . . ."

"Coco. You need to own your drama," she says sternly.

She's right. Being the opposite of the old me means being loud(er), without caring about the consequences or worrying that I don't deserve people's attention.

I take a deep breath. "I totally quit. And Ethan cheated on me and we're taking revenge tonight!"

"That little shitweasel," says Julia. "Are you okay? Why didn't you tell me?"

"There was nothing to tell . . . until now." I used to tell Julia everything, but she works so hard these days that she's never around. Besides, it's not like I *have* to tell her everything. I'm a grown-up. Adult. Whatever. "I think it's time for me to be wild. Whatever that means."

"Getting drunk," says Pia. "At work."

"Having casual sex," says Angie. "Also at work."

"Speaking your mind," says Madeleine. "No matter what."

"Telling your boss to fuck off," says Julia. "Or is that just my fantasy?"

"I already did that," I say. "Kind of. I mean, I didn't want to hurt her feelings or anything . . . Hey, how come you're out of the office before nine?"

Julia grins. "You know that deal I was working on until, like, three A.M. every night this week? It died. Hundreds of millions of dollars down the drain."

"Oh, shit."

"Are you kidding? Best news ever. I thought my boss was going to have an aneurysm. He's such a dick. And I'm not even tired anymore. I just want to get hammered."

Julie turns to Angie and Pia.

"I want a full makeover for the gig tonight, I want a montage to cheesy music, and I want to pregame. It's the weekend. Fivies!"

"Party Julia is here!" shouts Angie happily. "You can start with this."

She hands over her martini, and Julia takes a slug and chokes.

"That is disgusting. I'll have a beer."

"I'm not drinking. I have to rest my voice," says Madeleine. "Yes. It's a thing."

Pia reaches out, takes Angie's martini, and tips all of it back into her mouth. She hands back the empty glass and smiles. "Okay, ladybitches. Let's have some goddamn fun."

CHAPTER 6

As you might expect from a group of twenty-something girls, we spend the early part of the evening on an extended makeover session in Angie's room, with alcohol. I mostly watch until Angie suddenly grabs me and puts bright red Chanel lipstick on my lips.

"It looks amazing on you," Angie says when I protest. "You have perfect skin and teeth, and the *best* lips I have ever seen. Red lipstick should be part of your signature look."

"What's my signature look?" asks Julia.

"Corporate whore," says Angie.

"Better than fashion victim," Julia shoots back.

"I am many things, sweetie, but I am never a victim." Angie smiles.

"Would you two stop flirting?" Madeleine rolls her eyes.

"Holy shit." Julia looks at herself in the mirror. "I would totally bang me, if I was a dude. Do you think I should wax my—"

"Whatever the end of that sentence is, the answer is almost certainly no," says Angie. "There is nothing wrong with a little grass on the playing field, understand?"

"Since when do you like pubic hair?" asks Pia.

"Since I realized it's fucking weird to make my vagina look like it did when I was eight."

Everyone ruminates on this for a moment. It *is* weird, when you think about it like that. But I just waxed myself in the bathroom with one of those home kits I bought ages ago. I don't even know why I did it, it's just . . . that's what you do. You know?

"Isn't it . . . cleaner?" Pia speaks up tentatively.

"If you think it's dirty, then you have issues, ladybitch. Vaginas are perfect. Dudes don't wax their balls, and yet they ask us to nuzzle up to them at the drop of a damn hat."

Everyone pauses again, I guess to think about nuzzling hairy balls. Retch.

"Fine." Pia sighs. "I'll stop waxing. There's no one to notice anyway, since my boyfriend lives in another time zone and I never get laid."

"You know, I never get laid either," Julia points out. "Sex is not like water, you won't, like, die without it."

"I am so sick of talking about how much sex everyone is getting or not getting," says Madeleine. "Come on. I need to get to Potstill so I can set up with the band."

As we walk to the bar, the girls talk on and on about Aidan and Sam and sex, and my mind turns to my big Ethan plan for this evening. I feel my stomach lurch with nerves. Maybe I'll secretly text Ethan and cancel. I don't think I can go through with it, I really don't.

But I have to, I remind myself strictly. It's the first step toward being the new me. The wild me.

I've walked by Potstill a hundred times and never gone in. In the rich and varied landscape of Brooklyn bars and, more specifically, South Brooklyn bars, Potstill is . . . well, it's a dump.

It's dirty, for a start, with dusty smeared windows and cracked windowsills, and not in a charming Wild West kind of way, just in a forgotten kind of way. I don't think it's changed since the early '80s, at least. Most places around Gowanus have been hipsterfied by now, but Potstill is still—almost refreshingly—a total dive.

The front part of Potstill is very narrow, opening up to a weird cavernous space at the back where Madeleine's band is setting up. There's a bottle-crammed bar along one wall, and the whole thing is lit by harsh fluorescent bulbs, making everyone look sallow and dull. The walls are green and entirely bare apart from a handful of askew photos of the bar in its heyday thrown up haphazardly in cheap rusted frames.

We walk into the bar and pause, taking it all in.

"What a dump," comments Angie.

"Maddy, shouldn't you go help the band set up?" says Julia.

"I can't . . ." Suddenly, Madeleine can hardly speak. "I'm so nervous. All I can do is drink coffee, but I think I overdid it. Look." Madeleine holds up a visibly shaking hand. "Ugh. I feel sick."

"Eat some salty potato chips," says Julia. "Sodium works to counteract the caffeine, and the carbs release serotonin to calm your adrenals. They have some in the bodega on the corner."

"Is that true?" asks Pia, as Madeleine runs off to the bodega to find potato chips.

"I made it up," says Julia. "I figure it's probably all in her head, right? So if she thinks she's calmer, she'll be calmer . . . anyway, fuck, potato chips won't kill her. She's too goddamn skinny."

Madeleine's band is called Spector. It does hard rock covers of girl group classics from the 1960s, you know, stuff from the Supremes and the Ronettes. Maddy was with another band, but after she stepped in to help out Spector at a gig a few months ago, they recruited her, and that was that. Kind of funny how she's an accountant by day and a singer by night, huh? It's like she's leading a double life.

"I feel so much better," says Madeleine when she returns, stuffing chips in her mouth. "Maybe that was just nerves. The owner of this place, Gary, also has two bars in Williamsburg. If he likes us, we could get a regular gig with him. But I bet no one even turns up . . . Amy is going to be *pissed*."

Amy is the guitar player and unofficial leader of the band, a tall girl with pink hair and black-red lipstick who scares the crap out of me. She's been over to Rookhaven a few times to rehearse with Madeleine.

"Mad! Thank God! I need you!" calls Amy, and Madeleine skips back to where Amy is setting up with Hoff, a stoner/guitar player that was in Maddy's old band too, and Drum, their imaginatively nicknamed drummer.

"Where the hell is the bartender?" says Angie, sitting down on a rickety barstool. "And how shitty is this joint?"

"Very," says Julia, taking a seat next to her and pulling a mismatched stool over for me. "Shitty McShitterson."

Looking around, I frown. I don't think it's *that* shitty. The actual bar itself, you know, where the drinks are mixed, is kind of cool. Very old but beautiful wood, with cracked varnish worn down from years of drinking. It's the crappy green walls and the falling-down plasterboard ceiling that's the real problem. It's just a bit dirty, and not cozy or welcoming. And it's too hot and the lighting is just way too bright and white to flatter anyone.

Okay. Maybe it needs a little work.

"It's not old enough to be old-school-adorable shitty and not new enough to be hipster-chic shitty," says Pia.

"It's not even ironically shitty," says Angie. "It's just . . . it's a piece of shitty shit."

"Thanks, ladies," speaks up a deep voice, seemingly from nowhere, and we all shriek.

A guy appears from practically underneath the bar. Very tall. Messy dark hair. Stubble. Eyes that are too bloodshot to see what color they are.

Pia and Angie shriek again, enjoying their hysteria. I think they're a little tipsy from our makeover drinks.

"Jesus," the guy says, pronouncing it *Jaysus*. "I'll get you a drink if you promise to stop screaming. And stop swearing. You're like drunk sailors."

"Yes, sir," says Angie obediently.

"We'll have three vodka, lime, and sodas, please, young man," says Pia. She must be a little drink to be flirting like that.

"This is a *whiskey* bar." His accent is Irish maybe, or Scottish, I can never tell the difference. "I can offer you a whiskey, more specifically an Irish whiskey, or a whiskey-based cocktail. Or beer. But beer is boring, don't you agree?"

"Beer is cheap, you mean," says Pia, arching her eyebrow. The bartender winks at her.

"Here," he says, grabbing some shot glasses and a bottle of whiskey. "Let's drink these and see what happens. On the house."

Pia and Angie glance at each other and shrug. "Sure thing."

We all do the shot, including the scruffy bartender. He smiles wolfishly as we all make the predictable "oh, my God WHISKEY!" sounds.

"Tell you what, sugarnuts, why don't you rustle up a whiskey cocktail surprise for us," says Angie. "Something refreshing that'll take the edge off."

"You got it, princess. But the name is Joe Nolan. Not sugarnuts."

"Right on." Angie is looking at her phone now, ignoring poor Joe entirely. I guess when all guys give you special attention, you don't need to care.

"Are you from Ireland, Joe?" asks Pia politely.

"Ireland by birth, Cork by the grace of God," Joe deadpans, grabbing bottles and ice and glasses, moving with the fast efficiency of a professional. He slices, pours, and shakes with a sort of cool, detached precision, and we all find ourselves mesmerized, watching him.

"My boyfriend is half Irish," Pia says. "But he didn't grow up there."

"Poor bastard," says Joe. "Ripped from the motherland." He glances at Angie to see if she's listening. She's not. He slams down four icy-cold mason jars full of a pale yellow liquid. "Cold Hard Toddies."

"What's in this?" says Pia, sniffing it.

"Jameson Irish whiskey, apple cider, ice, lemon, and a slice of apple."

"Mason jar. Nice touch," says Pia.

I see her make a note in her phone: *Mason jars. Recyclable. Discount on next order when you bring it back.* Pia is always working. I can't imagine loving a job that much.

We all take a swig of the Cold Hard Toddy. It tastes worryingly unalcoholic. The kind of drink that you devour with thirsty abandon and then realize you can't see straight. Or think straight. Or walk straight.

"May I please have a glass of water?" I ask, but I'm drowned out by Pia and Angie.

"That is amazing!"

"What's in it again?"

"Whiskey, cider, apple, lemon. Do you want me to write it down?" Joe fills up a glass with ice and water, handing it to me.

"Thanks," I say in surprise. I didn't think he heard me. He's barely taken his eyes off Pia and Angie, with the kind of lazy grin that you see only on New York City guys who have a *lot* of casual sex.

"I'm going to the stockroom," says Joe. "Can you girls be trusted not to steal from the bar?"

Angie shrugs, eyes still on her phone. "You think we think this place made more than ten bucks today? Let's be realistic."

"Harsh," mutters Joe, walking away.

Julia turns to me. "Coco, let's talk about your future career."

I sigh. "Oh, let's not."

Angie snorts, but Julia can't be dissuaded that easily.

"I was thinking about it on the walk here. You'll get another job easily," she says. "You just need a regular babysitting gig over the summer and to apply to more preschools by the end of August. Let's get you on one of those sitter sites. I'll help you write a killer résumé and set up all the interviews."

"Julia . . ." I don't want to be rude, but I really don't want my sister to "fix" this situation for me in that loving bossy way. She'll just tell me what she thinks is best without wondering what I want.

Then Julia smiles at me so nicely, and I suddenly realize she doesn't know how bossy she is being. She genuinely thinks she's helping.

It's not like she's being unreasonable either. Working with children is what I am trained to do. But the idea of spending the next few months babysitting, shepherding someone else's children through the scorching New York summer, from park to pool to playdate, makes me feel very tired. And then back to a preschool? For how long? The rest of my life?

"I don't think . . . I don't think that's I want," I say, my voice barely above a whisper. "Working in a preschool, I mean. I don't want that."

I'm supposed to be the opposite of old Coco, right? That means speaking my mind. I clear my throat, and my voice comes out stronger.

"I don't know what I'll do, Julia, but I know it won't be that."

"Okay, well, let's think about what you do want to do, then," says Julia. Always Little Miss Fix-it.

Pia grabs her phone, ready to make notes. "I'll help! What are your strengths and weaknesses? Let's brainstorm."

"Fucking brainstorming . . ." mutters Angie.

My strengths?

I stare at them all, my mind a blank.

I don't have any strengths. I don't have any skills or talents or dreams or brains. I'm just me.

But I can't say that, they'd just think I have low self-esteem, and I really don't. I'm just realistic about my potential, i.e., it doesn't exist.

"Do you ever get the feeling Coco's doing all her talking in her head?" asks Angie.

"Yep," says Pia. She turns to me. "You like baking. How about a pastry chef?"

"Um, no," I say. "That's just a hobby." I don't say it aloud, but can you imagine how much I would weigh if I did that for a living? I know it's stupid, but that alone puts me off it.

"I didn't think anyone had a hobby since the Internet was invented," says Angie. "What about reading? I've never known anyone to read as much as you."

I shake my head. "I can't get paid to read books."

"You could be a librarian!" Pia says excitedly.

"I'm pretty sure libraries are an endangered species," says Julia. "They're all closing."

"Wow, that's depressing," I groan.

Some of my best childhood memories are getting books from the library with my mom. I was so impatient that I always started reading them in the car on the way home, my cheek resting against the warmth of the seat belt, trying to ignore the sick tummy I always got reading in a moving vehicle . . .

The memory of that feeling is so strong that I have to put my hands on the worn wood of the bar to remind myself where I am. I wonder if it's weird that I can remember my childhood so well. It's almost like I feel so close to my past that I can't accept that this life is my reality. Grown up and living in New York City, drinking in bars, unemployed and only qualified to do a job I hate, treated like shit by every guy I meet, with a long life ahead of me with nothing but more of the same in store . . . My God, I am tired.

"You like watching E!" says Angie, interrupting my reverie. God, she's right, I really do all my talking in my head. "Want to be a celebrity journalist?"

I shake my head, not trusting myself to speak without crying.

"Try this!" says Pia. "Close your eyes. Picture yourself in five years. Where are you? What are you doing?"

I close my eyes. Me in five years. Me, age twenty-six. At first, my mind is empty, blurry, messy . . . Then an image starts to form. At first I see Rookhaven, and the kitchen, and everyone else . . . but then I appear, curled up in a leather armchair, next to an open window, reading a book and sipping a mug of hot chocolate. My hair is longer, and I'm smiling while I read. The image is so clear, so real, that for a second I wonder if I'm imagining it or if it's from a movie or something. But no, it's me. It's really me.

My thoughts are interrupted by the sound of Julia noisily getting down from her stool.

"I don't think we should make any decisions about your future until we talk to Dad. Right! I'm gonna drain the dragon."

"You don't have a dragon," says Pia.

"Joe!" Angie slams her empty mason jar back on the bar. "Ten out of ten on the Cold Hard Toddy. What else do you have for us?"

"Anything you want, sweetheart."

"Joe, you're going to have to stop this flirting," says Angie matter-of-factly. "I have a boyfriend with whom I am desperately, passionately in love."

"And where is the lucky man tonight?"

"He's sailing in the Greek islands," says Angie.

Joe starts to laugh, then stops. "Sorry. I thought you were joking." He hands a drink over and Angie takes a big swig. "Amazing. Whiskey Sour?"

"With cassis," says Joe. "It's called a Sour Blush. Sweetness with an edge." He catches me looking at him and winks, and I quickly look away. Goddamnit. Why am I so self-conscious around guys? Especially the cool, self-confident, player kind of guys?

The band starts the sound check, and I take a moment to head to the bathroom.

Julia was right, Potstill is a total dump. The bathroom is down a dark hallway leading to a storeroom, and it's tiny and dingy as hell: two toilet cubicles behind doors barely hanging on to their hinges, a cracked sink, a dirty mirror, once-white grimy tiles, and a single hanging lightbulb. It stinks of cheap bleach, and the toilet seats look older than I am.

Ew. This is going to be a squat-and-hover pee.

I undo my jeans and go to peel them down, along with my underwear, you know, like you do.

But I can't. My jeans will come down, but my underwear is stuck.

What the heck?

Yanking them harder, I immediately squeal in pain. They won't budge.

I try again to yank, pull, and peel them off, but it's no good. They are soldered firmly to my . . . to my sugar, as Julia would say. To my ladygarden, my cha-cha, my fifi, my hoohoo, my, oh to hell with it, let's just be direct: my vagina.

They're not just stuck to the front either, but the entire thing . . . the undercarriage.

How on earth could that have—

Oh, my God.

I used that home bikini wax kit before I came out. And I guess I didn't use it properly.

Because hard wax is sticking my underwear to my entire vagina.

And I have to pee. Really. Badly.

CHAPTER 7

This would only happen to me.

Think logically.

Okay. I can't call the girls for help, I don't have my phone, and I can't just shout for them because they're all the way on the other side of the bar. Anyway, they'd find it insanely hilarious for *weeks* and Angie and Pia would tell everyone, including telling their boyfriends, and I don't want Aidan and Sam knowing that I did *this*.

I am never waxing again. Ever. Angie was right. Why the hell would we put something as destructive as wax on our most sensitive skin and rip out the hair and call it beauty? It's so weird! It's, like, über-fucking-weird!

Focus, Coco, focus.

Wax. What will melt wax?

I once read a Martha Stewart tip that when you get candle wax on your clothes, you should iron them with a newspaper over the top. The iron heats the wax, the newspaper absorbs it, and boom, problem solved.

But I can't iron my goddamn vagina, Martha.

Wait! The hand dryer! The hot air will melt the wax, right?

The hand dryer is all the way over next to the door, so I quickly shuffle out of the cubicle, take my jeans off one leg, then realize I don't want my jeans to touch the disgusting bathroom floor, so I take my jeans off entirely, keeping my shoes on so my bare feet don't touch it either. Oh, God, I need to pee, I need to pee . . .

Then, with one hand pressed against the door to keep it shut, I throw one leg up the wall like a ballet dancer stretching, and try to angle my underwear toward the nozzle.

Yes. I am trying to mount the bathroom hand dryer.

But I'm not flexible or tall, which means by the time the hot air reaches my . . . you know . . . it's not that hot or that intense.

"This is bullshit! This wouldn't melt an ice cube!" I cry out, and then quickly cover my mouth. Jesus. I need to shut up. What if someone comes in?

I now have to go so badly I could cry. Trying to distract myself with that little I-need-to-pee bobby-jiggle, I catch my reflection in the dirty mirror over the sink, and I look so ridiculous that I burst out laughing instead and nearly fall sideways, only righting myself at the last minute. Come on! Maybe the dryer will get hotter. I press it again, maintaining my ridiculous spread-eagle pose.

"Hello?" There's a male voice from outside. Shit! Before I can throw myself against it, the door pushes open.

Joe.

We meet eyes.

And then he looks down.

I can't move. It's like one of those dreams where you're cemented to the spot, unable to scream or run. But this is real. I was mounting a hand dryer and cackling like a madwoman.

I think I'm going to throw up.

Quickly putting both feet back on the ground, I hold my jeans over my body like a shield. OhpleaseGoddonotlethimseemythighs.

"What the hell—" Joe somehow gathers himself and quickly turns around, leaving the door open a crack for him to talk through. "I'm sorry, but what are you doing?"

"I . . . I um . . ."

Man up, Coco.

I mean, *woman up.*

"I administered a home bikini wax before I left my house this evening. And I need to go to the bathroom, but I seem to have leftover wax on my, um, and my underwear is now stuck to my—to my—to me." There. That was as matter-of-fact as possible.

There's a pause.

"I think I understand," Joe says.

"I don't know what to do, and the bathroom is so dirty. This is so bad, I'm, um, I'm freaking out."

"This bathroom is dirty?"

"Are you kidding? It's disgusting."

"Would you like some scissors?"

"Um . . . I don't see how that will help because it is *really* stuck. Tight. To my . . . all over . . . under . . . bits."

I close my eyes. Whywhywhy is this happening to me?

"Look, I don't want to get into a whole anatomy discussion with you, but I think perhaps you can use the scissors to alter your, uh, undergarments to relieve yourself of, hmm, your immediate urinary needs? And then deal with the rest when you get home."

"Okay," I say.

There is something so old-fashioned and delicate about the way

Joe is handling this, it's incredibly kind. If it had been Julia or Pia or Angie, they just would have screamed with laughter and made it even more of a *thing*.

He's back within thirty seconds, carrying scissors, and knocks politely at the door.

"Um . . . are you still in there?"

Where does he think I'll go?

I open the door an inch and he gives me the scissors, handle-first.

"Thank you!" I call.

"Anytime!" he calls back.

I suddenly start giggling helplessly. Anytime?

Still giggling, I carefully snip in a sort of H shape.

By the end, my underwear is in rags, there's a belt of elastic hanging uselessly around my waist, and I'm sweating slightly from stress, but I can finally pee.

Is there anything better than peeing when you've been waiting a long time? It's, like, painfully good.

Then I put my jeans back on, wash my hands and the scissors, and walk out. I currently have the remnants of a pair of underwear stuck to my vagina with hard wax. But I don't need saving. I don't need anyone to look after me. If I can handle this, I can handle anything.

I can sure as hell deal with Ethan when he turns up. That little asswipe.

I walk—no, I swagger, with the kind of arrogance someone with underwear rags stuck to her junk should not feel—back to the bar and slide the scissors down to Joe, who accepts them with a nod and a wink, just as the band starts its first song.

It's "Leader of the Pack," that hilariously dramatic song by the Shangri-Las. The drums and guitar dominate the opening chords, and Madeleine faces the crowd with a confidence that I've never seen in her before. Amy walks over and leans into the microphone.

Madeleine opens her mouth and starts to sing.

"Birds flying high, you know how I feel . . ."

It's "Feeling Good," the Nina Simone song. But with a rock-pop edge. Everyone is mesmerized.

Pia whispers: "We should put this shit on YouTube. She's a superstar." I nod. She totally is.

Tonight, more than ever before, I'm blown away by Maddy's voice. When Madeleine sings, you smile.

I look over behind the bar and see Joe checking his phone and uttering a soft "fock" under his breath. That's how "fuck" sounds in his accent: *fock*.

"Everything okay?" I ask.

I feel like we're war buddies after what we just went through together. He probably has post-traumatic stress disorder. I know I do.

Joe shakes his head. "My bartender was late and just texted to tell me he quit, and my boss has been hinting about selling the bar. Another shitty night and no staff would be the last straw. The end of Potstill."

I look around. Would anyone care if this placed closed? But I don't say that. "I bet you could easily get a job in another bar?"

"That's not the . . ." Joe sighs, picking up a lime and slicing it swiftly. "Potstill has been a bar, more than that, an *Irish* bar since 1891. It's got *stories*, you know? Nothing in Brooklyn has a real story anymore. Everything is new and shiny. I know Potstill is a shithole, but . . . it's got soul. It's worth fighting for."

I look around at the bar through new eyes. Maybe he's right. This really *is* a good bar. It just needs a little love and attention, that's all.

"I could do it." The words are out before I've even thought them through.

"You?" Joe looks up at me.

"I could be your emergency bartender tonight." This time, my voice is louder, stronger. I almost believe it myself.

"Really? Wait, what's your name again? How old are you? Do you have any bartending experience?"

"My name is Coco Russotti. I'm twenty-one. My only work experience is as a preschool assistant, but how can bartending be any harder than running around after small children?"

Bartending is much harder than looking after small children.

I discover that pretty fast.

But Joe helps me out. He shows me where the most frequently ordered drinks are, shows me how to work the register—though I screw that up more often than not—and where to stash my tips.

After an hour, I decide working in a bar is awesome. It's like a night out, without the stressful stuff. I get all the fun—Madeleine's band, Pia and Angie riffing each other, Julia high-fiving anything with a pulse—but I don't have to worry about saying or doing the wrong thing. In fact, I'm having more fun than I have on a night out, maybe ever.

When Spector finishes its first set and takes a break, Pia, Angie, and Julia are still on their barstools, acting like they own the place, holding court with some too-cool bearded Brooklynites.

"What is with the beards, you guys?" Angie is saying. "Are you aware that you all look like extras in a movie about the Gold Rush? I can't tell you apart with those things."

"What about the man bun? Do you secretly want to be a ballerina?" asks Pia. "And what's with all the plaid and the trapper hat? What do you call that, lumbersexual?"

"Maybe they symbolize that you don't work for 'the man'," says Angie, putting bunny ears around "the man." "Wow, you're all such independent thinkers. Except that you're identical."

"Harsh," mutters the guy with a beard and a man bun.

"Way harsh," agrees his buddy in the plaid and the trapper hat.

"I work for the man," says Julia, holding her drink up. "And I don't give a rat's ass—oops! Dropped my purse! Oh, thank you—" Julia meets eyes with a tall, cute, very clean-shaven guy in a suit who just picked up her purse. "Another corporate whore!" Jules holds her hand up. "Nice suit! What the hell are you doing in Brooklyn? Fivies!"

"Double fivies!" he replies, holding both hands up for a double high five.

"Hey!" Angie turns to Man Bun. "Being in touch with your feminine side doesn't mean touching my ass. Get lost."

Joe glances up from his frantic lime chopping. "Everything okay? That guy bothering you?"

"Everything is fine, Irish," says Angie, turning away from him just as the crowd clears a path for Madeleine to get to the bar. Funny, she has a little celebrity glow even off the stage. People are staring at her, and a couple of guys move in closer, trying to stand next to her. Wow. Madeleine has groupies.

"Can I get a Diet Coke, please, Joe?" Madeleine asks. "Coco? You're working here now?"

"Yes indeedy," I say.

"She's the best emergency bartender ever," says Joe. "So, Coco. You want to work here for real?"

"Yes." My voice squeaks. Goddamnit.

Joe frowns. "You sure you're up to it? The hours are long, the work is hard, and the patrons are scum." He grins at the crowd behind the bar, so charmingly that even calling them "scum" sounds like a compliment. "You need to be fearless. Are you fearless, Coco?"

I open my mouth to say yes, but then I look over at the front door of the bar and suddenly lose my voice.

Because Ethan, my boyfriend Ethan, my *cheating* boyfriend Ethan, has finally arrived.

He is smiling congenially in his smug little way, green rucksack on his back, tan windbreaker zipped up tight to the neck, hair fluffy as ever. As though nothing is wrong. As though he didn't cheat on me less than a week ago.

Forgetting to reply to Joe, I spin 180 degrees so my back is to the bar, and try to catch my breath. All week, while I've been hiding behind my phone, I never thought how it would feel to actually see him in the flesh.

It feels bad. It feels *really* bad.

But wait, why the hell am I freaking out like this? I *invited* him here. This is part of the revenge plan that Angie and I worked out on the stoop this afternoon. But I can't do it . . . I can't, I can't—

Yes, you can. You're in control.

That voice again. The spark.

You can handle Ethan. You can handle anything.

When I turn around, Ethan is standing importantly between Angie and Pia.

"Hello, mademoiselle!" Ethan calls, his voice unnecessarily loud and pretentious. "You're behind the bar? Marvelous! I'll have a chenin blanc!"

"This is a whiskey bar." My voice is barely more than a whisper.

Ethan claps his hands. "Excellent! Barkeep! A vat of your finest whiskey!" God, has he always been this much of a dick? What the hell was I thinking?

"What's your poison?" says Joe.

Ethan puffs up his chest, preparing for a speech. "Something Scottish, of course, Islay preferably—"

"*Of course?*" echoes Joe. "Ireland makes whiskey too."

"Irish whiskey?" Ethan wrinkles his nose, looking around the bar with sudden distaste. "I read a book—"

"Get out," I say, my voice suddenly loud and clear.

"What?"

"I saw you cheating on me." Everyone at the bar grows quiet, listening, all my roommates and Joe and a dozen strangers, but I don't care. "I saw you kissing a girl at the Jane Hotel last weekend."

"She—no—" Ethan stutters, blushing bright red.

"You *cheated* on me. I saw you. Don't lie. We're over, Ethan. I am breaking up with you."

My voice is shaking, and for some incomprehensible reason, my eyes fill with tears. I blink them quickly away. This is not a time for crying. This is a time for being angry.

My entire body tingles with shock that I'm doing this, high with the power of saying whatever the heck I want. "So get the . . . the *fuck* out of my bar and don't ever speak to me again."

"How dare you—"

"How dare *you*?" Julia turns on him. "You cheated on my perfect baby sister, you little dickslime."

"I—"

"Screw you, asshole." Julia throws her drink at him.

Splat. It hits him in the face, and for a moment, the entire bar goes completely silent. A split second later, before he can back away, Angie throws her drink at him too, and so does Pia. And then Madeleine's entire glass of Diet Coke. *Splat, splat, splat.*

Ethan doesn't even stop to wipe his face. He just picks up his rucksack and *runs* out of the bar.

The moment the door slams behind him, the entire bar erupts into applause.

"Jeez, people love a little bar theater," comments Angie.

I can't stop smiling. At this moment, I love everyone and everything in this bar. I love the world. This is what victory feels like.

Joe leans into me. "Nice work."

I grin at him. "Sorry about the drama."

"Don't worry about it. If you hadn't kicked that asshole out for cheating on you, I would have done it for badmouthing Irish whiskey."

Joe holds up two little glasses with a half inch of whiskey in them.

"A toast to breaking up. It's never a bad decision."

"Breaking up is never a bad decision," I repeat, taking the glass of whiskey.

"This is Kilbeggan. Smooth, warm, just sweet enough. Very easy for the first-timer."

I take a glass and try to maintain eye contact with Joe as we both drink.

The whiskey goes down easily. Then I start coughing helplessly. "*That* doesn't have a lot of fire?"

Joe grins. "You'll get used to it. Give it time. Welcome to Potstill. You're hired."

CHAPTER 8

"Guess who got laid last night?" Julia skips into the living room and flops down on the sofa between Angie and me. "Moi!"

"Ew," says Angie. "Have you showered?"

Julia throws her arms around Angie, rubbing her nose against Angie's cheek. "Nope."

"Dude. You stink of cock."

It's Saturday morning, and I've been watching TV and doing Facebook admin while Angie sews vintage buttons onto a jacket she made. It was so easy to defriend Ethan and everyone I met through him, it's like he never even existed. I can't believe I ever let him kiss me, I think, shutting my computer with a decisive good-riddance click and turning my attention to the girls.

I hear the front door slam, and Angie and I quickly look out the front window and see a guy bounding down the steps.

"That's him? What's his name?"

"Why didn't you ask your hook-up to stick around for breakfast?"

"Because I'm not that kind of girl. His name is Peter. And he was magnificent."

"Peter the Magnificent?" Angie snorts with laughter.

Julia sighs contentedly. She is red-faced from kissing, her hair a tangled nest, eyes glassy with happiness and hangover. "What are you making, Angelique? It's like being in little house on the goddamn prairie with all this sewing and peacefulness."

Angie smirks. "Seriously. Wash yourself. I could be pregnant just from sitting next to you right now."

"Gee whiz, is that how it happens?" Julia says, biting her finger in mock stupidity.

Angie arches her eyebrow and is about to say more when Pia and Madeleine walk in, fresh—or not so fresh—from SoulCycle. "Oh, God. Don't tell me how much you love your fucking spinning class. I don't want to hear it."

"Seriously, it's amazing, Angie," says Pia, who is glowing with good health. "Exercise is the best hangover cure."

Angie turns back to her sewing. "I grow weary of this shit."

Madeleine stretches, touching her forehead to her knees with remarkable ease. "I'm taking a shower."

"NO! I have to shower first!" shouts Julia. "I stink of cock! I stink of Peter the Magnificent!"

They both run for the hall, pushing one another. Madeleine easily wins, pounding up the stairs with glee. Rookhaven actually has two bathrooms, but only one shower is really good, and if both showers are on at once it does bad things to the water pressure, i.e., makes it disappear.

"Why are you smiling?" asks Pia.

I look up. "I am?"

I woke up thinking about Potstill and my new job and my new boss Joe, and I guess I've been smiling ever since. I'm in the best mood. My Ethan problem is dealt with. My job problem is dealt with. Which means I've taken the first steps toward changing my life.

But I don't say this out loud, of course. I'm just, you know, I'm not like that. Instead, I do a joyous wiggly dance in my seat, until Angie gives me a look and I stop.

Pia is now stretching in front of the TV with considerably less finesse than Madeleine.

"Why are you working out, Pia? You don't even need to lose weight," I say.

"Working out isn't always about weight loss, Coco. It makes me feel more in control of my life," says Pia, pulling herself up into a downward dog. "Maintaining a long-distance relationship and a career is hard. Working out regularly helps me handle my high-pressure existence."

Angie catches my eye and mouths "high-pressure existence"? I try not to laugh, but a bursting sound escapes me.

"Whatever, bitches." Pia lifts one leg back and up behind her, wobbling frantically. "The point is, I'm not thinking about Aidan. I'm focusing on my career. I have a big meeting today with that restaurant guy, Ray. He is considering partnering with me on a new food truck venture, so I'm taking him to this food truck festival thing, and—shit!"

Pia falls over with a squeak, and Angie laughs so hard she falls off the sofa.

This is what I love. I love all of us together, like nothing bad has ever happened or will ever happen. I love everyone being funny and silly. I don't want anything to change, ever.

At that moment, the doorbell rings. I skip to the front door to open it.

It's Vic, and a woman I don't recognize. She's in her forties— or fifties, I can't quite tell—and must be the daughter or maybe granddaughter of Vic's sister Marie, because she looks *just* like her: tiny, strong, and impish.

"Coco!" says Vic. "This is my niece Samantha, the smart one I was telling you about."

Samantha reaches out and shakes my hand. I'm never ready for handshakes; my hand is slippery and awkward.

"I was hoping we could talk to all of you girls. Is everyone home?"

"Julia and Madeleine are upstairs," I say. I don't add, "Julia is taking a shower because she smells like Peter the Magnificent's penis."

"We can wait!" Vic says. "Any muffins this morning, Coco?"

"I—oh, no, sorry, I haven't had time to bake this weekend," I say. For once, baking hadn't even occurred to me. "I'll get Julia."

I run up the stairs as fast as I can to Julia's room and open it without knocking. Julia is lying on her bed, wrapped in a towel, eyes closed, cuddling her old teddy, Dolch, to the side of her face. My mother always said Julia couldn't pronounce "doll" when she was little, so Dolch it is.

"Julia! Vic is here. With his niece."

Julia sits bolt upright, staring at me. "What? Oh. Vic. So?"

"They want to talk to us about something. I think it's important."

"Crap." Julia's hangover has eclipsed her postsex glow. She looks terrible. "I'm still waiting for Madeleine to finish. I'll be ten minutes. At least. I can't move fast, Coco. Don't make me move fast."

There's a knock at the door. "Shower's free!" shouts Madeleine.

"Entertain them," says Julia. "I'll be as quick as I can."

Ten minutes later we're all out on the back deck overlooking Vic's backyard, with cups of coffee and some old ginger snaps I baked last week. Strangely, my crippling shyness comes back around Samantha. I never feel this way around the girls or Vic, or even with Joe. Some people are just more intimidating than others.

"I can see the family resemblance, Samantha," says Angie, lighting a cigarette. "You have the same beautiful eyelashes as Vic."

Samantha laughs. I wish I could be as nonchalantly friendly as Angie. She's never shy. She just opens her mouth and says something cool and everyone thinks she's amazing.

"Hey, Vic, I'm picking up some lasagne later," says Pia. "Can I get you a—"

"Absolutely not!" says Samantha sternly. "He's having grilled chicken and steamed green beans for dinner and that's the end of it."

Everyone laughs.

Damn you, effortless small talk, why do you always evade me? I should say something. Stop thinking, Coco. Start *doing*.

I clear my throat.

Everyone looks at me.

But I have nothing to actually say.

Then, thank God, Madeleine comes out, her hair still wet from the shower, wearing a long-sleeve T-shirt and jeans, like always. Maddy doesn't wear tank tops even in the middle of summer.

"Hey, everyone," she says. "I'll just make myself a herbal tea and be right back."

"So, Coco. You work at a preschool, right?" says Samantha.

"Um . . ." I take a sip of coffee to stall and look up at the blue sky. It's that fresh premidday blue, when you know it's going to be superhot later on, but right now the day still feels sparkly and new. "I quit, actually. I work in a bar now."

"Preschool teaching is tough," says Samantha. "Everyone thinks it's all singing and sweetness, but it's not. It's intense and exhausting."

I glance at her curiously.

"I started as a preschool teacher," she continues. "I very quickly realized it just wasn't for me and went back to college and started again."

"You did?" I'm stunned. I never heard of anyone doing that. I mean, sure, there's grad school and medical school and MBAs and all that, but starting all over again from the beginning? "You mean like . . . a do-over?"

Samantha laughs. "Sure. A do-over."

"I don't even know what I'd do," I say. "Like, I don't know what I'd study."

"Ever looked into the options?" asks Vic, just as Madeleine comes back out with her tea.

Suddenly everyone looks at me.

Since when is this a counsel-Coco-on-her-career-choices session? I try not to answer, but they're all looking at me with such friendly openness, waiting.

But then, out of nowhere, comes the truth. "Um, well, I guess I would study literature or something. But it's so stupid. What job would I get after?"

Samantha smiles, throwing her hands into the air. "There are a million options."

"I don't want options," I say. "I want to *know*."

Samantha and Vic laugh as though I made a hilarious joke. "You'll figure it out as you go along, like the rest of us."

I gaze at her for a second, trying to digest this.

Figure it out as I go along? That's never been part of our family dialogue. According to my father, we have to know what we want and then make it happen. That's what Julia always does.

If we can't, then someone will tell us what we want and make it happen for us. I remember looking at colleges online—Smith, Vassar, Wellesley, Bowdoin—feeling the strangest mix of longing and fear. It was what I wanted most, and what I was most scared of. But my dad and Julia both thought it wasn't a good use of my time, that I needed something smaller, simpler, something that wouldn't stress me out.

But truthfully, they thought I wasn't smart enough. And I thought they must be right. Why did I listen to them? Why didn't I tell them what *I* wanted?

Because I didn't know how.

Maybe I *could* go back to college now . . .

But then I'd have to leave Rookhaven and my friends. Start over, in every possible way. I'd have to choose a college and share a room and meet new people. Oh, God, they'd probably just dismiss me straightaway. None of the girls would be friends with me, and I wouldn't get invited to parties. It would just be a more intense version of high school, a big clique from which I'll be excluded. I'd probably flunk out too, and the whole thing would be another huge mortifying mistake. And it would be all my fault.

How long have I been gazing into space, just thinking like this? Samantha and Vic are still looking at me. Angie is picking mascara out of her eyelashes, and Pia is texting.

I force a smile at Samantha. "Thanks. But I'm fine right where I am."

"Samantha!" Julia bounds out of the kitchen, her hair still wet from the shower, wearing shorts and a surprisingly booby tank top. "So nice to see you! Hi, Vic!"

"Julia," says Vic, smirking slightly at her bloodshot eyes and still-flushed face. "Late night?"

"Me? No." Julia can't meet his eyes. We Russottis are not good liars.

Samantha doesn't waste any time. "Well, girls, I'm here to ask your help. A group of my grad students are doing a study on millennials."

"Millennials?" says Vic.

"That's us!" Pia pipes up. "People born in the '80s and '90s."

"Right." Samantha nods. "And I'd like you and your friends to come in and tell us what it's like to be young, living in a big city, trying to start adult life."

"It blows," says Angie.

"Aren't your grad students in our generation too?" asks Julia.

"Yes, but they can't answer questions impartially and honestly," says Samantha. "Lying little bastards." We all look at her in shock.

"I'm kidding! Honestly, I'm just trying to get a good cross section of people. Plus, it pays a hundred dollars!"

"Is this a trap?" says Angie. "So you can paint us as a useless, self-absorbed generation of brats?"

"Angie!" Pia and Julia are shocked.

"Sorry, Samantha, but it's not my bag." Angie stubs out her cigarette and stands up. "I'm not a lab rat. You can't study me."

"That's really not the—"

"See you soon, Vic." Angie kisses Vic on the cheek, and a moment later she's gone.

There's an awkward silence.

"Um . . . well, I think it's cool," says Julia.

"Me too," says Pia, less convincingly.

Samantha claps her hands, a gesture that reminds me of Vic. "I'm glad you think so! Right, so, the study is taking place on a Friday in August—"

"I work on Fridays," says Madeleine. "And now I gotta go. I'm meeting Amy. Good luck."

A second late, Madeleine vanishes.

"Sorry, Samantha," says Pia. "Normally I'd love any excuse to talk about myself for an hour, but I have a job."

Samantha looks at Julia and me. "Looks like it's just you two."

"I can't do it either, I have to work, I—" Julia suddenly looks very pale, like she's going to throw up.

"Are you okay?" asks Samantha.

"I feel strange," says Julia, her voice soft and whispery.

Pia immediately takes her by the wrist to check her pulse, though I don't know why, since obviously if she was dead we'd know by now. "Have you eaten today?"

"I haven't eaten since . . ." Julia's voice trails off, as though finishing her sentence is too hard.

"Coco, get her a juice," says Vic quickly, and I run into the kitchen. By the time I've come back with the drink, Julia's lying flat out on the deck. She's breathing quickly, and her mouth and lips are a strange pale blue.

"She fainted!" Pia likes to make dramatic, obvious statements sometimes.

"I'm okay," Julia mumbles, her eyes closed. "I'm just not feeling too great." She takes a sip of Coke, then coughs, spitting most of it back out onto the deck. "It was a busy week . . . at work. Just . . . a little tired."

Vic shakes his head. "Julia, not for nothing, but not eating and not sleeping is about the stupidest thing you can do."

"My boss says sleep is a state of mind," murmurs Julia.

Samantha turns to me. "Which bank does Julia work at?"

I tell her.

Samantha purses her lips. "One of my neighbors' kids worked there. Had a breakdown. It's not normal to work that many hours a week. It's dangerous."

Within minutes, Julia's blue tinge has dissipated, and she looks normal again. Pale, but normal.

"Sorry, everyone. I'm fine, honestly, I'm fine. I'll just take it easy today."

Vic sighs, looking at his watch. "If you're really sure you don't want to go to the hospital, then Samantha and I had better get going. We're headed to Hoboken."

"I really would love to help with your study, Samantha, but I just don't have the time," says Julia. "Coco can, though."

I can? I instinctively want to say, "No, I goddamn can't, I have a life too," but I don't know why. So I just nod. Anyway, she's right. I have nothing else to do with my days. And extra cash sounds nice.

Samantha swaps numbers with me. "Excellent! Thank you so much. I can't wait!"

"Take it easy, little Julia, okay?" says Vic, standing up. "No more all-nighters."

When Vic and Samantha leave, Angie comes back out to the deck and lights up again.

"Smoking will kill you," says Julia.

"So if I quit I'll live forever?"

"I can't believe you fainted from too much sex," says Pia. "Like seriously. How big *is* he?"

"I didn't!" Julia starts laughing. "I hadn't eaten or slept!"

"Oh, mah Lord . . ." Pia puts on a Tennessee Williams voice. "Ah was *overcome* by the fluttahs of *exhaustion* after a nahght of *lurve*-may-kin' . . ."

"Ah'm *shakin'* from pleasure lah-ke a *magnolia* bush in a *summer* storm," adds Angie.

"Magnolias grow on trees, you moron," says Julia, grinning. "I'm fine. Drama over."

"When Ah'm around, the *dramah* is *nevah ovah*," says Pia.

Then my phone rings.

Joe. From Potstill.

I quickly turn my back on everyone else, let it ring four times—the way Pia taught me—and then answer as coolly as I can.

"This is Coco . . . oh, hi, Joe!"

Angie makes a whooping sound ending in an "ow!" as though Pia punched her.

"Hey, Coco. Can you work today around four?"

"Sure," I say.

"Cheers, Coco. You're the best. Well, after my mother. She's the absolute best. But you're a close second."

Moments later, I hang up, giggling, and turn back to the girls. They're all looking up at me expectantly.

"Sounds like someone's got a date!" says Pia.

"Better than that," I say. "I've got a job."

CHAPTER 9

The first thing Joe does when I get to work is hand me $20 and send me on a coffee run.

"Iced coffee, please," he says. "And some cake. Something that tastes homemade but looks manly, you know?"

"A manly cake," I repeat. "What does that mean?"

"No frosting," says Joe, like it's the most obvious thing in the world. "Maybe one of those crumb cake things you New Yorkers love so much. You know, the first time someone offered me a crumb cake, I was, like, a cake the size of a crumb, are you fecking mad?"

On my way to get us iced coffees and crumb cake, I take a quick detour to the old hardware store on Court, the one that's been around for generations, and buy the yellowest lightbulbs I can find.

Then I head to the old Italian bakery near President Street. There's no crumb cake, but I buy some biscotti, because they seem like the kind of tough cookie he was talking about. I return to the bar with my purchases, feeling exuberant.

"Biscotti are manly?" Joe looks doubtful.

"Yup," I say. "They're practically butch. Now. You need to get a better cleaning service, and we need to change the lighting."

"Why?" Joe bites into a biscotto. "Ouch. Are biscotti supposed to *hurt*?"

"Yes." I try sounding as self-assured as my roommates always do. "And Joe, girls want lighting that makes them feel pretty. This lighting is too harsh. We also like bathrooms that don't feel like they might give you the plague."

Together, we change the lights in the bar, and suddenly, like magic, Potstill is transformed from bleak and ugly to warm and charming. Even the chipped bar looks chic. (Well, chic-ish.)

"I feel prettier," says Joe, batting his lashes. "I really do. Do I look prettier?"

I try to think of a good comeback, but I just sort of giggle inanely instead. Goddamnit. Why can't I think of funny things to say when I need them?

Then we change the bathroom lights (while I try not to think about the underwear-waxed-to-my-vagina situation) and I add something else highly necessary I bought in the hardware store: a soap dispenser to affix to the wall. I'm fast running out of my pathetic savings from my preschool job, but to hell with it: I suddenly want to help Joe, to do everything I can so Potstill has a fighting chance at survival. And that means a decent toilet with nice soap.

"This looks so much better!" I exclaim.

"I found this the other day in the storeroom," says Joe, holding up a huge old-fashioned metal fan. "If we have this at the back of the bar, and we open the windows at the front, it might not be so stuffy, right? And it looks kind of—"

"Industrial chic." I try to sound like I know what I'm talking about. "Totally."

Next I sit at the bar, while Joe trains me in the art of bartending. The top whiskeys, the register, which glasses go where and what we use them for, how the ice machine works . . .

Then he invites me to join him behind the bar.

After confidently charging around the place changing lightbulbs and planning décor for the last hour, I suddenly feel strangely nervous. There's something physically and emotionally intense about being in this narrow little bar area with Joe when there are no customers here.

It's such a tiny space. I am acutely aware of how close he is to me at all times, of where I'm looking, what I'm doing with my hands, the fact that I seem to be constantly in his way, how tall he is, how . . . attractive. I mean, I don't like him like *that*. I really don't. And yet . . . I feel sort of giggly and shy around him, like I find myself smiling so much around him that my cheeks hurt. What is that about? Lame.

I clear my throat. "That's it? We only make five cocktails?"

"No, we make dozens of cocktails, but you can't learn more than five in a shift," says Joe. "Plus, now you and I have to drink the five we made. More than five and we'd be langered."

"Langered?"

Joe grins. "Irish slang. Drunk."

"Oh." I look up at Joe. His dark hair is clean but about two months overdue for a haircut and sticks up at weird angles. And he's wearing a plaid flannel cowboy-type shirt. (Actually, I think that if you're a dude, you have to own a plaid flannel shirt when you live in Brooklyn. Like, by law.)

" 'Langer' also means something else . . ." He points to his crotch.

"How confusing," I say, trying not to look at Joe's crotch.

"Indeed. Right, Let's start the demonstration." Joe grabs a glass. "Coco, may I introduce the Whiskey Sour? Now, we make our whiskey sours like the good Lord intended: fresh lemon juice, simple syrup, ice, and a good bolt of whiskey. Mix with anger, pour with love . . ." He shakes the cocktail shaker furiously and then delicately cracks it open and pours the frothy concoction into a chilled mason jar. "See? Go on, try it."

I take a sip, and gasp at the icy bitterness. "Wow. I mean, yum, but that is *sour*." I pause. "And I suppose, thus the name. Whiskey Sour."

"Right. My God, the brains on you. Genius."

I stifle a snort of laughter. Joe takes a slug, hands the glass back to me, then starts the next demonstration. I can't believe Joe is going to all this effort to make cocktails just for me. He's so hot and funny and—pay attention, Coco.

"An Old-Fashioned. Sugar cube, Angostura bitters, water, crush the cube, muddle . . ."

He is grinding the sugar with such an intense frown that I start laughing, and he looks up in surprise.

"Muddling isn't funny. Muddling is serious. Now, add the whiskey, squeeze the orange . . . voilà. Taste."

"Okay." I cough helplessly. It's disgusting. "Um, a little strong."

"You'll learn to love it." He mixes another in silence, while I look on and try to learn. "Try this. Rob Roy. Scotch, sweet vermouth, a little Angostura bitters, and a cherry."

"I love maraschino cherries!" I take a big slurp and immediately spit it right back into the glass. "Urgh! That's even more disgusting than the Old-Fashioned!"

Joe cracks up.

I am mortified.

"Oh, my God. I'm so sorry, that was just, um, automatic, I, um . . ." I'm babbling and I can't stop, shut up, Coco, *shut up*.

"You might like the next one better. A Whiskey Smash. Fresh mint, a quarter of a lemon, and simple syrup. Smush them down—"

"—is that a technical bartending term for anything smashed? 'Smush'?"

"Yes, smartypants, it is a highly technical term. You need to smush before you smash."

I giggle and hiccup at the same time.

Joe glances at me. "Are you langers already? You must be. I wasn't *that* funny . . . Strain, add whiskey, ice, voilà. Drink it."

I pick up the glass and take a long swig. It's very light and refreshing to gulp, and before I know it, I've drunk almost the whole thing.

"That's my favorite." I feel so light-headed and giggly. Drunk! At work! I *am* wild. According to Pia, anyway.

Joe holds up two limes. "I think you'll like the next one the most. It's a Rickey. Squeeze all the juice from both limes into the glass, add ice, whiskey, club soda, and . . . voilà!" He hands it over, and I take a sip.

"Nope, I like the Whiskey Smash more." I hand back the Rickey and pick up what's left of the Smash. "Yummy. Smash."

"I think you just like saying 'smash,'" says Joe.

"No, no, I like the mint. I grow mint in an herb planter in my kitchen. I like herbs."

"*Erbs?*" Joe takes a slug of the unloved Rob Roy. "In Ireland we pronounce the 'h.' *Herb.*"

"Herb? That's an old guy's name." My giggles are interrupted by hiccups. And then I start giggling again.

"You *are* langers." He smacks himself on the forehead. "Bad Joe. Bad. All right, make yourself another one. Go on. You're smart, you can do it. I'll watch."

I try to control my giggles long enough to make a Whiskey Smash. *Calm down, Coco.* I love the way Joe doesn't seem to take anything too seriously. And I like the way he said I was smart. For some reason, people thinking I'm smart makes me feel smart, and people thinking I'm dumb encourages me to make stupid mistakes. I wonder if that's normal.

"Why don't we do bar snacks?" I ask as I muddle the sugar and mint.

"No kitchen," Joe says. "I tried to convince Gary to get a popcorn machine, but he refused."

"That is an amazing idea!" I say. "I love popcorn. I put sea salt and dark chocolate chips on mine."

"What is sea salt, anyway?" says Joe. "I never heard of sea salt before about six years ago, did you? I mean, what did everyone put on their locally sourced hand-cut fries before sea salt was invented?"

"I think the other kind is called table salt," I say.

"*Salt* made from *tables*?!"

I don't think I've ever laughed this much around a guy. I can't tell if it's the Irish accent or the booze. Probably a little of both.

At that moment, an older guy walks in, and I can tell by the disinterested way he takes a seat at the bar that he's not here for a drink. Joe, suddenly nervous, quickly clears away the detritus from our cocktails and introduces us. It's the owner of Potstill, Gary.

Gary doesn't even meet my eyes, just takes his phone out and answers a text, sighing deeply, while Joe, unbidden, gets him a seltzer with lime. Gary looks like an ex-boxer who eats way too many subs. Bug eyes, receding pale hair, a nondescript goatee that isn't bushy enough for Brooklyn.

Gary takes a long drink, burps loudly, and finally looks up. "I'm closing the bar."

"What?" Joe is shocked. "Why? Last night was huge. This could be a great live music venue—"

"People who watch music don't drink whiskey," says Gary, with total confidence.

"We could offer other drinks, expand the bar—"

"There is no 'we,' Joe. There's only 'me.' I own the place. You just manage it. Don't forget that."

Wow, Gary is an asshole.

Joe takes a deep breath, clearly trying to stay calm, and finally asks, "When?"

"I'll put it on the market at the end of the summer. I'm going to my place in Nantucket until then. My wife's having another fucking baby. She refuses to stay in the city."

Did he just say *another fucking baby*? Charming.

"Okay," Joe is suddenly very interested in polishing already-clean glasses. "Thanks for letting me know."

Gary stands up, drains his seltzer, and, without even saying good-bye, leaves the bar. The door slams behind him.

There's a long silence.

"I can't believe that's it," mutters Joe finally. "Potstill is dead."

"Maybe someone will buy it and see the potential . . ." My voice trails off into nothingness.

"No one is going to look at the numbers and keep this bar open, Coco. They could make a lot more money ripping the guts out and building something new."

Joe sighs, rubbing the bridge of his nose, a gesture that reminds me of Julia. She texted earlier: she's recovered from Peter the Magnificent and is now out with Pia and Angie, while Madeleine rehearses with her band. I'd usually be with them, I guess, or maybe in the old days with Ethan while he monologued at me, teaching me things I didn't want to learn. I'm glad I'm here, though. This feels like the right place to be.

"If I could do one thing right now, it would be to make this bar a success," says Joe wistfully.

"If I could do one thing right now, I'd . . ." My voice trails off. I can't tell Joe the truth. He'd just think I was silly. And I don't want just one thing, I want three. I want to be thin. I want to fall in love. I want to figure out what I'm going to do with the rest of my damn life. And I have no idea how to do any of the above.

"You want another Whiskey Smash?" I ask.

Joe grins at me. "Sure."

As I make them, Joe takes his iPod out of his back pocket.

"You know what annoys me most about Gary? He doesn't even

like music. He agreed to let Spector play here because he owed someone in the band for helping him out with some pot deal." Joe reaches up to an ancient set of speakers and stereo system. "I don't particularly like pot. But I fucking love music."

A new song comes over the loudspeakers. "This is MGMT," he says. "Time to Pretend."

"It's great . . ." I say. But Joe isn't listening.

Then he looks back at me. "Let's get langers."

CHAPTER 10

So we do.

By the time the bar closes, we've sampled most of the whiskeys behind the bar, plus three more Whiskey Smashes (me) and four more Rob Roys (Joe).

A few more patrons come in, but each time, as if on cue, the previous patrons leave. Which means practically no actual bartending is done. Instead, we listen to music, talk, and, you know, drink. I can't think of the last time I had this much fun.

Later, sometime around midnight when the bar's been empty for over an hour, Joe makes the executive decision to close up. I go to the bathroom and realize I'm swaying slightly and feel deliciously fuzzy. Being a bit drunk is fun. But it also feels naughty . . . I mean, I'm at *work*.

"I thought it was illegal to be drunk behind a bar," I say as Joe locks up the stockroom and turns off the lights.

"No, that's behind a wheel," says Joe. "Jesus, I'm starving," he says, pronouncing it *schtarvin*. "How about a late-night snack?"

And as he holds open the door for me to walk out into the balmy June night, I realize something.

I'm on a *date*.

You know, kind of.

I'm with a guy and we're going for food after drinking cocktails. That makes it a date. Right? Right.

Funny thing about walking around in this happy tipsy state: it feels like it doesn't take long to get anywhere. We're heading to some diner in downtown Brooklyn. The whole time, Joe grills me about everyone in the house. I tell him about Pia's food truck empire, Julia's intense workaholism, Madeleine's accountant/rocker dichotomy, and Angie's fledgling fashion career. It's easy talking about my friends. So much more interesting than telling him about me. And I'm having the best time. I cannot stop smiling.

Eventually we reach the diner, a grubby little place with unflattering white lighting and torn faux-leather booths. We take seats at the counter.

"Two disco fries, two chocolate shakes," Joe tells the disinterested waiter. I raise an eyebrow. "What? I come here all the time. Can't I order for you?"

The old me would have just shrugged, accepted what he ordered, and then not really eaten it anyway. I never ate in front of Ethan; it made me feel really self-conscious and gross. But to hell with all that. This is the new me. And I don't want disco fries and a chocolate shake.

"I'm a grown woman. I'll order for myself," I say. "I'll have French toast with bananas and a black-and-white shake."

"What's a black-and-white shake?" Joe asks.

"Vanilla ice cream, chocolate syrup."

"Sounds perfect. I'll have that too, please, instead of my chocolate milk shake. But I'm sticking with the fries. Don't try to take an Irishman away from his potatoes. We'll fight you for them. Now, sir, do you have any cake?"

"No."

"No cake!" Joe cries out in mock horror. "The shame of it. Right, just the fries and the shake."

The waiter refuses to be charmed by Joe's banter and mooches off miserably. I am completely enchanted by it. I just have no idea what to say in response.

We lapse into silence.

Suddenly I feel very sober. Wow, this *is* a date. I broke up with Ethan last night and I'm already on a date!

Shit. I don't think I'm ready to eat in front of this guy.

"What's Angie's boyfriend like?" asks Joe.

"Sam? He's lovely." Joe's face falls. "Sorry! Um, I'm sure she'd be into you if it wasn't for him."

Joe shrugs. "Shit happens."

Never mind. This isn't a date. He likes Angie. Or would like her, if she was available. Which means he doesn't like me, not like that, anyway.

Well, at least that makes it easy.

"Story of my life," continues Joe. "I'm never in the right place at the right time."

"Neither am I," I say. "In fact, everything I've done with my so-called adult life is wrong. I'm twenty-one. And I've made so many mistakes already."

"I don't call them mistakes," says Joe. "I call them life experiences."

"Like what?" I can't stop myself from asking. "What experiences?"

"Falling in love with someone who didn't love me back."

Joe says it so easily, like it's not embarrassing. I guess that's confidence.

"Um, I've done that too," I say.

"Not a life experience to repeat, right?" Joe grins as our milk shakes arrive.

"I worked in a job I hated because my dad thought it was the right choice for me," I say. "That was not a life experience to repeat either."

"What did you want to do instead?"

"I don't know," I say. "I guess I would like to do something with books. But that just sounds kind of stupid."

"It doesn't sound stupid to me. *Someone* has to work with books. Otherwise they wouldn't exist."

"Did you go to college?" I ask, to take the subject off me again.

"I did indeed. Then, when I graduated, Ireland was a fucking disaster area . . . So I started working in bars to fund my traveling and ended up here."

"What did you study?"

"Engineering. But I don't want to be an engineer."

"Me too!" I clear my throat. "I mean, I wasn't an engineer, but I studied early childhood. But I don't want to be a preschool teacher."

"Sucks to be us."

"Yep," I say, then, trying to cheer him up, add, "At least you love bartending."

"Love bartending? No. I love that bar. There's a difference. That's why I've been trying to turn it into a music venue." Joe rubs his temples. "Probably sounds stupid, but I want to manage bands. When I hear a great band playing, my skin tingles, my heart starts beating really fast, and I think . . . I think . . . well, I don't know. Maybe everyone who loves music feels that way." He trails off uncertainly. "And everyone loved Spector, right?"

"Yes! It was amazing!"

"They have so much potential. They should be writing their own stuff, figuring out what they want to say, and I can help them do that . . . I mean, I think I can, you know, as their manager." Joe suddenly seems strangely vulnerable. I want to hug him. "Madeleine is the real deal."

"I totally agree," I say. "Do bands often employ managers?"

"Only the successful ones." Joe grins, as though I made a joke.

I feel embarrassed suddenly. I wasn't making a joke, I just didn't know that bands needed managers.

There is so much I don't know about how everything in the real world works. All I know is what my dad and Julia and teachers have told me, what they think I should know. And they don't know *everything*. I mean, they're not stupid, obviously. They're really smart. But the world is just too big and messy and complicated for *anyone* to know *everything* about it.

How can I ever know what I want to do with my life if I don't even know what jobs exist? How will I find my way?

"Fuck! I can't believe Gary is really going to close the bar." Joe presses his forehead to the Formica counter. I make a face. The counter isn't exactly sparkling with cleanness. "He won't change his mind. The earnings are shite."

"What if you impressed him with how successful it is over the next few months?" I ask. "Like, if you can turn around the financials, I mean, um, the finances, numbers, you know what I mean, then he'll have to reconsider, right?"

Joe grins. "What do you think I've been trying to do? I've worked my ass off on that cocktail list."

"Oh."

Then silence falls again as our food arrives, so we can get to the more important business of eating. At first I feel nervous about eating in front of him, but after a minute of taking tiny unsatisfying nibbles while Joe takes great big chomps, I relax. And then I realize how hungry I am.

"God, I love American food." Joe sighs happily.

"You love this?" I say, gesturing to the flaccid French toast and wilting fries.

"Yes. Love it." Joe takes a sip of milk shake. "Ahhh . . . black-and-white milk shake! Where have you been all my life?" He sounds so passionately grateful that I start laughing again.

When we're done—throwing my is-it-or-isn't-it-a-date? quandary a curveball—Joe won't let me pay. "I'm your boss. It's my job," he says, waving off my money.

"No," I protest.

"Too late." He places cash on the counter and takes me by the arm. "C'mon. I'll walk you home."

"You don't have to," I say.

"I'm your boss," he says again. "Safety first."

It's definitely, absolutely *not* a date. That's the clear message. He prefers Angie to me. He's my boss. And it's not a date.

We walk for a while. The summer air is soft and warm on my skin. I glance up at Joe, at his scruffy stubble and wild-man hair. He's so easy to be around. Maybe we'll be friends.

My first ever real male friend. Apart from Vic, of course.

"So, where do you live?"

"Carroll Gardens. Union Street," I say.

"You live in *brownstone* Brooklyn?" says Joe in mock admiration. "Jesus, do you realize how much better that makes you than the rest of us?"

I laugh. I've laughed so much tonight, I feel slightly euphoric. "My sister and I inherited the house. Rookhaven. We could never afford it otherwise. And it's kind of run-down, but we love it. It feels like home."

"That's how I feel about my apartment . . . Oh, wait. No, no, I do not feel that way about my apartment at all. It is a piece of shit. I think that the Craigslist ad for it actually read 'piece of shit.'"

I crack up again.

"The way you laugh reminds me of a movie star, you know, like from the '30s or '40s or something," says Joe suddenly. "I just can't think which one. One of those platinum-blond bombshells.

"Really!?" My delight manages to beat down whatever self-consciousness was edging its way in. "I love old movies."

"So does my mom. She makes me watch them with her whenever I'm home."

"Your father won't watch them with her?"

"My father is dead," Joe says.

For a long moment, I can't think of how to respond. His father died?

"When?"

"When I was ten."

We're on a quiet patch of the street now, and Joe's face is almost entirely in shadow, his voice low and expressionless. Suddenly he seems older, more serious. More tired.

"How did he die?"

"Car accident."

"I . . ." I pause. "My . . . my mother died."

"When?"

"When I was nine." The word gets stuck in my throat, like always. "Cancer."

I can't remember the last time I said this out loud to anyone. Most of the people I talk to already know about my mom. And with new people, I avoid conversations about mothers so I don't have to mention it. Ethan never even thought to ask, never cared.

As Joe and I turn the corner to Union Street, I feel all the space between us disappear.

So what if he's a player? And he's Irish and older than me and way hotter and cooler and funnier than I could ever be? I understand who he is, how he feels, what he thinks about in his darkest moments. I know, because he's just like me. I totally get him.

The thing about grief is you never really let go of it, you never forget it exists. You just get better at pretending everything is okay.

You get better at structuring your life so there's a dozen different layers of protection that prevent anything bad from touching you again. I've always hid behind my dad, my sister, my books, my baking.

Everything around me holds me together. Because by myself I would fall apart.

And yet . . . I don't have any of those things right now, and I'm still together. I'm not falling apart.

I wonder why.

The Brooklyn night around us is so silent, all I can hear is the soft strain of music from one of the brownstones across the street, and suddenly I realize we're home. We're outside Rookhaven.

I stop walking.

I have an insane, almost unstoppable urge to give Joe a hug. Almost. But I can't. It would be too awkward. Joe is about a foot taller than me so it would be like hugging a tree. And we only just met, and he's my boss (which he insists on reminding me of every chance he gets). And he's like this big, messy, overgrown wild man, he doesn't exactly seem like the touchy-feely type. And he may not want a hug. Unwanted hugs are the worst. And, and, and I just . . . I can't. I'm too scared.

So I drop my gaze, turn, and start walking up our stoop.

But just as I reach the second step, Joe grabs me by the hand, pulls me sharply around to face him, and wraps his arms around me, tight.

A hug. A real hug. The kind of hug you just *sink* into.

Joe is so much larger than me that his arms totally encircle me. I barely reach his chest. I'm trapped, held tight, unable to move away, my body pressed tightly against his. I can feel the heat of his body and my heart beating so hard and so loud that he must be able to feel it too.

"Oh, Coco . . ." murmurs Joe. His voice is low and intense, all traces of that showy jovial charm gone.

This is so surreal. Joe, my hot, smart-ass Irish charmer of a boss, a guy I met *yesterday*, for Pete's sake, is standing on my front stoop, *holding* me.

I can hear the rhythm of his breath, feel the warmth of his body through his shirt. I can smell the soapy cleanness of his clothes and the tiniest hint of something else. Aftershave? Shampoo?

I can't remember ever feeling this close to anyone before.

Then Joe pulls away slightly and looks down, staring into my eyes, his face so serious, more serious than I could ever have imagined him looking at me.

I gulp.

He's going to kiss me.

After what feels like an agonizing wait—seconds have never felt so long—Joe's head moves an inch closer, then another inch, and another. He stops, just a breath away, before our lips finally touch.

Pia once told me that kissing a guy is like kissing every other guy, except when it's really good, and then it's like you forget what it was ever like to *not* kiss him. I totally agree: this is a whole new kind of kissing. It's like I always imagined it should be but wasn't, the kind of kissing that makes all your senses tingle, that makes you simultaneously burn and shiver all over.

Eventually we break apart.

"Jesus, that was unexpected." Joe runs his fingers through his hair, slightly flustered.

"I've never kissed someone who knew how to kiss before," I say honestly.

Joe laughs, then pulls me in closer, wrapping his arms around me again.

"Do you want—" My voice is so quiet I can hardly hear it, and I can't quite believe I'm about to say it, but I can't stop myself. "Do you want to come upstairs?"

"Yes."

CHAPTER 11

Naturally, the girls bust me pretty much immediately the next morning.

I tiptoe into the kitchen, feeling light-headed from the sudden influx of sunshine through the kitchen windows.

I need water. And I need it bad.

Sex is exhausting, am I right?

I expected the kitchen to be empty, but instead I find Angie and Madeleine padding around happily in bare feet, fixing breakfast. Angie is having toast and eggs; Madeleine is making some kind of gross-looking shake with almond milk and chia seeds and spinach.

When I walk in, they both look up. Angie does an overly dramatic comic double-take.

"You had *da sex* last night!" shouts Angie.

"I did . . . not?" I'm the worst liar. I start giggling helplessly.

"You did," says Madeleine. "Your hair's a mess, you've got stubble rash. And you look happy."

"Okay," I admit, slightly embarrassed. I wasn't used to being on this end of the conversation. "I had the sex."

"*Da* sex," Angie corrects me.

"Da sex."

The girls scream with delight. "Details. Everything."

"Um, well, you know, Joe and I started drinking at the bar, and, um . . ." I raise my eyebrows innocently. "I guess it just happened?"

"Nice work," says Angie. "Sam is, obviously, my favorite flavor. But Joe has something."

"Yeah, he has something," agrees Madeleine. "The kind of guy who walks into a room and people notice him."

"He has that *thing*," says Angie. "That spark. Confidence without arrogance."

"He's confident because he probably sleeps with hundreds of women," I say. "I'm just another notch on his bedpost."

Angie shrugs. "All I meant was that he has charisma."

Madeleine takes a tiny sip of her shake and looks up at me. "So do you think it's serious?"

"Oh, fuck, no," I reply without thinking. "Fuck, I just cursed. Oh, shit, I cursed again." I clap my hand over my mouth before I can say anything else.

Angie laughs so hard she splutters coffee everywhere. "So you're just using him? Just a fuck buddy?"

"Um . . ." I pause. "I hate that word."

"Not delicate enough for you? 'Casual intercourse partner'? That better?"

I laugh, but my brain is racing.

Somehow, in the cold light of day, I know that I don't want to date

Joe. I know it without even thinking about it. I'm attracted to him, really, I think he's gorgeous, but it wasn't . . .

I don't know, it wasn't *it*.

Don't get me wrong, I like him. I understand him, completely. We have this strange, undeniable connection that comes from both losing a parent. And I want to hang out with him and maybe have sex with him sometimes, but that's it. I'm not even sure why I know, but I just . . . I *know*. It's too easy. Too relaxed. I don't get butterflies when I think about him. I always get butterflies when I like a guy. I'm, like, the queen of butterflies.

The point is, Joe is naked in my bed, but I don't want to date him, because this isn't love. It's lust. All-consuming lust. And it's exactly what I need to find the new me. The wild me.

I clear my throat. "Yeah. I guess I am using him. I mean, we're using each other."

At some point during the night—I think maybe at the moment he kissed me—I stopped wondering all that stupid is-this-a-date? and is-he-out-of-my-league? shit. I stopped wondering what he was thinking. I stopped wondering if he liked me.

I just thought, *I want him*. And I am going to, well, you know . . . *have* him.

So I did.

And it was absogoddamnlutely awesome.

I kind of wonder if this makes me a bad person. A fallen woman.

But why should it? Why do guys get to enjoy sex without guilt or love or relationships, and girls don't? What's the big deal? It's safe. We used condoms. It doesn't make me feel bad about myself. He wasn't taking advantage of me, and I wasn't taking advantage of him. He clearly has a lot of casual sex, he wasn't, like, exploiting me. We're not in some silly Nathaniel Hawthorne–inspired high school situation where he'll tell people and everyone will talk about it because they have nothing better to do.

We're grown-ups. We're friends. Joe isn't judging me, he clearly does this sort of thing all the time. No one is judging me except myself. There's a strange power in that.

And by the way . . . it was so *fun*.

We were in the dark, which made me so much more confident. And Joe kept complimenting my body, and was so funny and silly and sweet that I was smiling and laughing the whole time. It was so different from my first time with Eric that it was like having a different kind of sex altogether.

Urgh, sex with Eric. That entire experience is like bile in my memory. Not just because it was so cold and strange and awful—and it was, truly, it was awful, and I knew I was being used, even as I hoped with all my heart that he liked me, I knew I was being used—but because of what happened afterward. Abortion.

Even the word makes me feel bad.

If this was some lame after-school special, you know, or some lame TV show made by old men in suits who have never experienced anything but want to tell everyone else what to do, then the abortion would be a huge mistake that ruins my life. That's the only narrative that unwanted pregnancy is allowed to have. But this is reality. I talked it over with Pia and Angie so many times, and they really helped me get to the point where I can say: I will not be damaged by that experience forever.

I am still me.

No matter what happens, I will always be me.

And last night I felt so comfortable with Joe, and he knew exactly what he was doing, and that little fire deep in my gut just got bigger and stronger and brighter until—

"I totally came."

"WHAT?"

Shit. Did I just say that out loud?

Angie and Madeleine are shrieking when Pia stumbles in with swollen, bloodshot eyes. She's still wearing her clothes from yesterday and has bed hair to rival mine.

Immediately, there's a collective gasp of shock.

We just stare at her.

She ignores us, going straight to the refrigerator.

"Aidan is in San Francisco," says Angie, finally, in a very quiet voice. "Where have you been? And with who?"

"Whom," corrects Madeleine.

"Whatever."

Without answering, Pia pulls out the almond milk. "Who the fuck is lactose intolerant this week?"

"Was it Ray? It was Ray, right?" Angie is furious.

"Who is Ray?" whispers Madeleine.

"That ancient restaurant asshole," says Angie. "Not her boy-friend."

"I don't want to talk about it." Pia rests her forehead against the cool refrigerator, as though she doesn't quite have the strength to hold herself up anymore.

"I cannot *believe* you cheated on Aidan."

Pia grabs a bottle of Coca-Cola. "Don't fucking judge me, Angela."

"Don't fucking call me Angela."

Pia ignores her and takes a swig of Coke.

"Are you going to tell him?" asks Angie, raising her voice. "Are you going to tell Aidan that you cheated on him? Remember Aidan, your *boyfriend*? The guy who loves you and thinks you love him?"

"My boyfriend has moved to a different city, on the other side of the fucking country." Pia finally turns to face us. "He canceled three out of the last four weekends home, and he refuses to agree on a date for moving back . . . Would you call that a healthy relation-ship? We're on death row. If he gave a shit about me, he'd be here!"

We're all quiet. When she says it like that, it sounds kind of ter-rible.

Pia sighs. "I just wanted a little me time."

"A little me time with some cock!" shouts Angie, throwing her half-empty coffee cup in the sink so hard it cracks. "Aidan would *never* hurt you."

Pia's eyes widen. "*Excuse* me? I'm not taking advice from someone whose entire experience of a real relationship is six minutes on a fucking boat pier."

"Go fuck yourself, Pia."

Angie storms out to the deck. A second later I hear the familiar sound of her lighting a cigarette.

Pia slams the refrigerator door shut, and all my Aunt Jo's old serving trays that we keep on top of it promptly fall off, clattering loudly to the floor.

I scramble to help Pia pick them up. Tears are rolling down her cheeks.

"Pia . . . it's okay," I say softly, and put my hand out to stroke her shoulder. At my touch, Pia instantly collapses into a little ball on the floor, sobbing.

"I fucked up . . ." she croaks.

I exchange glances with Madeleine, and notice that her hair is all matted and wild. Who was *she* with last night?

But Pia's wailing jolts me back to the problem at hand. "I want to die . . ."

Madeleine rolls her eyes. "Oh, Pia, stop overreacting."

"Thanks, Maddy. You're *such* a good friend."

"You make everything so much more of a big deal than it needs to be."

"More of a big deal than cheating on the love of my life by screwing the guy I'm trying to go into business with?" Pia buries her face in her hands again. "Never shit where you work. That's the saying, right?"

(Did I do that? Crap.)

"Maybe you can still work with him?" I ask.

"With Ray?" I can hardly hear Pia now. "No way. He only met me yesterday because he wanted to hook up. I thought I was networking. I'm such a *dick* . . ."

Pia sobs loudly, and for once with Pia, it's not just ninety percent drama, ten percent anguish. This is genuine misery.

"We started drinking and I've been so lonely and it just . . . happened. Oh, God. I'm a terrible person."

"No, you're not," I say, at the same time as Angie. She must have been listening from outside, because she runs back into the kitchen and kneels on the other side of Pia, their argument forgotten immediately, as it always is between them.

"You're the best person." Angie wipes Pia's tears away. "You just made one mistake. Everyone makes mistakes."

"I thought you were pissed at me . . ."

"I just got scared. If you and Aidan, who seem perfect for each other, can't make it work long distance, what hope do Sam and I have?" whispers Angie.

"Poor Aidan . . ." Pia's voice is so faint I almost can't make out the words. "He's been texting me. I can't reply. Oh, God, I can't bear this. I can't. I feel so sick, my stomach is actually *aching*—"

"It's just guilt, P-Dawg," says Angie. "Just let it go. It's a pointless emotion."

"Why is it pointless to feel remorse for making a huge mistake?" asks Madeleine.

Angie snaps. "Seriously, Maddy? How the fuck is that gonna help?"

Madeleine gets up from the table. "Sorry." She rinses her glass, puts it in the dishwasher, and walks out of the kitchen.

"Just when I think that chick has stopped being a bitch," mutters Angie.

Pia wails some more.

"Pia. Ladybitch. Listen to me. Stop crying. I am taking away this guilt right now. Okay? It's gone," says Angie. "You can deal with everything tomorrow. But right now, go shower. It'll make you feel better."

It's weird hearing Angie be so motherly.

Pia wipes her eyes. "But I don't want to be alone with my thoughts."

"I'll sit in the bathroom while you shower," says Angie. "Okay? I won't look. I don't want to see your junk."

"My junk is awesome."

"My junk is better."

"Can I do anything to help?" I ask.

"Yes," says Angie. "Go jump on that hot piece of Irish ass again."

Pia sits up straight and looks at me. "WHAT?"

Just then, Julia walks in wearing her ancient Victoria's Secret pajamas done up on the wrong buttons, also with wildly tangled just-had-sex hair.

Wow, we're going to be using a lot of conditioner at Rookhaven today.

"Well, my vagina has never been so happy," says Julia cheerfully. "Why are we all sitting on the floor? Why is Pia crying? Why does Coco have stubble rash? Why is Angie the only person who looks like she didn't get laid last night? What the fuck is going on?"

"I hooked up with Joe," I say happily.

Julia's reaction shocks me. "Joe? The bartender? Tell me you're joking."

"Joking?" I say. "Why would I be joking?"

"Oh, honey. We can get you someone better than that."

"Joe is hot," says Angie. "I would totally tap that."

"Can we please talk about my crisis again?" asks Pia pleadingly.

By the time I get back upstairs, it's nearly noon. I creep into my dark little bedroom, carrying toast and tea for Joe—as he requested when I left hours ago (sorry, Joe)—and am hit by the salty smell of, um, sex.

"Coco?" asks a voice from the bed. "Is that you? Do you have sustenance? Please say yes. I'm wasting away here. It's my own little Irish famine, right here in Brooklyn."

Joe sits up, his wild hair flopping everywhere, his lanky arms and legs splaying out over the edge of my bed. I can't help laughing at almost everything Joe says. Sometimes I swear it's not even what he's saying, it's just the accent. Even though I know he'd probably rather be here with someone beautiful like Angie, even though I know he's way out of my league, it's just so damn easy to be with him.

Joe devours the toast with almost obscene glee, then grabs me again.

I'm actually a little sore down there, you know, like when you haven't ridden a bike in ages and then you start again and your body gets a little . . . achey. Yet somehow, the combination of crumbs and tiredness and giggling just makes it even hotter.

I don't know why I'm not more embarrassed to admit all this so openly.

I guess I just really want him.

"Wow. Sex is awesome," I say afterward.

"Yeah. More people should know about it," says Joe, reaching for me. "Kiss me again . . . Thank you."

"You're welcome."

"Do you have any cake?"

"What, like, on me? Right now? No. What are you, some kind of cake fiend?"

Joe grins. "Yes. I am a cake fiend. I like to roll up cake and snort it through a rolled-up hundred-dollar bill."

"Ew."

He stretches. "I have to open the bar in a half hour. If only I could get from here to there without having to actually, you know, move." He pauses, taking a moment to kiss me thoughtfully on the neck. "Fuck it, what's the point? It's closing, anyway. Gary is on his way to Nantucket. He'll never find out if I open an hour late."

"I think you should go open up," I say.

"Aw, really? Are you the responsible type? That's the last thing I want in a bar employee."

"Also, I've had an idea," I say.

"Is it something to do with sex in the shower? Because in that case, you read my mind, and—"

"No," I say, laughing. "Double ew. My roommates have to shower in there too."

"Kinky . . ." Joe waggles his eyebrows at me.

"Hush up and listen," I say sternly. "My idea is about how you can save Potstill."

"Go on."

"Throw a Potstill Prom party."

"A what?"

"A prom-themed party. You know? Spector will play, people can dress up in prom gear, like tuxedos and stuff, and we can have punch and snacks. Don't you wish you could go to prom all over again? I do!"

"I am from Ireland, Coco, we don't have prom. We have debs, which is like prom, but from the sounds of it, a lot less effort."

But I won't be dissuaded. "You could do it at the end of the summer, before Gary gets back. And we could put up flyers and sell tickets in advance at the bar. We can even do publicity online!"

"Sell tickets?" Joe is finally interested. "If we sell tickets, we could hire extra people to help out at the bar and with setting up . . . That might work."

"It *will* work," I say.

"Prom. Coco, you're a goddamn genius." Joe scrambles out of bed, reaches for his jeans, and puts them on so fast he loses his balance and falls over. "Can you work tonight? Come in at five. We can start planning. I'll text the Spector guys now and nail down a date for the end of August. This is going to be huge."

"Yes, boss," I say playfully.

"Thanks for a great night, tiger."

Joe opens my door, then stops and glances back at me and makes a tiger roar sound. I roar back. We grin dorkily at each other.

And a second later he's gone.

CHAPTER 12

The strangest thing about not going to work on a weekday is, well, being at home on a weekday.

On my first Monday morning after quitting the preschool and starting my job at Potstill, life starts just like normal. I'm a light sleeper, so as always I stir when I hear Julia's alarm. She leaves before six these days. Then I drift back to sleep only to hear—like clockwork—Madeleine, around seven, Pia, about half an hour later, and finally Angie, another hour after that.

Since I don't have any reason to get up, and for once in my damn life I'm not hungry, I happily stay in bed and do a little Facebook and Instagram and Twitter admin. Is it weird that I end up deleting more than half my social media posts? I get post-post anxiety.

This house is really badly soundproofed. I can hear Angie singing along to some angry girl music while she finishes getting ready.

Oh, God. Do you think that means everyone heard Joe and me having sex the other night? Because, ewww.

My phone beeps: a text from my dad to Julia and me: *Are you two available for lunch today? Unexpected meeting in the city. I'll be free at noon.*

That's unusual. He rarely flies all the way here from Rochester just for a meeting.

I reply right away: *Of course!*

Then Julia replies: *Can we meet near my office? Totally slammed today. But can't wait!*

I head downstairs to make some toast and then shuffle into the living room. I turn on the TV, but there's nothing to watch. The day-time soaps haven't started yet, and I'm not in the mood for the shouty chatter of a talk show. To top it off, I can't watch any good Netflix or Hulu shows because I have a complicated watching agreement with the girls, whereby we can't watch ahead without each other, unless one girl has opted out (Angie opts out of most teen shows, and Pia and I opt out of the violent stuff). Which is fine when we're all working days and watching TV at night but otherwise, lame.

I head over to our bookshelves. I decide to pick out a book at random rather than choosing a childhood favorite that I know will comfort me.

Choosing a book you don't know is risky. Pick something stupid, or nasty, or depressing, and it's guaranteed to ruin your mood, maybe even your day. And forget about scary books. I read two pages of *American Psycho* once and thought I was going to throw up. Don't read it. Really, don't, it'll make you want to sleep with the light on forever.

Standing right up against the bookshelf, I close my eyes, exhale the breath I didn't even realize I'd been holding, and let my fingers brush against the books until I find one that feels right. I pull it out and open my eyes.

Anna Karenina.

Tolstoy? It sounds way too serious. But why not, right? How hard can it be? It's not like it's still in the original Russian, for Pete's sake. So I take my toast and *Anna Karenina* and head out to the deck.

Two hours later, my toast is cold, I'm starving, and I need to pee so badly that I'm jiggling both knees.

But I can't put the book down.

Reading *Anna Karenina* feels like a friend is whispering in my brain—someone who understands life, and people, and, most of all, me. I won't tell you what happens in the book, I don't want to spoil it, except that it's about how people really feel, underneath everything.

I've never read anything like this. I feel like I really know the characters, know them like I know Julia and Pia and Angie and Madeleine, even though these people are imaginary and lived in Russia hundreds of years ago . . . It's that true and sharp and immediate.

In the book, one line is underlined in blue pen.

"I've always loved you, and when you love someone, you love the whole person, just as he or she is, and not as you would like them to be."

The words *so true* are scrawled next to it. I recognize my mother's handwriting immediately, and for a moment, it's like she's still alive.

When you lose someone you love and know so very, very dearly, sometimes it's like you can close your eyes and *feel* her. Even though she's gone.

I lay my cheek flat against the smooth page, smelling that good dry bookish smell. My mother held this page, this book. She read this, and it touched her so much that she wrote in it.

People should always write in books, should mark them so that when they're gone, their loved ones can feel a connection to them.

People die. But books are immortal.

I read the underlined section again.

I want to love someone just as I am. And I want him to love me, the whole of me. But he'd have to know me first. My mother always told Julia and me that anyone who truly knew us couldn't help but love us . . . but I can't imagine any guy ever getting to know me, not really. I can't even imagine being so completely myself with a guy. Being comfortable with Joe physically is one thing, but being comfortable emotionally, being open and honest so someone can really get to know you—that's another thing altogether.

How will anyone love me when nobody really knows me?

At that moment, my phone rings. It's Joe.

"Coco. How are you on this fine morning?"

Joe's Irish accent sounds much stronger over the phone, so I reply in my worst imitation: "I'm grand, thank you, Joe."

"Grand? Is it my accent you're making fun of now?"

"No, your syntax. It's a mess."

"I'll leave that, since I don't know what syntax is. Now! Can you please come to the bar early today?"

"Um, sure! No, wait, I forgot. I'm so sorry, I have to meet my dad for lunch."

"Oh, say hi to him for me."

I giggle. Even when Joe makes lame jokes like that, I laugh.

"Have fun, don't do anything I wouldn't do, and that includes heroin and karaoke, okay?"

"Yes, sir."

I'm still laughing while I'm getting dressed. I find a white T-shirt that I haven't worn in ages in the back of a drawer and pair it with skinny jeans and my brown satchel.

Then I hurry downstairs. Just as I'm about to go out the front door, however, I catch a glimpse of myself in the hall mirror. And, unlike usual, I don't immediately look away.

Instead I look closer. And I see myself, really see myself, for the first time in a long time. Possibly ever.

I'm not disgusting. I'm not fat. I look kind of okay.

But I look young. Boring. Like I'm on my way to high school. And I'm tired of looking that way.

So I run back upstairs, burst into Angie's room, and sit down at the desk she's fashioned into a sewing table. In the top drawer is her makeup bag.

I quickly look through her eyeliners—I know she won't mind, seriously, she is very relaxed about that sort of thing and anyway she has, like, fifteen of them—but I'm not sure I'm the eyeliner type. And I'm definitely not good at applying it.

Then I see, at the very bottom, that Chanel lipstick she put on me the night we all went to Potstill. It's red. Bright red, movie star red, Hollywood red. I've never really worn lipstick, only lip gloss, and as I put it on I start feeling weird. In a good way.

Because of the lipstick, I'm holding my mouth, and therefore my whole face, differently, and somehow, that makes me feel confident and self-assured. Don't laugh, but I feel like, well, a woman, not a girl.

Then I spy a tiny sample of perfume in the bottom of the bag, one of those little spritzers they give you when you buy a bunch of makeup from Saks or whatever. I take a quick sniff. It's Narciso Rodriguez's For Her. It smells sort of warm and sexy and nice. I spritz it on my wrists and under my ears, like my mom always used to, and then aim a spray above my head, just for good measure.

As I skip out of the house and down the stoop, a guy walking his dog down Union Street glances up at me and does the biggest double take I've ever seen. A double take at *me*. And for once, I don't assume it's because I have food on my face. It's because I look good. And yes, I know I shouldn't look for external validation and all that crap, but I don't care. I like it.

CHAPTER 13

I'm meeting Dad and Julia at a French bistro near Central Park, but naturally, as I get there, I get a text from my father: *Meeting running over. Reschedule for 2 pm.*

I can always tell when he's busy: he texts like we're colleagues instead of his daughters.

Julia replies: *No prob am slammed see you then x*

So I text Pia. She works somewhere in Midtown. *Are you having lunch? Want to hang out? xxx*

The reply comes straightaway: *Come to 41st and Fifth—look for the Italian Stallion!*

The Italian Stallion. That's the name of her new food truck. It sells, you guessed it, Italian food. Something different every day—like Mondays it's lasagne or minestrone, Tuesdays it's baked ziti or spaghetti pomodoro, and so on. But it's always hot and always delicious (sometimes she brings the leftovers home). A lot of meat, cheese, and carbs—very different from Skinny Wheels, her salad empire, but just as popular.

By the time I get to the steps of the New York Public Library, right across from the Italian Stallion, the lunch rush is dwindling, though of course, in New York City, someone's always hungry. I wait until the crowd is down to just a few people, and I come up to the window. Pia looks calm, but intensely focused, the way she never does at home.

"It's asparagus risotto or pasta with broccoli and sausage," she's saying patiently to a guy frowning at the menu. "No, we don't have anything else. Nope, no smoothies."

Pia glances up and sees me. I read, in the flick of her eyebrow, a message: *Can you believe this guy?*

"Nope, no hot dogs," she says. "No pretzels. See that guy over there with the dirty silver cart? He has hot dogs. We are an Italian food truck. We only have—thank you, have a nice day!" she calls after him cheerfully.

The guy is walking angrily away.

Pia and I meet eyes again and burst out laughing. She turns to the guy in the truck with her—one of her assistants. "Reggie, take over? I'm taking a tiny break." She turns back to me. "Are you hungry?"

I shrug. "A bit. But I have to eat with my dad later."

In a moment, Pia comes out of the truck, carrying a bowl of risotto and two spoons. We walk over to the New York Public Library steps and take a seat about halfway up.

"Are you happy to share a bowl? I'm not superhungry either. I was testing some new mozzarella suppliers all morning," Pia says. "Man, I love my job."

"Did you know you'd love it before you started it?" I ask.

Pia takes a bite of risotto, thinking. "I don't know . . . but as soon as I realized I could make a living doing this, I just felt a click. You know?"

I take a bite of risotto, trying to look like I understand what she means. A click?

"It was like I discovered food trucks, and I met Aidan, and the world just fell into place." Pia shudders a little laugh out, as though it's funny. But I can tell she's closer to crying.

"Have you spoken to him?" I ask softly.

"Nope," she whispers. "I just . . . I can't bear it. I've been texting. But he knows something is up, he must know . . ."

I nod. "I guess so."

"Do you think I should tell him that I cheated on him?" Pia turns to me. "Really. If you were me, would you tell him?"

If I was in love with someone who loved me back? And then I cheated on him?

I can't even imagine that ever happening.

"I don't know," I say. "What if it were the other way around? If Aidan cheated on you? Would you want him to tell you?"

"That's what I keep asking myself. Yes, I guess? But if it didn't mean anything, and it didn't, Coco, it really didn't mean anything, then . . . maybe not? I mean, it happened once. It'll never happen again. It's just . . . it's in the past now. I'm still me. You know? So what's the difference?"

I think for a second. I do know. That's what I was thinking the other day about my one-night stand with Eric. About my abortion.

But somehow . . . now that I really think about it, I know it can't be true.

"Maybe everything we do changes us," I say. "Just a little. Maybe that's what's supposed to happen. It's how we grow up. It's not bad, or good, it's just . . . it's what happens."

"Look at you, being all mature and shit." Pia is smiling, but her eyes are so sad. "So now that I know what it's like to make a giant fucking mistake, I'm a grown-up? But I'm also going to regret it forever? Is that all adulthood is? Remorse for the mistakes you made getting there?"

"No . . . that can't be right either," I say. "I don't know, Pia."

"I have to tell him," she says. "I do. I know I do."

I nod. "I think maybe you do."

She looks up at her truck. A sudden influx of tourists has boosted the line at the Italian Stallion. Her assistant looks stressed.

"I have to go back," Pia says, wiping her eyes. "My God, I cry a lot."

I grin. "Me too."

Pia gives me a big hug. "Thank you for helping me, Coco. You're a really good friend."

It's the nicest thing anyone has ever said to me.

CHAPTER 14

I still have time to kill before I meet my dad.

So I get the subway back up to Central Park and take a stroll.

The smell of grass in the hot sun is so distinctive, isn't it? It reminds me of my childhood summers, of drying off on scratchy grass after swimming, of birthday parties where everyone else was on the bouncy castle and I was too scared to join in because some of the boys were really rough. (Julia was really rough too.)

I've probably been in Central Park only four or five times in my entire life. That is pretty lazy of me given I live here now, but somehow it's easy to just stay in your own little area of New York City, even though everything else is just a subway ride away.

My first time coming to Central Park was with my mom.

She brought us into the city to see *The Lion King* for Julia's tenth birthday. We started out at Serendipity, for Frrrozen Hot Chocolates, which was officially my favorite dessert in the entire world until . . . actually, it's still my favorite dessert. Then we saw *The Lion King*, which was awesome and, at the time, a little scary. And then we walked over here to watch the toy sailboats on the lake.

My mom told us it was her favorite place in the whole world.

She said Central Park had a little bit of magic, that it opened the sky to the world below and vice versa, that you could stand in the middle of it and feel at one with everything around you.

We watched the boats for a while, before going to a playground to swing. After that we went down to this restaurant in Chinatown for dinner. Eventually we headed back to Aunt Jo's house, and Julia and I were so tired we fell asleep in the cab, and my dad carried Julia and my mom carried me up the stairs of Rookhaven and put us to bed. I can still remember the sensation of being carried by her, what it felt like to put my face into the soft crook between her shoulder and her neck, the smell of her perfume and shampoo. I remember her *momness*.

And then, suddenly, I realize I can't remember my mom's voice. No. No way.

What did her voice sound like? What was it *like*?

When I try to imagine it, I have like a blank fuzzy white noise in my head. I can hear Julia's voice, and Angie's voice, and Pia and Madeleine and Miss Audrey and Mrs. James and every other woman's voice I've ever heard. But I can't remember my mother's. What happens if soon I can't remember what she looked like, or her smile, or the feeling of her arms around me? It'll be like she never even existed! Why didn't I record her voice? Why? All we have is an old birthday video that my cousin made at Christmas once, and I'm, like, three or something. Why didn't we video every single day we ever had together? Why?

Suddenly, I'm going to cry. I know I am. The tears are already overflowing, blinding me, oh, God, this sadness is going to swallow me up.

Crying about death isn't like normal crying, it's not like crying over a TV show or a boy or whatever. I wouldn't say that to Pia, of course, I don't want to be all "you don't really understand sadness"— but truly, no one who hasn't experienced it themselves can understand. It's desperate and overwhelming, like drowning . . . It's like you're suffocating with fear. I try to not let myself cry about my mom because I'm scared that if I do, I'll never, ever stop.

Sometimes I used to wake up crying at night, like my body was holding in tears and would only let them out when I was sleeping.

Now, with every bit of strength in my body, I *will* the tears to withdraw, taking all of my sadness back into the center of my body where it normally lives. Then as I blink away the tears, focusing again on all the pigeons, I have a flashback to Julia's birthday.

We were standing next to the lake, and I was tired, when I saw this wild-looking woman—not a homeless woman, just one of New York's eccentrics—covered in pigeons. I totally freaked out. I started to cry and cry. And my mother leant down and said, "She's just doing her own thing, Coco. If she's not scared of the pigeons, you don't need to be scared for her."

Relief courses through me. I remember now.

My mother's voice was warm and reassuring and calm. It was like buttery toast. It was honey-colored. It was *Mom*.

I stare at the lake until I remember what I'm supposed to be doing today. Then I gather myself together and head to lunch.

An hour later, when I get to the bistro, I take a seat in the far corner and order a sparkling water while I wait for Julia and Dad to arrive. It's weird how I often think about my mom on the days when I know I'm going to see my dad. They still go hand in hand in my brain.

Where the hell is my dad already?

"Coco Russotti?" asks a voice, and I look up to see a vaguely familiar, extremely handsome face that I can't quite place. "Coco, is that you?"

"Yes? I mean . . . hi!" I'm drawing a total blank. Who the hell is this guy?

"It's me!"

The guy, the giant, gives me a big perfect shiny-teeth smile, all chiseled jaw and brown eyes and perfect dark skin, and I get the strangest flashback to seeing him in a football uniform. Huh?

"Topher Amies. I went to high school with you. In Rochester?"

I must still be staring at him blankly because he's starting to look confused.

"Um, I was a friend of Julia's? I mean, I'm still her friend, I just never see her anymore, she's like, socially elusive since she became the next big thing in banking . . ."

Suddenly I remember. Topher Amies! He was one of Julia's jock friends. He was part of the cool crowd. He dated a succession of pretty, toothy girls with long legs and bubble gum voices. His dad was a pro football player. He was en route to being a pro football player too until he broke his leg in a dramatic injury that left most of the cheerleaders in hysterical tears. He was scouted to be an Abercrombie and Fitch model, though it didn't happen, it totally could have. He was, in other words, a high school hero.

I can't believe he remembers *me*. I was nothing in high school. I mean, not nothing, but—never mind. Whatever. Julia wasn't in the so-called cool crowd either, exactly, but she was captain of the soccer team and everyone liked her, so she was accepted across different cliques. Anyway. Back to Topher. Who is standing right in front of me, waiting for me to speak.

"Hi!" My voice cracks. *Oh, Coco, you are so lame.* "I mean, hey. What a weird coincidence! I'm just about to meet Julia and my dad for lunch."

"No, I'm meeting your dad too," he says, taking a seat at the table.

"You're what? I mean, sorry?"

"My dad and your dad are golf buddies. And my dad wants me to get an internship with your dad's company, so he set this meeting up. Personally, I don't think I want to be a banker. But hey, that's my burden." Topher flashes a perfect smile, and I blink a few times. My God, he's so pretty.

I'm not exaggerating. He really is that pretty. The girls at school called him Hot Topher. Girls like me, who hung out on the edges of the cafeteria watching the cool people interact. Eric, that guy I had my stupid crush on for so many years, was in the cool clique too, but a much lower echelon, reserved for the guys who were friends with the cool guys back when they were all thirteen. Looking back, I think Eric had that tinge of desperation that the truly cool can sniff out a mile off. But I didn't mind: I crushed on Eric anyway. I would never have a crush on someone like Topher; he was too unattainable to even be an unattainable crush. I aimed lower.

Get back to the damn present, Coco.

"So . . . you live in New York now?" Urgh, stupid question. Obviously he lives here.

"Yup, I just finished freshman year at NYU," Topher says. "I know. A freshman at twenty-three. It's pretty . . . pathetic." His laugh is so open and infectious that I find myself laughing too. His teeth are so white. His eyelashes are so long. His lips are so pouty. "After high school I went to Duke for about four months, and I just, uh, hated it." He cracks up again. "So I took a few years off and went traveling around the world."

"Wow," I say. "That's so cool."

"Oh, no," Topher says. "Most of the time I was just broke and lonely. It was kind of tragic."

"Tragic is cool . . ." My voice trails off. Oh, man. That was a stupid thing to say.

"Now I live in a studio apartment uptown that my aunt owns.

It's tiny, but it's free. And I'm taking some extra classes this summer, you know, for credit."

"That sounds . . . fun."

"Does it?" Topher grins at me. "It's not. It's pretty boring."

He's so confident. So easygoing. No wonder everyone loved him so much in high school.

The waitress comes over. "Are you ready to order?"

Topher looks up at her and grins apologetically. "We're still waiting for two people," he says.

"No problem." She winks at him and walks away. Told you he was hot.

"I need the extra summer classes to help me graduate early," he continues. "For the next few weeks, my life is comparative literature."

"Cool!" I say. "It must be so much fun to just sit around and talk about books all day. I always thought that, anyway. Uh . . ." I pause, wondering if I sound like a total dick. "Sorry. I'm such a geek. I spent all morning reading *Anna Karenina,* and it was pretty much the best morning I've had in weeks."

Topher's eyes light up. "*Anna Karenina?* Are you kidding? That's such a coincidence! I—"

But before we can start talking about books, I glance up and see my dad and Julia walking into the café together. They must have arranged to meet up before coming here. They always do things like that: a united force.

I quickly stand up. "Hi, Daddy!"

"Little Coco!" exclaims my dad.

My dad looks just like Julia, if you can imagine Julia as a fifty-something guy with a slight bald patch and wire-rimmed glasses wearing a gray pin-striped suit.

He envelops me in one of his big rocking hugs, then leans back, looking at me. "Is that red lipstick? Wipe that off, sweetie. You look like a clown."

I frown, pick up a paper napkin, and quickly wipe off my red lipstick, feeling my skin prickle with embarrassment. I totally forgot I was even wearing it. Luckily, Topher didn't notice; he's too busy hugging Julia.

We all sit down. My dad doesn't even look at the menu, he never does, he always knows what he wants.

"Does everyone just want the roast chicken? That's what this place is famous for, right?" Dad waves over the waitress. "We'll take four roast chickens, please. What does everyone want to drink?"

"I already ordered a sparkling water," I say.

"Bad for your digestion," say my dad and Julia simultaneously, then grin at each other. "Jinx!"

Topher catches my eye and winks. I'm so surprised I don't even think to wink back, and by the time I've recovered myself enough to even consider winking back, the conversation has moved on and Topher isn't even looking at me anymore.

"I've been working so hard," says Julia. "That I realized the other day that I have more makeup in my desk drawer at the office than at home, and all my toothbrushes somehow ended up there too."

"That's my girl!" says Dad. "So, Coco. Quitting your job. Walk me through it."

"Um . . ." I look at Julia for help, but she's just smiling at me in this weird parental way she does when we're with Dad. I look back at Dad. He's going to grill me right here in front of Topher, a virtual stranger?

He looks back at me expectantly. Yes, yes he is.

So I tell him all about how I didn't like working at the preschool, how it wasn't what I wanted to do anymore, how I felt unfulfilled and depressed. Only I don't use the word "depressed," of course, it's not something we say in our house, I just say "down."

My dad nods the whole time and slowly eats three pieces of bread with butter.

As I finish my story, there's silence. I feel like I'm in trouble. But I'm twenty-one. If I hate my job, I should be allowed to quit, right? Why can't I just say that?

"Well, honey, we don't want you to not enjoy your work, of course," says Dad. "So let's figure out how we can make you happy."

"I think I just want to work at Potstill for a while," I say. "It's this really fun bar, and the manager is really cool. Plus, I can just work there at night and read during the day and figure out, um, figure out . . . stuff."

Total silence. Topher is concentrating on chewing his chicken, eyes on his plate.

"Figure out *stuff*?" Dad sighs. "Honey, a bar job is not a viable long-term career."

"I know," I say, though I'm thinking, *Why not?* Some people work in bars for their entire lives.

"I don't think it'll suit you," says Julia. "You know, rough patrons, drunk people, and you'd have to be on your feet all night."

"Little kids are way more intense and annoying than drunk people," I say. "And I was on my feet a lot in the preschool too."

"Coco, it's just not a job for a nice girl like you," says my father. "I think Rochester is a better place for you. You can live at home and work in one of the local preschools. They're great."

I nod, not trusting myself to speak without crying. He's going to force me to move back to Rochester?

My dad notices and puts his hand on mine. "You know I'd be happy for you to do a secretarial course, if you like. Or you could take a cooking course. You love to bake."

I look down at my plate. I don't want to be a secretary or a baker. I just . . . I know I don't. But if I say something right now, I'm pretty sure I'll burst into noisy sobs, and then Topher will think I'm even more of a loser than he probably already does.

"Don't stress, Cuckoo," says Julia. "We'll find you a job that you'll love."

Who is "we"? I suddenly wonder. Is she even including me in that "we"? Or does she just mean that she and Dad will decide?

She reaches over to grab my other hand. "Don't worry, okay?"

I hope that Topher can't see the tears filling my eyes. My dad and Julia are pinning my hands to the table, literally trapping me with their support.

The conversation tumbles on, but now I'm stuck inside my head. I can barely even eat. My dad and Julia think I'm incapable of determining my own path in life. They think I'm a loser. That I can't do anything by myself. And they know me better than anyone. So they're probably right.

My dad and Topher are talking about internships when Julia looks at her watch and jumps up so fast her chair falls over.

"Shi—I mean, yikes! I have to get back to the office."

"You just love saying 'I have to get back to the office,' don't you?" says Topher, laughing.

I crack up at this too. He's right. She does love it.

"Very funny," says Julia, hugging everyone good-bye. "See you at home tonight, Coco!"

"My flight back to Rochester is at four, so I better get going too," says Dad. "Coco, think about moving home. I'll start looking around for local jobs. It's really a good option for you."

He pays the bill, and no one objects. I wonder at what point you start paying for lunch instead of your parents. If I tried, my father would probably laugh at me.

Dad gets a taxi the moment we get outside, and I'm trying to think how to get away from Topher before he has to get away from me, a sort of preemptive good-bye, when he turns to me.

"Are you busy this afternoon? Come with me to my class. It's Russian Literature. You said you were reading *Anna Karenina*, right? You'll love it! And no one would even notice since it's a summer course for extra credit. You could just come and sit in—wait, why are you giving me that look?"

"I would love that!" I squeak. *Oh, God, Coco, be cool.* "I mean, that sounds great. Thanks!"

Topher smiles. "It's a date."

CHAPTER 15

"It took me awhile to get through *War and Peace*, but it was worth it," says Topher as we take the subway down to NYU. "We're also reading Pushkin, Gogol, Herzen, Gorky, Turgenev, Dostoevsky . . ."

I've never heard of anye of those writers, except maybe Dostoevsky, but I'm not even sure I could pronounce his name if I tried, let alonee spell it.

I am so sick of not knowing anything.

I never knew Topher was so chatty . . . like seriously, he never shuts up. He talks about classes he took last year, the problems he had, his apartment, his brothers, and even how much he's looking forward to working with my dad's company (though he hopes he doesn't have to just get everyone coffee all day).

It's kind of nice. Topher's monologuing means I don't have to stress about what I should say. I don't have to say anything at all: I just try to laugh at the right parts. Every time I look at him, I feel like my stomach is twisting into a tightrope. Wow, I must really like this guy.

Eventually, we get down to NYU. His Russian Literature class is in a big building just across from Washington Square Park. We take our seats—in the middle, to the side, the don't-look-at-me seats. I glance around the room. It's only about twenty percent full, I guess because it's just a summer class, and to my intense surprise, the other students all look extremely normal. They aren't at all the intimidatingly intellectual, cooler-than-cool types I had expected NYU students to be. And they aren't sitting in cliques like high school. Instead, everyone sits alone quietly, with laptops or notebooks, looking like they're just here to listen and think. They're dressed kind of dorky.

They're kind of like me.

But there is *something* unique about them, and it takes me a moment to figure out what it is.

They all seem very independent.

Then again, I guess they're living and studying in the middle of New York goddamn City. They *are* self-sufficient and independent. My roommates have that look too. I don't think I do.

My phone buzzes. Joe: *Can you pick up a dozen limes on your way in, sweetcheeks? We're out.*

I reply quickly: *You got it.*

Topher glances over. "That your boyfriend?"

"What? Oh! No! Joe. My boss."

My boss with whom I had casual no-strings-attached sex the other night, in a totally wild and out-of-character move. Just like coming to a college literature class that I'm not even enrolled in, with the most popular guy from my high school. Wow. New Coco has so much more fun.

I glance at Topher. He has a perfect profile. Like, just perfect.

He turns and meets my eyes. And gives me a smile of such easy reassurance that I nearly melt and explode at the same time. And then I realize that I am basically, in fact, entirely, probably, crushing on Topher Amies harder than anyone has crushed on anyone in the history of the earth.

"Good morning, everyone!" a voice booms.

An older woman with short black hair is standing at the podium, her deep voice carried throughout the room by the microphone. (Though really, I'm not sure it'd make much difference if it were turned off.)

"That's Professor Guffey," Topher whispers, nodding in her direction.

"Today we're talking about *Anna Karenina* and the depictions of women in Russian literature through the nineteenth and twentieth centuries . . ." she continues.

I smile. I think I'm going to like this.

Her lecture zips around, touching on different novels and events and politicians I've never heard of, but everything sounds interesting, everything sounds like it matters. I've never heard anyone talk about literature like this, as though it were an essential component of the world, a mirror that shows us who we really are, not just who we want to be.

For a second I have a small fizz of panic. I'm not smart enough to understand this. I'm just . . . I'm not.

Then she dives into discussing *Anna Karenina*. And what it meant to be a mother in the time before women had rights, what value love held when the law decreed that the husband was god, how Tolstoy presents the situation and the problem in a way that tears us apart, how Levin's love provides a purer, colder alternative, how we judge Anna compared to how contemporary Russian readers would have judged her.

Something inside me is waking up.

I want this to last forever. I want to ask questions, I want to say what I'm thinking, I want to find out more. I want Professor Guffey to keep talking all day, and I want to read everything Tolstoy ever wrote, I want to move to Russia, I want—I want—

"Who do you think Tolstoy sees as the true heroine of this book? Anna or Kitty?"

"Kitty!" pipes up a girl in front, one of those intimidating popular Connecticut types with perfect honey hair. "Anna dies. She makes a bad choice, loses her kid, and then dies. But Kitty ends up happy with Levin."

"I, like, totally agree?" says the girl next to her, the ubiquitous sycophant that popular girls need for reassurance when mirrors aren't available. "Anna never thinks about consequences. She's a loser."

"Bullshit!" I exclaim, and then clap my hand over my mouth.

Everyone in the entire class turns to look at me.

"Bull . . . shit?" repeats Professor Guffey.

"I'm sorry, I just, I think, um, I think . . . she just fell in love. But she didn't have independence, Russian law at the time gave women no rights . . ." My cheeks are burning. "Um, so, the cost of her adultery, falling in love with Vronksy, was that she loses access to her child, and to her newfound happiness, and then . . ."

I trail off. Why did I speak up? I'm not even supposed to be here. The professor is probably about to kick me out.

"*Exactly!*" booms Professor Guffey, pointing at me.

Everyone jumps.

"Independence!" she exclaims. "That's right. Exactly. Female emancipation. The desire, the right, to make your own decisions, to follow your instincts, to not just do what your father tells you, what your husband tells you . . . that's what Anna wanted. But she couldn't have it. Eighteenth-century Russian society wouldn't allow it. So Tolstoy didn't allow it either. Instead, he made the novel into a warning against love. Fall in love, he says, and lose everything. Your family, your happiness . . . Even your life."

Topher looks at me and winks. "Teacher's pet."

CHAPTER 16

"Nothing attracts a twenty-something like a two-dollar drink," says Joe, surveying the crowd at Potstill.

"If there's one thing I know, it's how to save cash in New York City," I say proudly. I put Potstill's happy hour on a couple of 'Broke in Brooklyn'–type blogs. And it worked. "People will go anywhere for a cut-price buzz."

"Yeah, must be real hard to save cash in the giant brownstone you inherited." Joe reaches out to pull my hair. I shriek and throw a piece of ice at him.

I can't believe how totally nonweird it was seeing Joe back at the bar tonight.

Considering all the things we did to each other's naked bodies, I should be all shy or embarrassed or *something*. But I'm not. I was a million times shyer around Topher today. Around Joe, I just feel totally normal.

I feel almost happy.

Maybe this is exactly what I need. I'll hang out with Topher at lectures all day and work in the bar with Joe all night. I'll be buddies with Topher, and fuckbuddies with Joe.

"What are you thinking so seriously about?" says Joe. "You're all frowny and adorable. Like a stoned kitten."

"How many kittens have you seen stoned?"

"Hundreds! Thousands. There's a real feline drug problem in Ireland. No, don't laugh, it's a nightmare."

I laugh so hard that he picks up half a lemon.

"Stop laughing at me, or I'll make you eat this."

"You will not!" I back away from him as he advances. For a petrifying—and, to be honest, thrilling—second, I think he's going to pounce on me.

"Calm down, lovers," says a voice. I look up. Angie! I feel like I haven't seen her in ages! Okay, it's only been one day . . . but I guess since I now work nights, and she works days, we'll be missing each other a lot. Which kind of sucks.

"Angie! How was your day?"

"Fun, tiring, bitchy, degrading, badly paid. You know, the usual lament of the junior fashion employee." Angie takes a seat at the bar. "Line me up some cheap drinks, bitches. Two for one, right? I will literally go anywhere for a cut-price buzz."

Joe and I exchange glances and start laughing again. That's exactly what I said.

Angie takes out her cell, assuming her default position. "God, you two really are in love."

"We are *not*," I say, shocked out of my hilarity.

"Actually, we are," says Joe. I glance at him in horror. "In fact, we're getting married. And we're going to have litters of children, like all good Irish immigrants."

"Gnarly." Angie arches her eyebrow at me, and I look away. I know she thinks there's something more going on between Joe and me, but we're just friends. With benefits.

"Pia and Julia are on their way. We're having an emergency house meeting about Pia's, shall we say, complicated love life, so we wanted to have it here so you could be a part of it."

"Thanks!" I'm so surprised and flattered.

"I texted Madeleine too, but she's rehearsing with Spector tonight." Angie pauses. "Something is up with that chick. Something more than usual. I can feel it."

Joe pours us all a shot of Lagavulin, which burns my throat like delicious fire. It still feels naughty to be drinking behind the bar, but I'm getting over it.

Imagine if Topher just turned up here right this second.

I must really have a crush on him if I'm already imagining him turning up, by surprise, to random moments in my life. If Topher was here right now, he'd make everyone laugh and pay special attention to me.

Pia arrives, and rather than parting the crowd at the bar with her confident stride like normal, she apologetically shuffles around people, like she just wants to be ignored.

"Is Pia sick?" asks Joe.

"Yes. Guilt is a sickness," says Angie. "It'll fucking kill you if you let it."

"Hi, guys," Pia's voice is a whisper. "Can I have a drink, please? Something strong. Very strong."

"For fuck's sake, put some makeup on," says Angie. "You look like a smallpox victim."

"Please, don't be mean to me. I can't take it right now." Pia reaches into her enormous bag and pulls out an entire box of Kleenex.

"Wow, you came prepared," says Joe, handing Pia a very large glass of whiskey.

Pia blows her nose and then takes a slug of whiskey.

"I did it," she says. "I told Aidan I cheated on him."

"And?"

There's a long pause. Then Pia looks at us, her eyes brimming with tears. "We. Broke. Up."

"Oh, shit!" Angie reaches out to give Pia a hug. Angie's become a big hugger since she met Sam. Love has made her all squishy. And yet she's still kind of scary. "Drink up. It'll help numb the pain."

Pia drinks her whiskey, eyes staring at us over the rim of the glass like a little kid drinking milk.

"Do you want to talk about it?" says Angie when Pia finishes gulping.

"Yes. No. I don't know. I can't think about it," Pia says. "I need to get drunk. Will you hold my hair back when I throw up later?"

"It would be an honor."

At that moment Julia charges in, all perky ponytail and smiles, still in her suit and little rucksack from work.

"Hi, gang. Whiskey Smash, please, Coco."

Julia arranges herself on a barstool, putting one of her bag straps under the stool leg so the bag can't get stolen, taking out her phone to check her work e-mails, and keeps up a steady stream of hyperactive chatter the whole time, oblivious of Pia's dramatic meltdown on the stool beside her.

"Well, I just had the best day. I'm working on this new deal. And it's going to be intense. It's like, the biggest thing *ever*. Way bigger than that other stupid one. So from tomorrow forward, say good-bye to Ju-ju because I will be Little Miss Workaholic for the next month or so, and then I'm going to make billions of dollars, get a promotion, and my ascent up the corporate bitch ladder shall commence."

I hand over a Whiskey Smash—a perfect one, if I do say so myself—and Julia takes a long slurp. "That is *excellent*."

"I told Aidan," says Pia dramatically. "We . . . we're over."

"That *sucks*," exclaims Julia. Man, she's hyper tonight. "You'll get back together. He'll get over it. You're the best thing that ever happened to him."

Pia bursts into loud sobs again. Joe shoots me a look, and I nod and pour her some more whiskey.

"Let's talk about something else," says Angie. "Julia, tell us more about your impending work hell, and why you look so happy about it."

"Yeah," says Pia, carefully wiping away her tears so that her eye makeup isn't smudged. "I don't like my friends being happy when I'm miserable. It's against the friend code. Like borrowing a piece of clothing before I have worn it."

Julia smiles beatifically. "It's Peter."

"The Magnificent," the three of us chorus in turn.

"Yup. We have a date tonight."

"Peter the Magnificent is a keeper," says Angie. "Well, I never."

"Peter and Julia. Julia and Peter," Pia enunciates slowly. "Yeah, I can see that. Julia Russotti and Peter the Magnificent."

Joe looks up, interested, from his drinks order. "You give your hook-ups nicknames? What am I? Wait—let me guess. Joe the Glorious."

"Right. Joe the Glorious. That's just what we call you," says Angie.

Julia takes another slurp of Whiskey Smash. "There's lemon in this, right? Good. Vitamin C."

Pia looks around. "Is it just me, or is the lighting in here better than it used to be?"

I grin triumphantly at Joe. "I told you! We're trying to make the bar better," I explain to Pia. "You know, so people actually want to drink here."

"It is way more crowded than last time we were here," says Julia, looking around. "Why don't you do it up all retro, like every other bar in New York City? You know, like a speakeasy."

"You mean a speak-cheesy," says Pia.

"Total cliché," agrees Joe.

"And so passé," says Angie. "I've been going to speakcheesies since, like, before I got my first period."

"Why do you have to bring your vagina into everything?" asks Julia.

Joe grimaces. "There is way too much estrogen in this conversation." He walks out from behind the bar to go collect dirty glasses.

Pia slams her empty glass back on the bar. "More whik-sey. I mean, whiskey. Please."

I hand over another.

"So, did you and Topher spend the whole afternoon together?" Julia grins at me and waggles her eyebrows.

"What?" I feel myself blushing. "No. I mean, yes. I mean, we just hung out and went to one of his classes."

"He's a great guy," says Julia. "Really smart. He's going places."

"You're so middle-aged," says Angie. "*Going places?*"

"I'm just saying, if Coco wanted to date him, it wouldn't be a bad idea."

My blush-rush doubles. "Don't be crazy. He's way out of my league."

"I totally thought he liked you today. And Topher is more in your league than some womanizing Irish bartender," says Julia, glancing at Joe disdainfully as he ducks into the stockroom. I frown. He can't hear her, but still, it's not a nice thing to say.

At that moment my phone buzzes in my back pocket.

Topher: *Want to come to my Rilke lecture next Monday?*

Maybe Julia is right. Maybe he does like me.

"Coco, did you just get a text from a boy?" says Angie, just as Joe walks back over.

"No," I say.

"Then why are you blushing?"

"I'm just, uh, it's hot behind the bar," I say, giving her a shut-the-hell-up face.

To my surprise, she does.

"Still heartbroken here, by the way," says Pia loudly. "Can someone please tell me everything is going to be fine?"

Angie steps up. "Of course it will. This is just a blip. Cheating is a symptom, not a cause, of problems. Aidan loves you. This is going to bring you guys closer together."

"But he broke up with me."

"It won't last!" Angie is smiling so widely, it must hurt. "I am sure of it. You and Aidan are meant to be. So you made one mistake! It's okay."

"The things you girls do for each other," mutters Joe. "She's clearly lying. That guy's not going to want to see Pia again."

"How do you know?" I whisper back.

"Because she cheated on him. That changes everything."

Shit. I hope he's wrong. I get busy serving drinks. Potstill is starting to feel like an extension of Rookhaven. It's just so homey. All of us here, just hanging out, conversations ebbing and flowing, someone having a crisis, everyone else helping her through it. Best of all, I can avoid too much attention, and just work away here behind the bar. Just like I used to when I was in the kitchen baking.

It's perfect.

And then Madeleine comes in, to complete the scene.

But she's not alone. She's with someone else. A guy.

Who the heck is he? He's kind of cute, wearing a suit, his tie undone, top button open . . . Is this the guy who gave her that unexplained bed head the other day? I never followed up on that, I wonder if she's dating him. Wait a minute, I know this guy, it's—

"Peter the Magnifi—Peter!" says Julia. "Hi! I mean, what are you doing here?"

"Julia?" Peter is swaying slightly. "I have some bad news."

"You don't want to go out with me tonight?" Julia looks like she might faint.

"No, I do, but—" Peter drops his wallet on the floor and bends over to pick it up. When he stands up, he seems to have forgotten where he is.

"I found him passed out on the stoop at Rookhaven," says Madeleine. "He got fired."

"He what?" Julia is horrified. "Why didn't you call me?"

"My phone belonged to the company. I had to leave it. My phone—my life. Everything." Peter suddenly looks so vulnerable and sweet, gazing beseechingly at Julia. "I wanted to tell you but I didn't know your number by heart. I don't even know my mom's number by heart. Isn't that insane?"

"Welcome to the twenty-first century, buddy," says Madeleine. "Okay. Now that I've dropped off your drunk boyfriend—"

"He's not my boyfriend," mumbles Julia.

"Whatever. I'm going to Amy's apartment to write songs. Later."

She leaves, and all of us turn back to Peter, who's still swaying on the spot, a small frown on his face as he tries to look sober and fails.

"Can I get a beer?" says Peter.

Joe glances at him. "No. You're langers."

"I think you should go home, Peter," says Julia.

"But . . ." Peter seems at a loss. "But we have a date tonight."

Julia shakes her head. "Call me tomorrow—oh, right. No phone. Hang on." Julia grabs a coaster and a pen from the bar, and writes her number on the back. "Get a phone tomorrow. Then call me."

Peter nods miserably. "You don't like me anymore because I'm the kind of loser who gets fired, right?"

"No!" she exclaims, though obviously that's exactly what she's thinking. I can tell. "Of course not. Um . . . Let's have dinner next week. It'll be ace."

Peter puts the coaster in his pocket. He seems more sober now. And kind of sad.

After he leaves the bar, Angie turns to Julia.

"You're totally going to dump the first guy you've liked in however long, just because he got fired?"

"I can't *dump* him. We're not *dating*," says Julia. "It was just a hookup."

"He likes you. You like him. It's just a matter of time and semantics," says Angie.

"Semantics? What a big word," says Pia. "Can you spell it?"

"B-L-O-W-M-E," says Angie.

Joe cracks up.

"I just don't see a future for us, you know. I'm totally . . . I'm just really focused on my career, anyway. That's not a bad thing, right?"

"Not bad at all," agrees Pia. "But . . ."

"He's good-looking. And he seems so nice," interjects Joe. We all turn to stare at him. I thought he was a womanizer. "Sorry, I've got a lot of little sisters." He shrugs. "I'm used to hearing this kind of chat."

"What do you think I should do, then?" asks Julia. "Just date an unemployed guy?"

"Hold your horses, he's been unemployed about six minutes," says Joe. "And he'll get another job. Like immediately. Cutbacks aren't personal. They can happen to anyone."

"My dad always says that companies cut back just to get rid of the dead wood," says Julia. "I don't want to date dead wood. I like people who are winning at life."

"*Winning* at *life?*" Joe looks incredulous.

For the first time ever, I wonder what effect our dad's high-handed approach to parenting has had on Julia. Maybe she was always this tough and driven. Or maybe he made her that way.

"Some people are going somewhere even when they look like they're standing still," says Joe. "Who are you to judge?"

"Whatever, Irish," says Julia.

At that moment, Pia starts to cry, apropos of nothing except perhaps her third drink of the night, and Angie and Julia agree to take her home. Everyone seems a little deflated now, and tension hangs in the air. And why doesn't Julia like Joe? She never dislikes people, not really.

I'm so glad I'm on this side of the bar. Safe from any kind of drama. Safe from everything.

Much later, when the bar is empty, and we're cleaning up and collecting the last of the glasses, Joe says, "So, let's talk some more details about your Potstill Prom idea."

"Okay," I say. "So, we have to pick a theme. Right? Like . . . um . . ."

"Enchantment Under the Sea," suggests Joe. "That was the name of the school dance in *Back to the Future*. Best movie ever."

"Okay, um sure," I say. "Then we decorate the bar to look like we're under the sea."

"So . . . an oil spill?" Joe is deep in thought. "Plastic bags. Crashed airplanes. Killer whales playing Ping-Pong with baby seals."

"What? Ew. No," I say. "Like sand, and starfish, and shells, and schools of little paper fish we can hang from the ceiling . . . Stuff we can make ourselves, homemade, you know? That would make it look extra legit."

"And very Brooklyn," says Joe, as we carry our trays of empty glasses back to the bar.

"Right."

"Are you arty? You look arty."

"No, but I'm a trained preschool assistant, cutting things into shapes and sticking them on the wall is pretty much my MO."

Joe laughs.

I'm on a roll. "We'll need sea-themed drinks, and a snack table, and oh! A bubble machine. And we can pin blue cellophane on the lights over the dance floor."

"So it looks like we're under the sea?"

"Yes. How did you know?

"Just a guess." I get the feeling he's making fun of me, but I don't care. Another prom! But this time it won't suck and the guy I like won't sleep with my so-called best friend.

"Maybe you and I can dress up as mermaids?" I say. "I mean, you can be a merman, and I—"

I can't talk anymore. Joe has come up behind me and is kissing my neck and, *boom,* my insides turn all warm and shivery. He swivels me around, tangling his fingers in my hair, and we kiss and kiss and kiss and—

"Wait." I push Joe away briefly. But his eyes focus on my lips, and he leans in and we kiss more—

"Wait!" I say again. "Joe, we're just—this is just—"

"Just what?" Joe moves my hair out of the way and starts kissing, almost nibbling, the skin behind my ear.

"I—oh, God, that's so nice, I—I just want to make sure we both know this is, um—" How can I say "I only want to have sex with you and nothing else" without sounding like a heartless hussy?

"This is casual." His lips are still on my skin, the words warm and husky. "I know. You just broke up with someone. You're not looking for anything serious. We're both grown-ups. I get it."

"Right," I say.

Ethan! I did just break up with him. I totally forgot. How could I forget? I should be analyzing and replaying the breakup over a million times in my head, just because that's what you have to *do* the first few days after a breakup. But I've been too busy enjoying my life. And of course Joe hasn't got a problem with just being friends with benefits. I mean, he's a total player, you know, and what a cliché, the hot Irish bartender who sleeps with everyone, I—oh, wow, Joe is good at kissing my neck, I can't finish my train of—

"But we can be friends," he murmurs.

"Friends . . ."

"Best friends," he says. "Best friends who get to see each other naked and have fun. Your place or mine?"

"Mine."

CHAPTER 17

I've been illicitly attending comparative literature classes with Topher for weeks now. Frankly, I'm starting to get pretty blasé about the whole thing. No one seems to care. No one even seems to notice.

It's just like my regular nighttime hookups with Joe.

It's totally my choice.

I don't even feel guilty, even though I know my dad would disapprove of just about everything I'm doing. He keeps e-mailing me links to preschool jobs in Rochester, like a helpful little career counselor . . . But I'm an adult, I can do whatever I want, and I don't want to move home to Rochester. I know it won't make me happy.

In fact right now, with the classes, the hookups, and the bar work and Potstill, I think I'm the happiest I've ever been.

A small part of me is niggling that this isn't enough. That I need . . . *more*. But I don't know what that "more" is. So what can I do about it? It's just a feeling. And maybe that feeling is one of those things my dad would call "endemic of my generation." The feeling that we should be totally happy, all the time.

Urgh. I don't know.

Topher and I are walking out of today's class when Professor Guffey stops me.

"Hello," she says, staring at me intently, her ice-blue eyes cold and steady.

Oh, my God, I'm busted.

I glance around for Topher in panic, but he's already out the door.

"Hello . . ."

"I really liked your thoughts about determinism and free will," she says. "I think you're getting a lot out of this class."

"I am." My voice is a whisper.

"Have you read any Flaubert? Sartre? I think you'd enjoy them."

"Umm . . ." My heart is beating wildly in my chest. Should I have read Flaubert and Sartre? Aren't they French? "No . . ."

Professor Guffey gazes at me for a second. "What's your name again?"

"Coco Russotti." The words are out before I can stop them. Crap.

"Coco." Professor Guffey frowns, as if trying to remember me from a course list. My heart speeds up frantically. Could I get arrested for attending class illegally? "Well, I'm teaching Contemporary Literary Theory in the fall. I think you'd enjoy it."

"I'm sure I would!" I say. "Sounds . . . so interesting."

"Wonderful."

She turns away. I am dismissed.

I run out of the building as fast as I can and see Topher waiting for me outside.

"Dude, I thought you were busted for sure," he says. "For stealing education."

"So did I." I feel giddy with relief and then start to laugh. "Stealing education. That's the first thing I've ever stolen."

"You're such a good girl," says Topher. I flinch at the words, but he doesn't notice. "Come on. My brain is hurting."

We settle down under our usual tree in the southeast corner, the same place we've been sitting after every class every day for the past few weeks. I've come to think of it as "our" place. And try not to pinch myself that I get to have an "our" with Topher Amies. We text every day. We e-mail and he comments on my Instagrams.

We're really truly friends.

Maybe more.

Maybe I'm about to achieve one of the three things on my Happy List.

Topher looks at me and grins. "So, I have a surprise for you." He passes me a brown paper bag.

I open the bag. There's a sandwich inside.

"Coco, meet my favorite sandwich in the world," says Topher seriously. "Peanut butter and cucumber."

I gasp. "That was *my* favorite sandwich in grade school! My mom always made it." I unwrap the sandwich. "Thank you. Really, thank you so much."

We both take a bite and chew in silence a moment.

"This is delicious," I say.

"Shh," he says. "Just chew. Honor the sandwich."

Giggling, I take another bite and chew away.

My God, Topher made me a sandwich. Julia keeps telling me how much he must like me, that Topher is totally the kind of guy's guy who only ever makes friends with guys, so if he's hanging out with me, it's because he's got a thing for me.

Maybe she's just telling me that to get me away from Joe. She still seems to dislike him, totally irrationally. Or maybe Topher really does have a thing for me.

I sure as hell have a thing for him.

So what now?

Peanut butter and cucumber sounds like a weird combo, I know, but I swear, it's so good. Fatty, salty, creamy peanut butter, cool, crisp cucumber, soft white bread . . . it's, like, the perfect combination. He didn't add flakes of sea salt, which I would have done, but then again, I add sea salt to everything. Seriously. If I could add sea salt to my toothpaste, I would probably do it.

"My brain hurts," complains Topher.

"Mmm," I say, chewing.

"I'm just . . . I think that I'm too stupid to get this stuff. I'm not as smart as you."

I nearly choke on my sandwich. "What?"

"I'm never as smart as everyone else." Topher's brow furrows adorably. "Like my brain just didn't work the way everyone else's did in high school."

"That's how I feel!" I say, and then I try to sound all cool and nonchalant. "Um, I'm not sure if this will help, but you can borrow my notes anytime. It's not like I really need to use them for anything."

"Really? Wow, that's a great idea!" Topher grins at me. He's so hot I have to break the gaze and look at my hands. Urgh, disgusting. My cuticles are a mess.

"If you need anything, just ask," I say, to my nails.

"Really? Would you consider reading over my assignment? Tell me what you think?"

"Of course. Tolstoy is just so incredible. It's like he knows people, like, humanity, better than any other writer ever. And he presents them with their flaws, but it feels like he still loves them . . ." I trail off, realizing Topher isn't listening.

Instead, he's digging in his bag for his assignment and hands it over to me with a big grin.

I start reading. Right away I can see that he hasn't planned this paper properly. The structure is a disaster. The first paragraph lasts an entire page, and he doesn't even outline what he's going to talk about in the rest of the paper. His punctuation and grammar are a mess. And one sentence both begins and ends with "anyway."

"Um . . . do you have a pen? I need to mark a few things," I say.

"Damn. I left it in class." He frowns.

"Well, if you like, e-mail me the assignment and I'll make notes in, you know, track changes or whatever."

Topher grins at me. "Really? That would be incredible. I'll buy you dinner to say thanks." He winks at me.

"Sure!" I say, my chest lifting with joy. Dinner! A date!

"You're the best, Coco." Topher leans over and puts his hand on mine. "Thank you."

I can't say anything. All I can do is gaze at his hand and think *DO YOU LIKE ME? AND I HOPE YOU ARE NOT LOOKING AT MY NASTY-ASS NAILS.*

Instead, I nod. And, thank God, Topher just starts his usual monologue again.

"So . . . how about that Pushkin, huh? Is it just me, or does he sound like an asshole? He challenged everyone to duels, like all the time. He was, like, are you talking to me? You wanna fucking duel?"

"He was the Raging Bull of Russia in the 1800s?"

"Exactly."

Then Topher starts talking about his internship at my dad's company, asking if I thought my dad would pay him even though interns don't usually get paid. His eyes are so beautiful, I have to stare at his eyebrows or else it's like staring into the sun. Or look away entirely, at Washington Square Park, where everyone is taking their little break from the New York City madness to just *be* for a few minutes . . . I see some pigeons flocking to some old guy throwing crumbs, and for a moment my mind skips to that pigeon lady and to my mom, *Don't think about her right now, Coco, not now, not now—*

"Coco?"

I turn. It's Vic, my neighbor, and his niece Samantha.

"Hey!" I stand up and quickly hug them both, and introduce Topher. He does the standing-up-to-shake-hands thing. I love that.

"What brings you all the way over here?" I ask.

"Samantha works here, remember? We meet for lunch once a week," says Vic.

"How's that millennial study thing going?" I ask.

Samantha sighs. "Not great. We're pushing back the interviews by a few weeks, but don't worry. I'll be in touch."

"Millennials?" says Topher.

"Yeah. My sociology grad students are doing a study, but we're having trouble getting candidates to take part. Even though we're paying a hundred dollars per interview. It's insane."

"Are you kidding? I'll do it!" says Topher.

"Great!" Samantha gets a card out of her bag and hands it to Topher. "E-mail me. It'll be toward the end of the summer."

"What are you going to ask us about?" asks Topher.

"Your thoughts on life, careers, love, the future—"

"The simple stuff," interjects Vic, chuckling.

"Right." Samantha grins.

"So I guess we'll let you get on with your, uh, your date," says Vic.

"Oh! No, this isn't a date, ha!" I try to laugh, so Topher knows I would never think that, though obviously, I totally would. "We're just, you know, we're hanging out and stealing education," I say quickly.

Topher laughs. Phew.

"Stealing *what*?" Vic's voice rises about two octaves.

Topher stops laughing.

"Um . . . education," I say. "That's just a figure of speech. I'm not really stealing. I just come to Topher's classes with him. It's not a big deal. I'm not . . . hurting anyone, you know, I just have nothing better to do—"

"You think learning is for when you have nothing better to do?" Vic is incredulous.

"No! No, that's not what I meant—"

"Wait . . . are you enrolled?" Samantha is confused. "How are you graded?"

"I'm not writing assignments or anything. I write notes but that's just because, um . . ." I'm rambling now. "I mean, I just, you know, I work nights and I don't know what else to do with my time—"

"Really? You're reading all the books and taking notes and attending classes at New York University because you don't know what else to do with your time? *That's* why you're doing it? Do you have any idea how crazy that sounds?"

Vic can barely contain his disbelief.

And I don't blame him. It's so lame. Why *am* I doing this? Because I'm bored and lonely? Because I have a stupid, pointless crush on Topher? Because I'm a big fat loser who does stupid stuff like this?

Then suddenly the truth dawns on me, and tears rush to my eyes.

Because I'd never get in to NYU any other way.

I'm not as smart as everyone else. Not really.

Vic and Samantha are staring at me expectantly. But if I say anything out loud right now, I know I'll cry.

Then, unexpectedly, Topher rescues me.

"Coco is fine," he says, and Vic and Samantha glance at him in surprise. "She's just figuring out her next move. She's not hurting anyone. She's not lying to anyone. She's just hanging out, reading books. I don't see why that's a problem."

I smile at Topher gratefully. My crush just ratcheted up tenfold.

Vic stares at Topher. "Is she helping you study too? Taking notes for you sometimes? I thought so. Great side benefit for you, huh?"

"I'm not cheating." My voice is tiny. "I'm just—"

"Yes you are," Vic interrupts. "You're cheating yourself."

There's a long pause.

"Isn't that my problem, not yours?" I say finally.

It's the rudest thing I've ever said to Vic. It's maybe the rudest thing I've ever said to anyone.

"Okay, little Coco," Vic says sadly. "You're right. It's your life. C'mon, Sammy."

Samantha smiles and takes Vic's arm, urging him along, and they walk away.

Topher turns to me. "You okay?"

"Fine," I say, though I feel ice-cold inside, like I'm in trouble.

But I'm a grown-up. I mean, adult. Whatever. I haven't done anything wrong! Right? What did he mean by I'm "cheating" myself? How is that even possible?

I can't just sit here thinking about Vic, though. I have to go home and get ready for my shift at Potstill tonight.

My favorite thing about my life right now? Between days in class with Topher and nights in the bar—and bed—with Joe, I don't have much time to think about anything.

CHAPTER 18

Friends.

With benefits.

Best. Idea. Ever.

The bar was dead tonight, so we closed before midnight and came back to Rookhaven. (Frankly, I think both of us just wanted to get laid. Ahem.)

"Do you have any cake?" Joe whispers, cuddling into me in the dark. It's really too hot to cuddle, but I don't care. The tiny ancient air conditioner gives out more noise than air, so we usually keep it off.

"Cake?"

"Manly, postcoital cake?"

I grin into the darkness. "Alas, I do not. I haven't baked in weeks. I can offer you peanut butter on toast."

"My dad hated peanut butter," Joe says softly. "He was old-school Ireland, you know, thought peanut butter was newfangled American madness. So whenever I want peanut butter now I think, *Sorry, Dad . . .* Is that strange?"

"No," I say. "I get it. Random stuff always makes me think of my mom."

"Yeah. It's like he's always somewhere in my head, ready to step into my thoughts."

Neither of us needs to explain ourselves any further. We both totally understand what the other means. I start kissing him again. I'm sleepy and sticky, but right now, I don't care. I just want to kiss him more. I never thought I could feel so relaxed and in control when it came to sex. My virginity was such an albatross for years, and then my first time with Eric was just the worst. But sex with Joe is just . . . it's *fucking great.*

Joe pulls away. "Can I ask you a serious question?"

"Sure."

"Will you marry me?"

"What?" I choke the word out, suddenly very awake.

"I need a Green Card to stay in the States. I don't want to go back to Ireland, but my visa ends in a few months, so I figured—"

I sit up so fast that I nearly fall off the bed. "No! I mean, I can't—"

"Relax, I'm just messing with you," Joe says. "Maybe I'll go home to Ireland. I'll board the plane and be welcomed by the dulcet tones of the Irish air crew. I'll fall in love with the one named Colleen. We'll have eleven children and live happily ever after . . ." Joe sighs. "I'd rather stay in New York."

"If Potstill Prom makes enough money, I bet Gary will get you a visa," I say, lying back down. There's enough light coming in my attic window from the streetlamps outside that I can just make out the outline of his face

"Right. Like our little party is going to turn everything around," says Joe, defeated. "Coco, face it. The bar is dead."

"Don't be negative. The prom will be a huge success, Gary will rebrand the bar as a music venue, and he'll ask you to be the music venue guy—"

"I don't want to be the music venue guy, I just want to be a music guy."

I smile, pulling him closer. Joe reaches out, tracing a line with his finger from my lips, along my jaw, down my neck, and then we start kissing, and . . .

I know what you're thinking, but Topher doesn't even cross my mind. Lust is different. Everyone always talks about your heart versus your head. With me it's more like my heart versus my, uh, vajayjay.

Maybe it's strange to crush on one guy and sleep with another, but I can't help myself.

I like being with Joe.

I'm having a good time.

And he is too. He's a big boy.

He knows the rules of this game: we're just using each other temporarily. Men like him are always using women, right? Like how Eric used me. It's just the way it is. So now we're just using each other. This way, no one gets hurt.

Just as things get, uh, intense, Pia crashes through my door.

"Coco? Oh, shit!" She immediately U-turns, cracking up. "Sorry! Coco, I need your help."

"It's fine!" I immediately push Joe off of me, sit up, grab a T-shirt from the floor, and switch on my bedside lamp. "Just give me a minute to get dressed."

Joe gasps at me in pretend outrage, mouths "what about this?" and points at his, uh, you know, erectile nondysfunction. I try not to laugh and mouth "later." He mouths back "when?" and I start giggling uncontrollably.

"Are you two done?" says Pia.

She turns around. Joe grabs the sheet to cover himself just in time.

"Jesus. Do you always barge in here at one A.M.?"

"This is about Aidan, you guys. I need to win him back." Pia is very dramatic when she wants to be.

"Why do you want him back?" asks Joe.

"Why? What do you mean, *why*?"

"Well, you cheated on him. That tends to be a sign that something is wrong."

"Don't you dare judge me, Irish!" Pia's face is suddenly lit with fury. "I love Aidan. I made a mistake. I'm a dick. Okay? It will never happen again, ever. I need him to know that."

"Are you sure?"

"Totally sure," says Pia. "I've been crying almost nonstop ever since we broke up. I feel sick with grief about hurting him. He won't even answer my calls. I just want a second chance—"

"Second chances never work," Joe interrupts. I look at him in surprise. I've never heard him sound so harsh. "I've been cheated on. I gave her a second chance. And she cheated on me again."

Pia's voice cracks. "But that's not me. Hurting him is the worst thing I've ever done. Knowing that he's in pain because of something I did . . . I almost can't bear it. But he's in New York just for one night, for a work thing, and I want to ask him to forgive me. And I need everyone's help to do it. Angie and Madeleine are coming, and we're picking up Julia on the way. But I need you two too."

Pia sounds so earnest. I nudge Joe with my shoulder. He glances at me, and I can read the message in his eyes. But she's my friend. And he should trust me.

Joe sighs and looks back at Pia. "We're in."

Within half an hour, we're all in Pia's food truck, Toto, driving across the Brooklyn Bridge. It's a crappy old former ice cream truck, a sort of cartoon pig pink color, and these days she has far nicer food trucks to drive. But she still loves Toto best.

Joe and I are riding up front with Pia, and Madeleine and Angie are in the back.

"Is it safe to have them back there?" asks Joe. "Are there seat belts?"

"Oh, grow a pair." Pia changes gears with a clunk, and steps on the accelerator. She's become extremely proficient at driving food trucks this past year and does it with a sort of Formula One laid-back aggression.

Joe changes tack. "Can we put the air on? It must be a hundred degrees."

"Do you whine like a little bitch in bed too? Open the window."

Joe gives me a mock scared look and winds the window down.

There's a thump on the wall behind us.

Pia changes gears again, pumping the clutch like she's stamping out a fire, and makes a sharp turn up, taking us up toward Midtown.

"Man, I want a cigarette," Pia mutters. "I'm so fucking nervous."

"Do you want me to get you one?" I say. "I can buy some. Stop at a bodega."

"I can't smoke in the food truck! I'm a responsible adult and shit."

Out of the corner of my eye, I see Joe smirk.

Pia pulls up to a corner, and Julia bounds toward us, still wearing her work clothes, complete with her building security pass around her neck. I calculate quickly: it's after midnight. That means she worked about eighteen hours today, at least. She opens the truck door and seems surprised to see Joe and me sitting in front.

Julia's face falls. "What is he doing here? I thought it was just us."

"He is the cat's mother," says Joe.

"He's with me," I say protectively. Julia raises an eyebrow.

"So I have to sit in the *back*? In my *pantsuit*?"

"What, are you and your *pantsuit* too good for my food truck now?" Pia rolls her eyes.

"No . . ." Julia glances behind her. "I just don't want anyone I work with to see. They're brutal about shit like this."

She does a quick 360, making sure no one is watching, and runs around the back of the truck. I hear the door opening and closing, and moments later, a double thump indicates we're good to go.

"Aidan is staying at the Ace Hotel," says Pia. "It's on Twenty-ninth."

"Are you going the right way?" Joe looks doubtful.

Pia arches an eyebrow. "Excuse me? I basically drive around Manhattan for a living. Evens go east."

"Huh?"

"You drive east on Manhattan streets with even numbers—twenty-eight, thirty, thirty-two. And you drive west on Manhattan streets with odd numbers. With exceptions." Pia shifts the truck into gear. "Pay attention, little man. You might just learn something."

Joe shoots me an alarmed look, and I fight back the urge to giggle. I feel like Joe and I are in this together, somehow. Like he's my partner in this group adventure.

Once we get to the Ace Hotel, Pia reverse parks with skilled precision.

"Okay, team!" she shouts. "Let's move it."

Joe and I get out of the food truck just in time to see Angie step out of the back, walk straight out to the middle of the street, stop, and put her hand out right in front of her.

A yellow cab screeches to a halt, stopping inches from her knees.

"What the fuck is wrong with you?" The cabdriver is irate.

"Thank you so much!" Angie calls sweetly. "Can you help us out? I need someone big and strong to lift these speakers up on top of my friend's truck!"

Madeleine and Julia are pulling out a microphone and stand from the back of the truck. *Huh?*

"Did we bring an extension lead?" Julia is saying.

"What the hell is going on?" asks Joe, just as Pia charges up to us. "I thought you were apologizing to him—"

Pia interrupts. "Joe. Coco. You need to go inside, get Aidan's room number, go to his room, and convince him to come downstairs. But don't just call him. He'll hang up. You have to convince him in person."

"Why are we doing this in the middle of the night?" says Joe.

"Because I only thought of it an hour ago, and he leaves tomorrow." Pia's face is serious. "Look, I know this seems stupid. But I have to try. He's ignoring my e-mails and my calls, and I couldn't turn up and just beg. I need to *show* him how sorry I am."

Joe stares at her for a second and then nods. "I understand. We'll get him."

"This reminds me of something," I say, as we walk into the cavernous, dark lobby. "Oh! I know! Courtly love, you know, knights in shining armor writing sonnets and doing brave deeds to demonstrate their devotion. Only I guess that makes Pia the knight and Aidan her damsel . . ."

I am slightly out of breath. Joe has frog-marched me all the way to the concierge desk.

"Good evening to you both," says Joe, his Irish charm out in full force. "My name is Aidan, and this is my brand-new fiancée, Coco."

The hipster-model hybrids working the desk burst into applause.

"And we accidentally dropped our room key card in the Hudson. You see, I proposed on a boat."

I smile ecstatically, trying to look drunk and engaged. "We just had so much champagne . . ."

"What room number are you?" asks the concierge, just as Joe pretends to answer his phone.

"Um . . . I can't remember, so much has happened today! The last name is Carr?" I try to smile with newly betrothed joy. "My new last name! Or maybe not. I mean, it's kind of old-fashioned to take your husband's last name, don't you think? Besides, I like my name. Plus, I have a career to think about."

The concierge—already sick of us, just more annoying drunk people in his life—nods and takes out a key card for me. "Twelve twenty-four."

Joe grabs the key card, dips me into a kiss, winks ostentatiously at the concierge, and whisks me away.

" 'Plus, I have a career to think about' is one of the most hilarious ad libs I've ever heard," whispers Joe, as we wait for the elevator.

"Especially since I don't." I sigh. "I have no career."

"You will, my lovely wife-to-be," says Joe, brushing some hair out of my face. "Just give it time."

I grin up at him, and he winks.

A nervous flutter rushes up from deep in my tummy.

No.

No no no no no *nooooo* . . .

I know this feeling. It's that thing. That nervous fluttery thing. The thing that makes me think I like Joe, I mean, not just like him, but *like* like him.

As we walk into the elevator, my brain is suddenly in free fall.

Was our whole casual sex thing leading to something else, something bigger and better? I felt that strange *together* feeling in the truck. Is that what this is? Do I *like* like Joe? More than Topher?

Oh, shit.

I feel shy. I feel tongue-tied. I can't speak. I can't look at him.

Joe plugs the key card into the security slot and presses twelve.

"What's that?" I ask, my voice shy and whispery.

"Security," Joe explains. "You can't get to your floor without your key card."

The moment the elevator doors close, Joe grabs me with a little growl.

"Just in case they're watching on the closed-circuit camera."

Joe pushes me against the side of the elevator, holding my hands against the wall, and kisses me very slowly and deliberately.

Wow. This is hot.

"I wonder how much it is to get a room here . . ." he mutters.

The elevator stops, Joe pulls himself away from me, and I nearly fall over.

He takes my hand as we walk down the hallway, and I suddenly wonder how it is I've never noticed his hands before. They are very large, with long fingers and a wide, flat palm. They are the sexiest hands I've ever seen in my entire life. . . . Oh, God, my palms are sweating, I wonder if he can tell.

We get to room 1224 and knock loudly a few times.

Aidan answers, wearing a T-shirt and pajama pants, squinting in the light.

"Coco?" he asks, confused. "What are you doing here?"

No wonder Pia wants him back. Even pale and sleepy, Aidan is tall and handsome and kind of perfect.

But next to Joe, he's almost *too* perfect. Joe is taller and bigger than Aidan, and significantly scruffier. Aidan never has a hair out of place. He's impeccably groomed. I can't imagine him ever losing control. But I prefer Joe's look. More real. My God, I think I like Joe, I really, really like him—

Pay attention, Coco, for Pete's sake.

"Hi, Aidan!" I say cheerfully, then realize I need to look serious. "Um, good evening. You need to come with us. Pia needs to see you. It's urgent.

Panic flashes across his face. "Pia? Is she okay? What happened?"

"She's fine!" I say quickly. "I promise. She just . . . she has to tell you something."

Aidan sighs. "Oh. Look, I don't want to be an asshole, but I don't want to see her."

"Please?" I say. "She feels *so* bad, and she really . . . she loves you, I think, I mean, I know she does, and, um—"

Joe interrupts. "Aidan. I'm Joe."

Aidan looks at Joe. "Hi."

"I know you feel like shit, I've been where you are. I told her not to bother to ask for a second chance. I wouldn't give her one either."

Aidan raises an eyebrow. "Are you trying to make me feel better?"

"Look. Just come downstairs with us and listen to what she has to say. Then you can come back to your lovely posh hotel room and sleep on your eight-hundred-thread-count sheets."

Aidan rubs his temple, nods, and grabs his slippers and room key.

"This is your key, by the way," says Joe, handing it over.

Aidan gives a half laugh. "I wondered how you made it up here."

We head back to the lobby, Aidan wearing his pajamas and slippers with the kind of blasé self-assurance that reminds me of Pia and Angie. That's the definition of confidence: wearing pajamas in public without batting an eyelid. When we get out to the street, it finally dawns on me what is about to happen.

Pia is standing on top of the food truck. The microphone stand is set up in front of her, and the speakers are on the truck. She's going to *sing*? Pia is scared of singing in public! A crowd has gathered: the doormen, hotel guests, people walking past, cars that have stopped. All waiting to see what's about to happen.

"Are you kidding me?" Aidan stares up at Pia incredulously.

Pia looks so alone and vulnerable up there. I can see her hands shaking. Why the hell is she doing this to herself?

Because she loves Aidan, I suddenly realize. She loves him, and she'll do anything to get him back.

Pia clears her throat.

"Aidan, I am so sorry I hurt you. I will never hurt you again, I just want to be with you, I . . . it was the biggest mistake of my life, and . . . and you're the, you're the only one for me, I, um . . ."

Her voice is hardly audible. Oh, God, she's freaking out. I try to send her a message via ESP. *Breathe, Pia. Breathe . . .*

What if she loses her shit and has a panic attack? It's happened before!

I look around for the girls. Madeleine, Julia, and Angie are all standing in front of the taxi, next to the speakers. Madeleine pointedly elbows Julia in the ribs, Julia glares at her, pressing Play on an iPod.

The music starts, and I hear the opening notes to . . . wait, I know this song, I'm sure I know this song.

Pia clears her throat, and starts to sing.

CHAPTER 19

"Imagine me and you . . ."

Pia starts softly, stammering over the words. There are more and more people now, coming out of nowhere: hotel guests, from bars and restaurants on the street, from the cars and cabs backed up as they try to pass.

Pia is staring at Aidan, and suddenly her eyes flick to Joe and me, and out of the corner of my eye, I see Joe give her a thumbs-up. That's all it takes. Pia's voice grows louder, stronger, more confident, building slowly until she belts out the chorus and—

Wait! I know this song! My mom and dad used to sing this in the car. "Happy Together," by some old band called the Turtles.

I glance at Aidan and see his face crack into a huge smile. He loves Pia. He can't help it. The chorus starts, and led by Julia, Angie, and Madeleine, the entire crowd, everyone outside the Ace Hotel in the middle of New York City joins in, shouting joyously.

"I can't see me loving nobody but you for all my life . . ."

Joe grabs me and dips me into a huge Hollywood kiss, and I smile through our kisses as the whole of New York sings "Happy Together," all around me, and all I can think is, *My friends are the best.*

Aidan forgives Pia, of course. I can see it happen the moment she hits the chorus.

And the crowd is on her side. Everyone is singing along, and most of them are filming it on their phones. This is going to end up on YouTube, for sure.

When the song is over, the crowd cheers wildly as Pia gets down from the truck, looking as scared as I've ever seen her, and walks up to Aidan.

"I'm so sorry . . ." she whispers, her eyes big and pleading. "I will never hurt you again. Please forgive me, please. I love you."

Aidan stares at her, then *boom.* They start kissing, and crying, and kissing, and crying some more.

"Well, this is all very emotional and dramatic," remarks Joe.

I grin, gazing up at the city around us. The night is so warm, and the lights are so bright, that it doesn't feel like the middle of the night. At moments like this, New York City feels timeless, hourless, limitless. Like the entire universe begins and ends here.

I glance over to see Madeleine climbing up to the roof of the truck, her eyes glittering intently. As soon as she grabs the microphone, music starts pumping out of the speakers again, and Madeleine throws her fist in the air and belts out the opening lyrics to "Just a Girl," that '90s song by No Doubt.

"Take this pink ribbon off my eyes . . ."

A ripple of interest goes through the crowd. Pia's song was romantic and cute—an adorable only-in-New-York anecdote to tell their friends. But Madeleine's voice and stage energy, or charisma, just plain old talent, whatever you want to call it, is undeniable. She's wearing jeans and a black top, yet somehow it's like a light is emanating from her. And to say her voice is *extraordinary* doesn't begin to do it justice.

"It's not just me, right?" says Joe, staring at her proudly, his arm slung around my shoulders. "She's really got something."

"It's not just you," I say. "She's the best."

"What's her name?" says a voice behind us.

"Madeleine." Joe glances at the guy and then does a double take. "Ian James? I'm a huge fan. Joe Nolan."

They shake hands while I check out Ian James. Is he famous? He must be, right? He's short and tanned, and is wearing a weird little hat. He's one of those people who look like they *should* be famous, if you know what I mean. New York is full of people like that.

"Is she signed to anyone?"

"Not yet," says Joe. "She's with a band called Spector. I'm the manager."

"Well, the name has to change."

"Oh, totally." Joe nods quickly. "It started as a covers band. You know, old Phil Spector stuff, with a noise rock edge, uh . . ."

Ian nods. "Great."

I can see Joe is about to say something else, when Ian's phone rings, and he quickly answers it and walks away.

"Fuck me, Ian James . . ." says Joe under his breath. He glances at me. "Music producer. Big. Huge."

We both gaze expectantly at Ian James's back, but he walks down the street without pausing. He's already forgotten Madeleine.

"I should go after him. I should ask him for advice. I should . . ." But Joe is rooted to the spot.

"Go!" I say. "What's the worst that can happen?"

"He says no and laughs at me," says Joe. "Isn't that always the worst that can happen?"

Madeleine finishes the song, to more rapturous applause and whistles, and climbs down.

People in the audience are shouting, "More! More!" I cheer and clap and scream until my throat starts to crack. My friends, taking over New York, helping each other. We are all in this together.

Joe pulls me in for a quick kiss, just before he bounds over to the food truck and reaches for the microphone.

"If you guys want to see Madeleine playing live with her band Spector, check out the Potstill Brooklyn Web site!"

But now that the show is over, the crowd has lost interest, too jaded and busy to care.

I head over to the girls, who are congratulating Madeleine.

"That was incredible!" Angie is saying.

Madeleine grins, looking shy but euphoric. "Julia's idea."

"You are amazing! Fivies!" Julia is in hyperactive mode now, everyone's little cheerleader. Everything she says has an exclamation point. "I expected someone to come up and give you a record deal immediately!"

"Totally." Madeleine rolls her eyes to let us know she's joking. She looks over to Pia and Aidan, who can't keep their hands off one another. "Well, at least Pia's plan worked out."

"Seriously," Angie says. "I don't know what you're doing wasting your time as an accountant."

"Raking in the Benjamins," replies Madeline.

"You mean counting someone else's Benjamins."

"That too."

Joe walks up, grinning. "I love New York. At any moment you could run into people who are really *doing* something with their lives, you know?"

"Yeah, it's a fucking nightmare," says Angie, lighting a cigarette. "We're so close to everything we want, but so far away."

CHAPTER 20

Later, back at Rookhaven, Joe and I are upstairs in my room when I'm suddenly overcome by shyness. That nervous flutter in my tummy is bigger than ever.

I like him.

Joe is lying stretched out on my bed. He's such a big guy that his feet hang off the end, and his long arms easily reach the sides.

I perch awkwardly next to him.

"I'm hot," he says. "Can you put the air on?"

"It is on," I say. "Sorry. It's kind of old."

"No problem."

Joe reaches up, taking his shirt off over his head. I eye his broad shoulders and muscled arms and am suddenly stabbed by desire. God, I want him.

"You want to lie down?"

Joe moves over an inch so I can lie down on the pillow next to him. We're so close that I can feel the heat from his body, and I'm having trouble breathing. I reach up to turn off the bedroom lamp, but Joe grabs my hand.

"Leave it on?"

Then he leans into me, and slowly, so slowly I'm almost aching, kisses me.

How can kissing, fully dressed, with a lamp on, somehow feel more intimate than having real actual sex in the dark?

Because we just had such a weird, crazy adventure, the kind that only my friends can have?

Or because I can pretend to be someone else in the dark? Because in the dark you can just forget yourself in desire?

I don't know.

All I know is kissing Joe is making me forget how to breathe.

Then I wonder if he's looking at my nose and thinking that it's ugly, or that I have a double chin, so I prop my head up on one hand, elbow resting on the pillow. I hope this is a more flattering pose. Then Joe does the same, and suddenly we're face-to-face, eye-to-eye. He grins at me, and I grin back, but I'm so tense right now, it's more of an awkward grimace.

"What's that book?" Joe asks, squinting at my nightstand.

"*Anna Karenina*. I'm rereading it."

"What's it about?"

"Um . . . love," I say.

"Stealing education again? Why don't you just go legit, enroll in college and use your prodigious reading ability to earn a degree?"

"I'm not smart enough," I say, trying to sound offhand about it.

"Course you are," says Joe. "You just have to believe in yourself."

"I've never believed in myself," I say flippantly. "Sometimes I think I'm imaginary."

"I believe in you. I believe that you can do anything you want to do."

That's the nicest thing anyone has ever said to me.

I glance up and we meet eyes. Joe smiles, and I smile back, and then look away, my insides cramping with nerves. I pretend to sigh and close my eyes again, like I'm really sleepy, and secretly look down through my lashes at his body, the sinews of his muscles, and his flat stomach with those little hip curves that lead to—

"Can I ask you a question?" asks Joe, interrupting my about-to-be-R-rated train of thought.

"Yes."

"The first time we, you know, made sweet, sweet love . . ." He pauses as I snort with laughter. "Was it your first time?"

Midsnort, I start coughing awkwardly. Why is Joe asking that? Because I was so terrible at sex?

"You were amazing," he says, reading my mind. "Truly. The skill of Mata Hari."

I laugh despite myself. "Um, okay, well, no. That wasn't my first time."

"Was it okay for you?"

"It was lovely," I answer honestly. "Why?"

"I don't know . . . Sometimes I feel like there's a barrier up, like there's a part of you that you're holding back. Something in reserve. I wondered . . . I don't know."

There's a long pause.

"There was one other person," I say finally. "His name was Eric. I thought he was my friend and, um, he wasn't. And I didn't want to have sex with him, but we did."

"He—he forced you?" Joe suddenly looks furious.

"No! No, I mean, not exactly . . . It just, you know, it happened and I didn't really expect it to. It wasn't how I would have wanted it."

"What a fucking asshole," Joe growls.

"Worse than that. I, um . . ." The words come out before I can stop them. "I got pregnant."

"Shit," says Joe.

I take a deep breath. "I got an—an—you know."

"I know."

I gaze into Joe's face, trying to read if he's judging me, or hating me. But he's not. All I see is understanding.

"My sister had one," says Joe. "She went to England for it. It's still illegal in Ireland."

"It's *illegal*?"

He nods. "Of course, it still happens. It always happens." He sighs. "It's not fair. It takes two people to do it, but the girl deals with the consequences alone."

"Not always alone," I say. "I bet some boyfriends are supportive."

"Probably." Joe doesn't sound like he believes it. "My sister's boyfriend dumped her the night before she had to go to England."

"That's awful," I say.

"I got him back," says Joe. "I saw him in a bar in town a couple of weeks later. I punched him. Broke his nose."

"You're a nice brother."

"I wish I hadn't had to do it."

"I wish I hadn't had to do it too," I say. Suddenly, I know I'm going to cry. I close my eyes, and the tears roll down my cheeks. "I was stupid. I was so naïve. It wasn't even a year ago, but I've changed so much since then. If I could go back in time, I would never have gone home with Eric. I wish— I wish—" I can't talk anymore.

"It's okay," says Joe, brushing his hands against my cheeks to wipe away the tears. "It's really okay."

Joe wraps his arms around me and I snuggle right in to him. He's so warm and lovely, and I feel so safe that I stop crying. I take some big, shaky breaths, calming myself down.

"You okay?"

"I'm okay. Talk to me about something else. Tell me stories about the hundreds of women you've slept with."

"Okay," Joe says, says, stroking my hair. "Would you like to hear about the wonderful events of my first time?"

"Yes."

"Last year of school. My girlfriend. And she had to tell me I wasn't putting it in the place that I, uh, thought it was in."

I crack up.

"It was fine! I found all the right bits eventually. You know. Trial and error. It was nice. Special. For me, anyway." Joe pauses. "Then she cheated on me."

"Bitch," I say. "What happened?"

"The usual. She went away for college, met someone else, couldn't bear to break up with me. I found out because someone else I know posted photos of a party on Instagram. Some guy was kissing her."

I make an involuntary *urgh* sound. "That's bad."

Joe shrugs. "She was just young. That's what I think now. We both were. Shit happens. It's all part of growing up."

I nod. "That's what I think now too. About Eric, and everything after. It's just part of my past. Like everything else, good and bad."

We lie in silence for a moment. Then I run my fingers along the muscles on his back.

When I touch him, he takes a deep breath and makes a peaceful little *hmmm* sound, and I get that nervous flutter again. It's the same feeling as when I'm with Topher, but somehow . . . warmer, safer.

I gaze at up him, willing Joe to open his eyes and look at me, to feel what I'm feeling.

Bizarrely, he does.

We stare at each other for a moment.

Without warning, Joe shifts and pulls me under him so he's pinning me to the bed with the entire length of his body. He looks serious, more serious than I've ever seen him and, my God, so perfect.

He kisses me slowly.

Then he pulls back and looks into my eyes. I feel totally exposed, emotionally naked, if that makes any sense, lying here, nose-to-nose, so close, in the lamplight.

Joe smiles. "Beautiful."

I frown when he says it. He clears his throat and says it again, his voice low and intense.

"Really. You are. You're so beautiful."

Then we start kissing. Real kissing. Kissing with intent. The kind of kisses that make your entire body tingle and your lips feel swollen. We undress each other, still with the light on, and I try my hardest to cover myself, especially my thighs, but then—

"So perfect," Joe says, almost under his voice, running his hands down my thighs. "Soft and smooth. Your body is incredible. Just the way women are meant to be." Then he says that word again. The word I've never thought about myself. "Beautiful."

"I . . ." I can't find the words to contradict him. I look down at our naked bodies and think, *Maybe he's right.* His body is long, hard, muscled. My body is soft and smooth and voluptuous. It's meant to be like this.

And then we . . . well, you know.

This time it's different. This time I feel like I'm here, really here, present in the moment. My body, my soul, my brain: all acting in unison. I'm not just using him for his body, and I'm not closing my eyes and pretending I'm someone else. I'm here.

We're here, together.

An hour later, when we're lying half-draped over each other, sticky and sated, Joe moves his head to my stomach, and I absently stroke his wild man hair. My nervous tummy is finally gone.

I am perfectly content. "Oh, Coco," Joe murmurs. "That was amazing."

I don't even know what to say. It was more than amazing. It was sex like I always imagined sex would be.

"Thank hell we became friends, right?"

My chest clutches for a second. Is he making a joke? I can't tell.

"Friends . . ." I repeat. "Of course. That's us. Friends."

"Friends who get to see each other naked and have fun, isn't that what you said?"

"Yup." My voice is barely a whisper.

Joe must sense that I thought there was more between us. He's warning me there's not. So I don't get hurt again. Because he's just a womanizer, a total player, the kind of guy you can be friends with, hook up with, but never date.

And *boom*. My happiness is shattered.

We're just friends.

I was stupid for thinking I felt anything else. I will never make that mistake again.

CHAPTER 21

I love walking the Greenwich Village streets around New York University.

Even now, on a sunny midsummer morning, when most students are on vacation, it feels special. A huge college, with over fifty thousand students, in the middle of the best city in the world. Isn't that wild? I always thought of college as something isolated way out in a small town in the middle of nowhere, you know, where you're just stuck all the time and the food sucks and the locals hate you, but NYU is in the middle of downtown Manhattan. It's so cool.

Topher e-mailed me back the assignment and asked me to proofread it one more time, print it out, and drop it off at Professor

Guffey's office for him. She's requested that everyone print them out and deliver them in person, rather than e-mail them.

I finally get to her office, on the top floor of a nondescript building on Greene Street, just a couple of blocks from Washington Square Park. There's a plaque on her door. ROSEMARY GUFFEY. PROFESSOR OF LITERATURE, PROFESSOR OF SOCIAL AND CULTURAL ANALYSIS. She won't be here—she has a class on the other side of campus. I checked. (I'm not stupid.)

I slide the assignment under the door, stand up, and walk down the hall.

"Coco?"

My entire body seizes with panic.

I turn around. "Professor Guffey!"

Professor Guffey smiles and stoops to pick up the paper. Without looking at the paper, or the name on the front—*Topher Amies*—she beckons for me to come inside.

"I was hoping to talk to you," she says. "Come into my office."

Oh, my God, I'm so busted.

Why isn't she in her class?

I follow her in, feeling icy dread in the pit of my stomach. She hasn't looked at the name on the assignment yet, and as she walks behind her desk, she opens a file, drops it in, and closes it, all without glancing at the name.

She doesn't know I just handed in Topher's assignment and not my own.

Yet.

The walls of her office are lined with books. My eyes nervously flick around.

"Wow, you have so many books," I blurt out. "I mean, of course you do, but, um . . ."

"I'm a book person," she says. "I know it's old-fashioned, but I can't see myself on a Kindle anytime soon."

"Oh, me too," I say. "If I'm getting the train home to Rochester, or whatever, you know, it's a long journey, and books are so heavy, then maybe I'll use the Kindle app on my iPad. But I like the feel of books. I like the permanence of them." I'm gabbling now, my eyes darting around the shelves, desperately searching for something to distract her. "The smell. The weight. The whole thing."

"Exactly," she says. "Now—"

"Oh, look! *Jane Eyre,* I love that book, and *Little Women,* of course, I know that one by heart, I've read it what feels like a million times. I first read it when I was, like, eight years old," I know it's rude to interrupt, but I can't bear for her to ask me if I'm really a student here. I can't lie to her face, but if I don't, Topher might be expelled, right? "Um, and we studied *A Doll's House* in high school, but I never really clicked with it."

Professor Guffey laughs. "High school has a way of destroying any real love for the written word. I hated Shakespeare in high school, truly, I did. I thought it was overrated, at best. Then I read *Much Ado About Nothing* of my own accord when I was twenty-three, and I just . . . got it."

I grin. "I never got Shakespeare either. Maybe I should try him again in a couple of years."

Professor Guffey nods. "Maybe you should."

She pauses, thinking.

My breath catches in my throat. Then she leans over to her laptop, taps a few buttons, and walks over to her printer. A moment later, it prints out a sheet, which she picks up and hands to me.

"I was thinking about you last night. I made a list of books you should—I mean, might like to read," she says, leaning against her desk.

"You did? Why? I mean—thanks, but why?"

"The summer course list is a good start, but it's Russian-centric, of course, and there's so much more out there. Particularly novels by women, about what it felt like to be a woman in eighteenth-century London or nineteenth-century France or New York or . . . well, you get the gist."

I am not sure what to say. No teacher has ever taken a special interest in me before.

"This isn't for studying," she adds quickly. "And it's not compulsory. This is just because I think you'll enjoy them."

"Um . . . thank you. Seriously, so much."

I look at the list. I've never read the books on it, even if I've heard of them. *Indiana* by George Sand. *Villette* by Charlotte Brontë. *Ruth Hall* by Fanny Fern. *The House of Mirth* by Edith Wharton. *The Coquette* by Hannah W. Foster. *The Awakening* by Kate Chopin. *Evelina* by Fanny Burney. *North and South* by Elizabeth Gaskell. *Middlemarch* by George Eliot.

"I'll read them, but I probably won't understand them," I say, trying to joke.

But Professor Guffey frowns. "Of course you will. They're not difficult. They're just stories. There's nothing intimidatingly intellectual to understand . . . you just need to feel them."

"But . . ." I pause. "I'm just not smart enough."

"Coco, I know you're smart. It's in everything that you do, what you say, how you say it—"

I laugh, despite myself. "That's not what my father says. And my high school grades were not exactly stellar—"

"High school is nothing," interrupts Professor Guffey, snapping her fingers to emphasize her point. "It is *not* an indicator of the rest of your life. Your teachers didn't encourage you like they did some other students? So what? That's their mistake. Don't make it yours. High school teachers are not the masters of the damn universe. Neither is your father. He doesn't decide your fate."

I am stunned by her intensity. She really seems to care. "Okay, I will. I'll read them. Thank you, Professor Guffey."

I stand up to leave.

"I'm sure you'll like those books," says Professor Guffey. "Even if you're not at NYU studying them, you'll enjoy them."

Something goes clunk in my stomach.

She knows.

I can't bear to turn around and meet her eyes. I walk out, closing the door behind me.

She knows I'm not a student here.

She knows I'm stealing education.

She knows I'm a liar.

But why should I care? I won't get in trouble; I can't get kicked out of a school I don't even go to, right? And Topher can't get into trouble either. She doesn't even know that I practically wrote Topher's assignment. I mean, I could have been just dropping it off for him, right?

It still feels wrong. I feel guilty. I feel like a bad person. I'm never a bad person.

Maybe deep down, I'll always be a good girl.

My brain whirring, I walk in the blazing sunshine all the way down to SoHo, stopping for a coconut water, and then all the way down Broadway to City Hall and over the Brooklyn Bridge. I walk and walk and walk.

As I walk, I think back to my stupid Happy List.

My Happy List
1. Be thin
2. Fall in love
3. Figure out what to do with the rest of my life

I thought I'd made such headway toward happiness this summer: having casual fun sex with Joe, hanging out with Topher, working in a bar for cash, learning for free during the day.

But I'm no closer to achieving any of those things than I ever was.

I'm still not thin, I'm still not in love, and I still don't know what to do with the rest of my life. I'm still the kind of good girl who feels bad for getting in trouble with a teacher, and she's *not even my teacher*.

I worry about Professor Guffey all the way home.

But I stop at BookCourt on Court Street and pick up *Middlemarch*, and then go home, walk right up to my attic room, and read.

CHAPTER 22

Much later, but what feels like mere moments, I get a text.

It's from Joe. *The bar is boring without you. Send me a selfie. You know the kind I mean.*

I smirk. *No. Use your memory. Or your imagination.*

He replies: *Now I am picturing you wearing fairy wings and knee-high pink rain boots and NOTHING ELSE.*

Laughing, I look out my bedroom window. It's nighttime already, and I didn't even notice.

Somehow, hours passed while I was reading *Middlemarch*.

It was like time travel, or something, just jumping into a different world, becoming totally immersed in an alternate reality . . . This is the best book I've ever read, better than *Anna Karenina*, better than anything, ever. I want to make every page last forever.

My stomach growls, and I head down to the kitchen. To my surprise, everyone's there, seated around the table.

"What up, ladybitch?" says Pia. "I brought home some leftover chicken cacciatore from the food truck kitchens. Hurry. Julia's eating all of it."

"I am not." When Julia is in a bad mood, she completely loses her sense of humor. "I had one tiny bowl."

"It's good," says Angie, mopping her bowl with a piece of bread. "It needs a little more salt."

"It has plenty of salt."

"Well," says Angie, "I guess I just like more salt."

"Well," Pia mimics her, "have fun retaining water."

They both crack up.

I make myself a bowl and take a seat.

Despite my elation about loving the book, now that I'm back in my own reality, I feel kind of down.

Okay, very down.

But why? I didn't get busted by Professor Guffey, I mean, not really. She *kind* of let me know she knows I'm not a student, but nothing *happened*.

It's not because of Joe and everything that happened the other night. I knew I didn't *like* like Joe, then I thought I might for, like, a nanosecond, then I realized I didn't. So I'm right back where I was. He's my friend with benefits. Nothing more.

What else do I have to feel down about? Family? No. My dad is off my case about the job thing. Ever since his visit to New York, he's been totally cool about me working at Potstill, and by "totally cool" I mean he has not mentioned it.

Money? No. I used to be always just *this* close to being broke, you know, even though Jules and I don't have to pay rent because we inherited the place . . . I was constantly tallying up additions and subtractions in my head. New York is such an expensive city, it's insane. I used to get cash from an ATM on Monday and make it last for a full week, leaving all my credit cards at home so I couldn't make any accidental spends, that sort of thing . . . But I've been working long hours at Potstill, and it's been increasingly busy. With tips, I'm earning more than double what I used to earn in the pre-school. Plus, the tips are tax-free, and cold hard cash. Bartending is more profitable than educating. How about that?

Weight? No. I used to spend days thinking bad things about my body. Just sort of ruminating on it, in a negative way. Sensing my thighs rubbing together, my jeans too tight around my stomach. Oh, the hell of feeling fat and hungry, and loathing and craving, in equal measure, everything you eat. I don't even think about that stuff anymore. I just stopped.

There's nothing to worry about. Yet I still feel dejected.

Why?

It's Professor Guffey. It must be. Even though I've been trying to tell myself it's okay, thinking about her makes my chest thud with shame. I feel like I let her down. I lied to her. And when she caught me, I just ran away.

It was wrong. Even though I'm not a real student, and it's not like anything I do matters.

Oh, my God. My brain needs to shut up.

Sighing, I look around the kitchen.

Pia is cheerful. She's eating the chicken with a dreamy smile on her face, staring into space. After her singing-on-the-cab performance, she and Aidan got back together, and he's now back in San Francisco and has apparently sworn to spend every weekend with her from now on, and do everything he can to move back to New York as soon as humanly possible. That is love, I guess. I wonder if she would have forgiven him as easily if he'd cheated on her . . . or if we would have encouraged her to? I don't know. I'm just glad she's happy.

Angie is happy too. She finished all her bags for Serafina, and they chose three to go into production. And Sam is on his way back to New York. He's sailing right now, somewhere between here and Europe. Right now she's eating a block of cheese with the enthusiasm of the naturally skinny, sketching in her notepad.

Madeleine is . . . I don't know. I can never read her. She's thinking about something, that's for sure. She's barely responding to anything anyone says, but she seems to want to stay here in the kitchen with us, like being around us is comforting her in some way. I wonder if I'll ever figure her out.

And Julia is miserable. Though I'm not sure why. She keeps saying she loves work, but maybe it's one of those things you say so you'll believe it. She's looking incredibly tired, huge dark rings under her eyes. This is the first time she's been home before midnight in ages.

Sometimes it seems like we can't all be happy at once. Maybe that's the law of averages: in a house of five girls, someone's always going to have something bad happening in her life.

"Are you guys all coming to the Potstill Prom?" I say out loud.

"You're really doing that?" says Angie in surprise.

"Yeah!" I say, trying to sound positive and enthusiastic. "Totally doing it. It's going to be huge. You know, if the prom is a hit, then Gary won't close the bar, and maybe he'll help get Joe a Green Card."

"The band is playing too," says Madeleine. "We're totally psyched."

She's so deadpan, I have to stare at her for a second to see if she's being sarcastic. I think she is, but in a low-level way, which is okay.

"Who are you guys taking as dates?" asks Pia. "I'll bring Aidan! He'll be here then!"

"A date?" I echo.

I seriously hadn't thought about it.

I have to get a *date*?

My first thought is Joe. But he can't be my date. Joe doesn't like me. Joe's just a friend. Anyway, I can't ask him, or he'll think I like him, and I don't, I mean, I did, for a moment, but then I realized I was wrong, totally wrong.

"Sam might be back by then," Angie smiles happily. "Yay."

Madeleine shrugs. "I'm singing. I don't have to bring a date."

"Are you going to ask Peter the Magnificent?" Pia asks Julia.

"No. Forcing us to bring a date is fascist," says Julia.

"Saying that's fascist is an insult to the true victims of real fascists," says Angie.

Julia gives her the finger. Pia starts giggling.

But I can't laugh. I'm freaking out. I've never asked a guy out on a date in my entire life. And there's only one person I can ask.

Topher.

I have to ask Topher.

He's the perfect date for the new grown-up, wild me. The old me, in high school, went alone to prom. I was sick with excitement and nerves, and in the end, I just came home alone and cried all night, because my so-called best friend slept with Eric, and I thought I was in love with him. In a way, that was the moment my entire life took a sharp turn downhill. My self-esteem hit rock bottom. Instead of getting turned off him, I became desperate to have Eric like me back, and that's why, years later, in New York City, I slept with him. Stupid, stupid, stupid.

Taking Topher to the Potstill Prom would be like righting all those wrongs. Like everything had a point.

At that moment, Julia's phone beeps. She glances at it and purses her mouth in a little line that means she's stressed about something.

"What is it?"

"Peter."

"What does he say?"

"He says 'no problem.'"

"Why is he saying that?"

"I texted him earlier. Told him I was probably too busy to have dinner this week."

Everyone shouts at Julia at the same time.

"What the fuck?" says Madeleine. "You told me you liked him."

"Just because he was fired? Everyone gets fired! I've been fired a dozen times!" That's Angie.

"He is a nice guy, Julia. You liked him so much. How can that be just *kaput*?" Pia sighs.

"Okay!" exclaims Julia. "Everyone back off. The guy is *unemployed,* okay?"

"Everyone's unemployed until they get a job," says Pia.

"Real deep, Pia."

"Jules, you can't be so hard on people," says Angie.

"I'm only as hard on everyone else as I am on myself." Julia crosses her arms, the ultimate defensive gesture.

"Maybe you should be a little kinder to yourself too," says Pia gently. "There are no points for being a hard-ass. No one is keeping score."

"Says the person who never played a team sport in her life," says Julia. "Someone is *always* keeping score."

"Oh, for fuck's sake," says Angie.

Madeleine interrupts. "Look. All we're saying is, in New York City, it's really hard to find someone with whom you actually want to spend time." I've never heard her be so thoughtful and passionate about something. "When it happens, you don't *question* it, Julia. You just *go* with it."

Julia stares at her for a moment. "Fine! I'll text him. Tell him my schedule cleared up."

"Attagirl."

Julia frowns at everyone and reluctantly taps out a text. A moment later, she gets a reply.

"Wow, he's not playing hard to get, huh?" says Angie.

Julia reads the message and grins. She really does like him. She can't help it. Then she looks up at all of us. "Okay, everyone. Show's over. Julia and Peter are back on. For now. He better get a job soon, that's all I'm saying."

I still haven't said a word. My brain is stuck on a loop saying, "I have to ask Topher to prom, I have to ask Topher to prom, I have to ask Topher to prom."

But later, when I'm alone in my bedroom, I practice it in the mirror.

"Do you want to be my date to prom?"

Wow, that was hard to say. Even to myself.

I clear my throat, shake my hair, and try again.

"So there's this lame prom thing at the bar? Do you wanna, like, come?"

Too low-key. And a little too Valley.

"We're throwing this party at the bar where I work. It's prom-themed. You should come."

Perfect.

CHAPTER 23

After our next afternoon class, Topher and I take our usual spot on the grass in Washington Square Park.

I'm going to ask him to be my date to prom.

If I can work up the courage.

I just need to summon up the nerve.

Then he looks at me, and I feel a little thrill run through me. Gosh, it's nice being here with him. All those times in high school when he was hanging out with the jocks and I was hanging out in the library, who would have thought we'd end up here, together, like this?

"What makes you happy?"

The words are out before I can stop them. Where did that even come from?

Topher looks up in surprise.

"Happy? Me? Um, a free place to live, that makes me happy. Getting paid for my internship, that makes me happy." I smile. I spoke to my dad about it, and Topher's now getting a stipend, plus expenses. "Hanging with my buds, you know. The usual stuff." He pauses, and then grins. "Blow jobs."

I laugh in shock. It wouldn't shock me if Pia or Angie said that, but for some reason, Topher saying it to me shocks me. That's weird.

"What makes me happiest of all is going out and getting hammered. There's a big party tonight at Mel's place. Remember Mel Arnett?"

Of course I do. She was one of the popular crew back in high school. Not actually pretty, if you get down to it, but white-blond hair dye, a well-padded bra, and sheer force of personality made everyone think she was the hottest thing around. She lives in New York now too? That really annoys me, for some reason. How dare she move here, to *my* New York City?

"Um . . . yeah . . ." I frown, like I'm trying to think. "I think I remember her."

"It's gonna be wild." Topher looks at me and grins. "You like wild parties, Coco?"

"Sure, I . . ." I'm about to say I love wild parties. And I'd love to go with him and what time and where and what should I wear and should I bring my own alcohol or will it already be there and is that okay or should I pay someone for it, when Topher's phone rings. He glances at it and smirks, then picks up.

"Hey, fuckface! What up?"

He pauses and then cracks up, and turns to me, mouthing, "I've gotta go!" and grabs his backpack.

I smile and wave good-bye, but Topher is already walking quickly away, deep in conversation, laughing hysterically at jokes I can't hear.

Wait, so did he invite me to that party tonight?

He didn't really, right? He just said, "You like wild parties, Coco?"

Yeah. I like wild parties, goddamnit. I really like them.

That could be my big chance with Topher. We're such good friends now, you know, I bet if we just had a few drinks, something would totally happen. Maybe. And even if it doesn't, at least I can ask him to be my date to the Potstill Prom.

But where's the party? I can't go if I don't know where it is!

By the time I get back to Rookhaven, I've decided.

I'll tell Joe I'm sick and can't work tonight.

And then I'll text Topher and ask him about the party tonight. Totally casually. And then, totally casually, ask him to be my date to the Potstill Prom.

I just need to figure out how to do that without throwing up from nerves.

I texted Julia to see if she knew where the party was, but she replied: *Mel Arnett is a fucking idiot, why would I go to her party?*

So annoying. Julia had very set views in high school on who she liked and who she didn't like, and the sexier girls who weren't as smart as her and didn't join every club like she did were not her favorites.

Maybe I'll just text . . . *Hey, Toph, so about that party, can I come?*

Urgh, no.

It is very hard to nonchalantly get yourself invited somewhere. Even harder than asking someone to prom. I mean, not prom, but, you know, a prom-themed party.

I pick up my phone, willing Topher to text. *Text me Topher, text me, text me . . .*

My cell beeps.

Oh, my God. It's Topher!

It's like we have ESP. Or something.

Thanks again for your help. You're the best.

I'll text back later—after waiting the requisite amount of time so I don't look too eager, of course—and say, *My pleasure. So, about that party . . .*

I text Joe first: *Hey! I'm sick. My throat hurts and I have a fever. I probably shouldn't come in tonight. So sorry . . .*

I'm even bad at lying in a text message.

Screw it, I'll just send it.

And as soon as I work up the nerve, I'm texting Topher to find out where this party is.

I walk downstairs to the kitchen and out to the deck. It's a gorgeous summer evening, warm, blue-skied, and quiet. Angie's out here too, smoking a cigarette and tapping on her phone.

"It's Sam," she says, without looking up. "He found WiFi."

She smiles at the screen. *Taptaptap.* Practically levitating with happiness. Her thumbs tap frantically, and she just raises an eyebrow now and again as she reads his responses. They're so in love.

I wonder what that feels like, to be genuinely in love with someone who genuinely loves you back.

Pretty goddamn nice, I bet.

"You okay?" I say.

"Fine." *Taptap.* "I saw my dad and his girlfriend today. She's knocked up. It's weird and I hate it. Sam is calming me down."

"Oh," I say. "So, what would you do if you wanted to get the address of a party you weren't officially invited to?"

She doesn't take her eyes off her phone. "If I wasn't officially invited, the party probably isn't worth going to."

And there you have it. Cool in one sentence.

I'm texting Topher in two minutes.

Maybe three.

The front door slams and then I hear Madeleine's voice. She's with someone. Amy, I guess.

"Hi, Madeleine!" I call out.

There's no response, just the sound of them going up the stairs, and eventually I hear Madeleine's door slam. Angie's still taptaptapping away.

I need to just ask Topher about the address for this party and then go there and ask him to prom and then my life will be perfect. Right? Right.

I'm so stressed, I should bake.

But no, I know that won't make me happy.

"I don't bake my feelings anymore," I say, almost to myself.

To my surprise, Angie was actually listening.

"Well, no wonder you've lost weight."

"What?" I double-take. "Say that again."

"You've lost weight." Angie finally puts her cell down to look at me. "Your clothes are loose."

I actually laugh out loud. "I have been waiting to hear those words for, like, twenty years."

"You didn't *need* to lose weight, Coco. Are you eating enough?"

"I think I am . . ." My voice trails off. Am I?

Maybe I'm eating less. My life used to be punctuated by food. It revolved around three square meals a day with three or four (or five) snacks. I just don't think like that anymore. I eat when I'm hungry, not when I'm bored or lonely or worried. It's that simple.

"Are you going to become anorexic?" asks Angie seriously. "Because I remember some girls in a little thinspo club at college. They were like ugly little sticks. The hair on their heads fell out but they got this weird fluff on their faces. They stank like nail polish remover." She pauses. "Do you feel me, Coco? No. Anorexia."

"Promise," I say. "Besides, I'm not *that* thin."

Angie shakes her head. "My God, you're so hard on yourself. Where did you learn to treat yourself like that?"

"Uh, have you met my sister and my father?" I say lightly.

Angie smirks, but then her phone beeps, and *boom,* her attention is gone.

I look down at my body. It does look a little different. But I feel like I'm just the right size for me.

I like having boobs and hips and a waist that goes in and out. Joe told me I was beautiful the other night. My body doesn't make me unhappy anymore. It just . . . it doesn't. The realization is like a huge weight off my shoulders. In fact, I love my body. Just the way it is.

I make a mental note to cross the first item off my Happy List.

Now all I have to do is fall in love and figure out what to do with the rest of my life.

My phone beeps. It's Joe, replying to my text telling him I was sick. *Poor baby. Take it easy. Want me to come over later and play doctor?*

"Angie, do you think what I'm doing with Joe is bad?" I say. "You know. Because I'm sleeping with him and I don't want anything else?"

"As long as he knows that, and it's all he wants too, I think it's fine."

"He knows," I say. "But do you think everyone else thinks I'm . . . um, you know . . . a slut?"

Angie pauses, midtap, and looks at me. "I think 'slut' is a stupid word used to hurt women. I think that anyone who believes that a woman's worth is dictated by her sex life is a Neanderthal. And most of all, I think that what you do with your vagina is your business and nobody else's." She stares at me for a second, and I'm almost frightened by her intensity. Then she turns back to her phone. "But hey, I'm a feminist. That's just my thing."

I'm thinking about this, wondering if I'm a feminist too, because that seems like something I should have decided by now, when my phone rings. It's a strange number. Maybe it's Topher calling from someone else's phone to invite me to the party!

"Hello?"

"Is that Coco? Coco, it's Peter. I'm, uh, I'm—I'm your sister's, uh—"

"Peter the Mag—er—"

"Yes. *That* one. Look, I'm with your sister, I mean, she's fine, but she's, uh, she's—"

I grab Angie's arm to get her attention. "Peter! What happened to Julia?!"

Angie drops her phone and looks at me. "What? What happened to Julia?"

"Nothing, nothing, she just collapsed, we were at dinner and we had a couple of drinks and she—"

"She collapsed?"

"She's been hitting the Adderall a little hard. I'm with her now. St. Luke's. They say it's exhaustion and dehydration, and—"

"I'm on my way," I say.

My brain is spinning so fast, I almost can't see straight. I'm exploding with thoughts that just tumble down, one after another . . .

Julia fainted from working too hard? Can that even happen? What if she actually has a brain tumor and that's why she fainted? What if she dies? What if she had an epileptic fit and dies from working too hard, like that banker guy a couple of years ago? How much Adderall has she been taking? Why is she even taking Adderall? Where did she get it? What if she has an aneurysm? What if she has a heart attack? What if, what if—

Stop!

It's that little voice again. I haven't heard it in weeks. I gulp, taking a deep breath in and out. I need to stop freaking out.

"We have to go to Manhattan," I say to Angie. "Julia's in the hospital."

CHAPTER **24**

Losing a parent when you're just a kid teaches you that there are no guarantees. More than most people, I know that sometimes everything is *not* going to be okay.

My mom will never hug me again. She'll never kiss the top of my head or hold me tight when I'm sad or scared. And other people I know will die too. It's inevitable.

Death is waiting for all of us. One day, you're here, the next you're gone. The same sun is in the sky, the same houses are on your street, the same food is being served at your favorite restaurant, the entire world continues perfectly without you in it. But you're dead. Or you're still alive. And someone you love is dead instead. Which is another kind of death altogether.

It's something I try not to think about, because once I start, I can't stop. I've played out a hundred deaths in my head for everyone I know. I guess that sounds macabre, but it's true. It's like my brain thinks I should prepare, just in case. I think about if my dad died suddenly, how Julia and I would survive, or if we wouldn't, if we'd just disappear, drowning in the sadness, tumbling into a vertigo terror of grief. I think about my friends dying, my cousins, our neighbors from Rochester. How I'll feel, what I'll do.

And sometimes I think about Julia dying. But that's the one I can't handle. That's the one when I always think, *If it happens, I'd want to die too.*

"I'm so scared," I say, my voice a tiny squeak.

"It's okay, Coco," says Angie, grabbing my hand when we finally walk out of the subway near the hospital. "She'll be fine."

I meet her eyes and nod. I hope she's right.

As we walk into the hospital, my heart pounds erratically in my chest, and I start getting flashbacks to being in the hospital with my mother.

At first, Julia and I would go with mom to her appointments after school, and because she didn't want us to hear what the doctor said, we'd just sit in the waiting room reading ancient issues of *American Girl,* both of us feeling sick with fear but unable to express it, even to each other. Then, when she started chemo, she scheduled it during our school days, so that in the afternoons she could rest at home while we played or did our homework. I took over making dinner and baked cakes and cookies to try to get her to eat more.

I didn't go back into a hospital until much later, when things were so bad that my entire soul was shriveled into a tiny walnut of horror deep inside me.

Oh, God, that overwhelmed feeling is back, I can't get any air into my chest, I can't—

Breathe.

Yes. Breathe.

Focus on this moment. Nothing else matters but this moment.

When we reach Julia, she is lying in a curtained-off hospital bed, talking animatedly to Peter, who is covered in what looks like blood, but proves, on closer inspection, to be spaghetti sauce.

Julia is hooked up to an IV drip, oh, my God . . . She's pale and waxy-looking, her hair wet with sweat.

But she's also very, very, very hyper.

"Coco! Angie! Hey, you guys! It's fine, nothing really. We were at dinner, and I was having slight palpitations, and you know, I felt a little shaky. Nothing I haven't felt before after an all-nighter! It was fine, *totally* fine, and then suddenly it was like someone switched gears in my heart and my chest was like bangbangbangbang and then it felt like someone was sitting on it and I was, like, holy shit-balls, I'm having a heart attack, you know? So funny."

Angie nods, frowning. "Right. A twenty-three-year-old girl having a heart attack. Hilarious."

Julia nods, continuing to smile and talk like some kind of pepped-up cartoon.

"And I couldn't breathe, it was literally like I'd forgotten how to breathe. And actually, you know, that happens to me sometimes at work, it's like I'm holding my breath for the longest time, and I suddenly think, *When was the last time I actually exhaled?* Then I tried to speak, but suddenly I felt like I couldn't say more than a couple of words at once. And then I stood up, but I felt like I couldn't walk more than like two or three steps. Then the air went all numb, that makes no sense, but—"

"She fainted," says Peter. "And because she's Julia, she fainted in the loudest, most energetic way possible. She knocked over the table we were sitting at. Pasta everywhere. Wine bottle broken."

"Thus the tagliatelle stains," says Julia, smiling at Peter. He smiles back and reaches over to take her hand. What the hell? Is this meant to be some kind of romantic anecdote? "So the moral of the story is, don't work all night and then drink four espressos before heading out for spaghetti and wine."

Oh, my God. Julia doesn't even think this is bad.

She's acting like it is no big deal that her boyfriend had to take her to the hospital.

She could have had a heart attack. She could have had an epileptic fit. She could have died.

And why is she talking like that? When did she start monologuing aggressively at warp speed? Is that the Adderall? Or is that just the way she is these days, now that she's the next big thing in banking?

"Why were you taking Adderall, anyway?" I say. "I thought you only took Xanax."

Julia flinches.

I've just broken the unspoken promise between us to never mention her Xanax in front of anyone else. I know—in the way that you just know things about your family even when you've never talked about them—that she wants everyone to think she's too smart and tough to possibly need medication, but fuck it, I don't care. None of the girls ever asked how I got the Xanax that time at the dinner party, but whatever. I stole it from Julia, obviously.

"The Xanax was left over from years ago!" Julia glances quickly at Peter. "Coco, you know that."

"But you don't need Adderall, you don't have ADHD." I'm aware of how naïve I sound, but I don't care.

"It helps me concentrate. My work day is really long, and sometimes I need to pull all-nighters, you know, the usual stuff. Everyone does it."

"That's crazy! That's completely crazy!"

I glance at Peter, who looks away guiltily. He must have taken Adderall too, I suddenly think. Back before he got fired. Then I look at Angie, but she doesn't seem fazed either. Maybe she takes Adderall. Maybe everyone takes it. Everyone except me.

"It just helps me concentrate, Coco," says Julia. "It's not a big deal."

"So how long till you're out of here?" asks Angie, changing the subject.

Is everyone just taking drugs to help them achieve their dreams now? That's the new norm? Fine.

What about my dreams?

I want to fall in love. Joe will never love me. And I don't care, I don't want him.

I want to fall in love with Topher.

Suddenly, almost without thinking about it, I turn around and walk toward the exit of the ER.

"Where are you going?" shouts Julia after me.

But I don't reply.

She doesn't need to know.

I'm going to Mel Arnett's party. I'm going to see Topher.

And I'm going to kiss him.

CHAPTER 25

The party is at Mel's apartment in Murray Hill. I texted Topher as soon as I left the hospital. It was so easy.

What's Mel's address again?

So perfect, right? Low-key, totally indicates I used to know Mel's address because of course we're in touch all the time, even though she was in Julia's year in school and we never spoke and I haven't seen her since I was fifteen and she wouldn't even remember me.

Topher texted me the address a second later. Which is practically like being invited.

As I'm waiting in the lobby of her building for the elevator, I apply red lipstick. My armor.

Just as the elevator arrives, two guys I know from high school walk into the building. Zack Ober and Jay Mitchell. They were in the year above me and below Julia and Topher and Mel, firmly in the cool group, the guys that messed around in class and played the most practical jokes. They're living in New York too? Did everyone move here after college, or what?

I hold the elevator door open for them.

"Thanks," says Zack.

I smile at him slightly, feeling too nervous to respond. He never spoke to me in high school.

"What floor is it?" says Jay.

"Um." I clear my throat. "Eleven."

Oh, my God. I'm actually going to a party with the most popular people in school. The same people who always made me feel invisible, deficient, and self-conscious just walking the hallways. I remember constantly wondering: did they all get handed a "how to be cool" handbook when they turned twelve? Everyone seemed to know rules that I didn't. Everyone seemed to know what to say and when to say it. I was just . . . I was so clueless. Sad and clueless.

When the elevator stops, Jay holds the doors open and indicates I should exit first.

"No, no, you go ahead," I say quickly. He held the doors open for me! So nice.

Jay and Zack leave the elevator and walk down the hallway toward an open door. The music is so loud that I can feel it in my teeth. Then we walk in.

Everyone from high school is here.

They look over at us, greets Jay and Zack, totally ignoring me. Wait, do they just not remember me? Seriously? I was in the same school as them for years.

I'll find Topher. And take it from there.

I walk though the hallway into a small living area. The tiny kitchen counter is covered in open bottles of booze and Coca-Cola and red plastic cups. It's crowded with people dancing and drinking. Mostly drinking.

A scream catches my attention, and I look up to see a couple of girls I remember as football groupies, drinking tequila straight from the bottle and falling against each other.

This is fine! This is totally fine.

Topher won't mind me dropping in. He never seems to mind anything. Though it's kind of hard to know exactly what's going on in Topher's head. He's always smiling.

Maybe it's impossible to ever really know another person, inside and out, you know? Even my friends and my sister . . . I'm not sure I will ever know what's going on inside their heads. Like, why is Julia so slammed at work that she has to turn to prescription drugs to keep up? Why does Madeleine seem to be retreating even farther into herself? How can I ever guess when I don't know what they've been through in their lives? I don't know what they're most scared of or want more than anything. How can I ever know someone else when I barely even know myself?

Shut up, Coco.

I need to stop thinking, find Topher, and kiss him. And my heart needs to stop beating so fast. Why am I nervous? I'm just at a party. It's totally normal.

"Coco, hey!"

Topher. Over in a dark hallway just off the living room.

"Hey!" I smile at him, relief overwhelming me.

Topher reaches out to hug me hello. It's the first time we've officially hugged, I think, and I can smell a lemony shower gel.

"Glad you texted me. I didn't know you were coming," he says.

"Um . . . I just . . . I was in the area."

Behind Topher, all huddled together in the hallway, I see a bunch of the guys he was friends with in high school: the jocks. Some of them are already so drunk their eyes are half closed as they slump against the wall. It's not even nine o'clock.

184

Topher hands me a glass of brown liquid. I take a sip. Cheap whiskey. Not nearly as good as the stuff I've been drinking at Potstill all summer. But I don't say anything. I take a long sip, looking around.

Didn't any of them make any new friends since graduation?

So this is what happens at a party with the popular crowd. Seems like a pretty average party to me. Our housewarming for Rookhaven last year was way wilder.

The bathroom door right next to us bursts open, and four girls stumble out, all giggling and chatting over each other, pushing through the drunk guys. The last girl to walk out is Mel Arnett.

"Hey, T-bone!" she says to Topher, then her gaze lands on me. "You. I know you. Do I know you?"

"I'm Coco," I say. "Thanks for—"

Mel sniffs and rubs her nose. "Hi, Coco! Nice to meet you! Are you guys okay? Toph, do you want anything? I can get you anything you want. Anything at all. Oh, my God, there's Jessica! I have to go! Byeee!"

Topher meets my eye as she hurries away, and winks.

"Bottoms up?" he says, and we both finish the cheap whiskey in our glasses. "Damn. Let's have another."

"Sure!" I say. "Do you have any Kilbeggan?"

"What's that?"

"It's an Irish whiskey, kind of honeyish, um—"

"All I know is, if it's brown and it gets me loaded, I like it," says Topher. "Scotch, rye, bourbon, Canadian, I don't give a shit."

I smile. "I love whiskey. I think—"

But he doesn't hear me; he's already gone back to the bar to refill our drinks.

While I wait for him to get back, I look around at the party. So many people I haven't even thought about since high school. I can't believe they're all still hanging out like this.

Maybe it's just me, but there's a really weird vibe at this party.

Actually, it's not weird.

It's boring.

Then I realize: no one is laughing. Everyone is just here to be here. They're either looking at each other, or being looked at, or too drunk to see anything. Isn't that bizarre? At the parties we've had at Rookhaven, all you can hear is people laughing and talking and shrieking with joy—the sound of *fun*.

"Coco . . ." A male voice speaks up behind me.

My chest freezes in horror. I know that voice. It's Eric.

Holding my breath, I turn around.

"You look great!"

I hate him.

I hate his stupid hair and bad skin and sleazy smile. I don't know how I could ever have thought I liked him. I don't know how I could possibly have had sex with him.

"Um, thanks . . ." I say, my voice barely audible above the music.

I hate him. I really, really hate him. He never even called me after that one time we slept together. I tried to tell him about what was going on, about the abortion, but he wouldn't even return my e-mails. He's that kind of guy. He's scum.

"Come with me!" Eric says, grabbing my hand. "I need to talk to you about something in the bathroom."

"No, uh, no thanks . . ." I pull my hand out of his grip.

"C'mon, don't be boring!"

"She said no, man," says Topher, coming up behind me. "Back off."

Eric obediently backs off, going into the bathroom with a couple of the other guys he used to hang out with at school. Topher hands me another cup of cheap whiskey.

I look up at Topher, overwhelmed with gratitude. He protected me from Eric. I feel like nothing could ever go wrong while I'm with him.

"Don't mind Eric. He's a fucking douche," he says.

"He totally is," I say. "A complete fucking douche."

Topher leans in to me, rubbing his shoulder against mine. "I'm glad you came."

I can hardly breathe. "I'm glad I came too." I look up at him. His lips aren't that far from mine. Maybe if I tilted my head, just like this, and gaze at him, he'll lean down and kiss me.

Kiss me now, I think, as forcefully as I can. *Kiss me please kiss me kiss me kiss me now.*

But he doesn't.

How can I get him to kiss me? Do I just lean forward and kiss him? Do I gaze at him until he kisses me? How did I first kiss Joe? I can't remember. It just happened. Damn, that was a good kiss. No, don't think about Joe, that makes me feel weird. Should I just try to kiss Topher? Fuck it. Why not.

So I twist my body to face Topher, get on my tiptoes, lean my face into his and—

"Toph!"

The most beautiful girl in the world is standing right in front of us.

Long brown hair and long brown legs and long brown eyelashes that *must* be extensions, *seriously,* and a teeny-weeny little black dress.

Oh, no.

"Maggie!" Topher puts his arm around her waist, pulls her tight against his body, and kisses her passionately. I can see their tongues.

I inhale sharply. My God, she's like a Bratz doll. Her legs are so thin I'm surprised they can hold her up. Is she Topher's girlfriend? He's never mentioned a girlfriend, has he?

She's pressing her body against his so hard that I feel like I'm intruding on their personal space, so I look down at the floor.

Maggie's wearing four-inch platform heels, the kind that Angie always says are "urgh, so basic." Her toes are pretty. She has a predictably perfect pedicure in the kind of shiny apricot-blush-nude color that I can never find at the nail salon, ever, no matter how many bottles I swatch before choosing a color. I glance at my ancient sandals with my three-week-old half-cracked purple pedicure underneath. Why did I choose purple? It's the worst color. My toes look like dead grapes.

Finally, Maggie and Topher pull apart, and her eyes swivel around the room, eventually landing on me. "This must be . . ."

"An old buddy from Rochester," says Topher. "Coco, Maggie. Maggie, Coco."

"Oh, right! Coco! You're just like Topher described!" She smiles at me. Her eyes don't seem to move or crinkle like they should and her forehead is all plastic and hard. I stare at her curiously. Does she have Botox? Is that already a thing?

"You're the reason Topher passed his class, I hear."

"I am?" I say. "Oh, um, you mean because I helped edit his paper?"

"You didn't edit it. You wrote it."

"Are you calling me stupid, Maggiemoo?" Topher kisses her again. Wow, he likes to use a lot of tongue.

"Um, so, how do you guys know each other?" I ask.

"Maggie and I met last year," says Topher. "She lives in L.A., but her parents live here, on the Upper West Side—"

"Central Park West," she corrects him quickly.

"—so she visits a lot," he finishes, not minding her interruption at all.

They lock eyes for a moment, twinkling prettily at each other, like something out of a reality TV show.

"Um, what do you do in California?" I ask just to fill the space.

"I work for a movie producer." Maggie has just enough brag in her voice to make me immediately sure that I hate her.

"Maggie and I are heading to the Hamptons tomorrow to take a couple of weeks off before fall semester starts," says Topher.

I tried to kiss him and he has a *girlfriend*.

What was I *thinking*?

"Can you open this?" asks Maggie, handing Topher an expensive-looking bottle of white wine. "You know I can't drink cheap alcohol."

"Sure, baby. Another drink, Coco?" says Topher.

"No! I mean, um, no thanks," I say quickly, draining the rest of my whiskey. "I have . . . to work! Yeah! I have to work!"

"Oh! Where do you work?" Maggie asks, smiling prettily.

"A bar in Brooklyn." I drop my bag twice in my hurry to leave. "Bye!"

"Nice to meet you, Coco!" She calls after me.

As I'm walking away, I see Eric again.

"Coco!" Eric reaches out for me, a full plastic glass of beer in one hand.

I grab it from his hand and, *splash,* throw the beer right into his face.

"What the hell?" he splutters.

"Go fuck yourself, Eric."

I walk out of the apartment and slam the door behind me. Then I rush to the elevator, and as soon as I'm out on the street, I hail a cab. It's going to cost a lot to get me all the way to Brooklyn, but I don't care.

I'll never fall in love. I'll never figure out what to do with the rest of my life. I need to distract myself from everything that is real, I need escapism in the true sense of the world, and no, a book won't fucking cut it tonight.

CHAPTER 26

After a couple of hours in a very crowded Potstill, speed-drinking Joe's best concoctions, I'm feeling ohhhhhh so much better about everything.

"Everything okay, Coco?" asks Joe for the eighth time. The bar is unexpectedly busy tonight, and I should probably offer to work. But I don't want to work. I only want to drink.

"Is everything okay?" I repeat. "That's a great question, Joe."

My sister is in the hospital because she's abusing prescription drugs. I crashed a party and tried to kiss Topher. Topher has a girlfriend, and everyone else I idolized in high school is weird and boring. Joe just wants to use me for sex and I was stupid to ever think anything else was possible. I get everything wrong. I am such a *dick*.

"No, everything is not okay."

Joe frowns at me. "I thought you were sick?"

"Give me another Whiskey Smash. Smash me!"

At that moment there's the sound of a guitar from the other side of the bar. I look over, squinting one eye to help me focus. Spector is setting up. Madeleine is checking the microphone, Amy is tuning her guitar, and there's a new drummer, who is adjusting her stool to be just the right height.

I hiccup. "Fuck, yeah! Maddy!"

"You're so cute when you swear," a blond woman next to me at the bar says. I look over. She grins at me flirtatiously.

"Wrong tree, wrong dog barking, my friend," I say. "Wait. That's not what I . . . never mind. I didn't know Spector was playing tonight!"

"It's a surprise set," says the woman. "Just for friends, and friends of friends."

I look around the bar and suddenly realize that every single person in here, apart from Joe, is female. And young. And hot. And gay.

"Well, at least I'm not going to go home with some random guy and get pregnant, am I right?" I say.

"Damn straight," says the blond girl next to me, reaching over for a high five.

I take out my phone and text Angie.

At Potstill. Come down! Madeleine is playing a gig!

Then I add some emoticons: the woman in the red dress, the octopus, and a flag. Just because I think they're funny and I'm drunk.

"I'm drunk!" I say to Joe.

"I know, honey," he says.

"I'm not your honey."

"You will be later."

I roll my eyes and turn back to the stage. Maddy is talking intensely with Amy, the pink-haired punk guitar player, and there's something about the way they're talking—faces real close together, half smiling at each other—that strikes me as unusual for band mates. Then Maddy throws her head back, bursting into laughter. I've never seen her so relaxed and happy.

Amy leans over and whispers something, and Maddy looks at her with this funny glint in her eye, and smiles, it's like—I mean, it's like . . .

Oh. I get it.

Madeleine is gay.

"Well, that makes sense," I say to no one in particular.

Moments later, the band starts, the lights go out, and spotlights— since when do we have spotlights in Potstill? Joe must have done it—light up the entire band.

Then, with a big drumroll intro, Spector starts playing a cover of "I Saw Her Standing There" by The Beatles.

And the entire bar is suddenly a dance floor. Everyone is going crazy. I shimmy along from my barstool, cheering and whooping for Madeleine.

"Okay, my friends. Go grab shots for the next song!" shouts Madeleine. "They're on the house!"

Joe must have been primed, because there are fifty shot glasses lined up on the bar, and he's pouring out a lethal-looking mixture from a huge mixing jug.

"What's in that?" I ask.

"Rye whiskey, Peychaud's bitters, sugar, lemon peel, and a smidge of absinthe."

"A smidge?" I repeat.

"A smidge."

"How can we afford to give out free booze? We're broke, remember?"

Joe shakes his head. "Everyone here for the gig paid twenty dollars to get in. We can afford it."

"Why didn't Maddy tell me about this gig?" I ask. "I was supposed to be working, you know, I would have found out . . ."

"I was going to send you home before the gig started," Joe admits after a moment of deliberation. "Maddy asked me not to tell you."

Why would she do that? I'm her friend!

The crowd charges the bar to get shots, and I don't want to miss out, so I take two and down them in quick succession.

Then two things happen.

The absinthe hits my brain.

And Spector starts playing a fast, dirty amped-up version of "Wild Thing."

"I LOVE THIS SONG!" I scream.

No one pays attention. So I do another shot and scream it louder. Then one more. And then . . .

Blackout.

CHAPTER 27

I wake up looking into a bucket that shows signs of having contained vomit very recently. My head pounds. My stomach aches. I'm lying across my bed, my head and right arm hanging over the side . . .

I look down.

There's vomit on the floor too.

I try to groan, but no sound comes out.

Oh, God.

"Are you awake? Jesus, finally, I was about to call the paramedics."

Joe.

Joe is lying next to me. Naked. Then I realize I'm naked too. And nothing is covering my ass.

I grab the sheet with one arm to cover myself, but the movement gives me immediate motion sickness, so I lean over and retch into the bucket. Nothing comes up. My stomach cramps with empty pain.

"Drink." Joe hands me a coconut water.

I choke down the coconut water, shaking slightly with the effort, and then two seconds after I've finished it, I vomit it all right back up into the bucket. Some of the puke dribbles down my chin.

I collapse onto my pillow, feeling tingly with nausea.

"Poor little bunny . . ." Joe takes a Kleenex from my nightstand and wipes my vomit-strewn mouth. "What am I going to do with you, huh?"

Why didn't I remember that I'm not good at drinking? Why do I ever drink at all? What made me think that was a good idea? Why does anyone ever drink when this is what happens?

"I hate alcohol." My voice is barely a whisper. "I'm never drinking again."

"Heard that before."

"I mean it." I close my eyes. The effort of talking is too exhausting to bear. "This is hell. I am in the fiery pits of hell."

"But Coco, you were amazing last night. The life of the party."

"Please leave the room," I whisper. "I need to be alone with my shame."

Joe pulls on a pair of boxers and walks out, still laughing.

Oh, God.

Every time I close my eyes, my bed gives a terrifying lurch, without me actually moving. Like seasickness and vertigo combined.

So I keep them open, staring at my bedroom ceiling and the glow-in-the-dark stars that don't glow anymore, the same ones my mom used to look at. Oh, God, I hope she can't see me now. For the first time I hope that there is no afterlife or heaven or whatever, so she can't look down and see me and know what a pathetic moron I am.

Memories from late in the night float back in snatches, a montage of crazy.

I danced. I danced on the stage. I danced on a chair. I danced on the bar.

I smoked a cigarette.

I ordered more shots.

I made out, just briefly, with the girl who came on to me earlier and then told her that I regrettably had to stop kissing her because I am straight, and that I just—oh *God*—"really love penises," but that I fully supported her right to sleep with and marry anyone she wanted, with or without a penis.

I made out with Joe in the bathroom (which is disgusting, seriously, that bathroom is cleaner than it used to be but still *ew*). In fact I maybe, yes, I did, I definitely did, have sex with Joe in that bathroom.

I threw a glass of Whiskey Smash on the floor and shouted, "whiskey *smash*!" and laughed so hard I fell off the barstool.

Why can't my memories stay in my blackout where they belong?

I tried to sing onstage with the band, I suddenly remember with an extra lurch of horror. I tried to play the drums. Madeleine had to force me off the stage. I bought everyone—*everyone*—drinks. I know it's stupid to regret being generous, but seriously, did I have to get nineteen rounds of cocktails and insist that Joe take my cash even when he tried to refuse?

Why, why, why did I drink so much?

Because I was upset about Julia being in the hospital.

Because she's changing from my sister into a workaholic type-A New Yorker who I don't even recognize.

Because I was embarrassed about trying to kiss Topher, the guy I liked so much that it was almost an ache, practically in front of his thin, perfect Bratz doll of a girlfriend.

Because of that one night I thought I liked Joe and he never, ever, would or could *ever* like me back.

Because no one will ever love me, and most of all, because I'm completely aware of how pathetic it is for me to think that and want to weep with self-pity.

My phone beeps.

A text from Pia: *How's your head this morning, Ace?*

Did I even see Pia last night?

Then I see a lot of texts that I don't even remember sending.

To Pia: *Maddy is GAY! And I might be too. Not really. I love Topher! Come party! xxxxxx*

To Angie: *I'M DRUNK! It's sooo fnnnn xxxxx*

To Pia: *I dancin ON THE BAR xxooxxooxx*

To Joe: *Meet me in bthrrrom for SEX xxxx*

To Pia: *I want you to call me Ace from now on okay?????*

To Angie: *Call me ACE!*

To Topher: *How's yr night?*

To Topher: *I hope it SUCKS. Kidding!! Ace xoxoxox*

To Topher: *You should date MEEEEEEEEEE*

To Topher: *I didn't really try to kiss you I was just kidding*

To Topher: *But if you want to kiss me that would be fine oxoxox-oxox*

Oh, no.

OhJesusGodpleasenowhywhywhy . . .

I outed Maddy to everyone. I had sex with Joe in the bathroom of Potstill. And Topher—I can't even bear to think about what Topher must think of me. He must think I am such a loser.

And none of them even replied. Like, not a single text.

Unless I deleted their replies?

I can't remember.

Joe returns and I quickly hide my phone under the pillow.

"Well, I have to go to Potstill," he says, pulling on his clothes. "I need to prep the bar for the band." He kisses me quickly on the forehead. "You okay?"

"I'm so embarrassed," I say. "I was such an idiot."

"Of course you weren't! It's healthy to go a little wild sometimes."

After he leaves, I stare at the ceiling again. I am too hungover—and frankly, too full of shame—to move. Then there's a knock at my door. It's Julia, carrying a huge bottle of ice-cold Coke.

"Thought you might need this," she says. "I ran into Joe on his way out. He told me you partied hard last night."

"Thank you, oh Ju-ju, thank you . . ." I almost drop the bottle in my haste to get it to my lips. "When did you get back from the hospital?"

"Last night. I told you, it was nothing."

Julia puts one hand on her hip and watches me as I guzzle half the bottle and then let out a guttural belch. Normally, burping is practically a sport with her, but today she doesn't even crack a smile.

"I think it's time you grew up, Coco."

"Excuse me?" I whisper.

"This whole wild child act is just so not you. You need to calm down."

I can't respond for a second. Is she *serious*?

Then I find my tongue. "Don't tell me who I am. And don't tell me to calm down. You're the one who ended up in the hospital last night."

"That was because of *work*, Coco," snaps Julia.

"You can't keep working so hard!" My voice is still nothing more than an angry rasp. "It's not healthy!"

I never tell Julia what to do. Her eyes widen with surprise and annoyance. "Well, you can't keep working in a dead-end bar and sleeping with your loser boss."

"Joe is not a loser." I'm hot with fury. "How dare you call him that?"

"Because he is a loser! Why the hell won't you just go out with Topher? He's so much better for you."

"Topher has a girlfriend. And that doesn't even matter, because who do you think you are, telling me who to date? Why do you think you know it all? Look at you and Peter. He's the nicest guy in the world, and you were going to dump him."

"Fuck off, Coco." Julia offers a disparaging laugh, her attempt to get the upper hand.

"No, *you* fuck off," I say. "I am so sick of you telling me what to do! You're not in charge of my life." I make my voice as loud and strong as I can. "Fuck. Off."

I've never said *fuck off* to anyone before, ever, and now I'm saying it to my sister, the person I love more than anyone. Nothing makes sense anymore.

Julia is red with anger. "I'm going to work. Because that's what grown-ups do."

"Have fun snorting Adderall on your way there."

"Have fun staying home like the petulant boozy loser baby that you are?"

I throw myself back on my pillow and close my eyes so Julia can't see the tears that are almost overflowing, and thank God, a moment later, she leaves, slamming the door behind her.

CHAPTER 28

"Nice texts last night, ladybitch," says Pia.

Angie looks at me and cracks up.

For a moment, I almost feel better. Being around Angie and Pia always makes me smile.

But then I remember last night, and the fight with Julia. I stayed in bed all day, having hangover dreams that tasted of regret and vomit. Now it's evening, and about ten minutes ago, I came down to the kitchen where Pia and Angie are playing cards. I'm eating buttery toast, very slowly.

"Please don't tease me. I can't take it. I'm hanging on to sanity by a tiny thread, and I swear, it's this close to breaking. I was such a penis last night."

"You were not! Your texts were hilarious. Everyone needs to go crazy sometimes."

"No . . ." I shake my head, then quickly stop, because it really hurts. "I tried to kiss Topher, and he's dating a Bratz doll—"

"Wait. What? Start from the beginning."

So I tell them the whole story. About Julia fainting ("That girl is on a one-way track to a quarter-life crisis," comments Pia), about trying to kiss Topher seconds before his girlfriend turned up ("And he never mentioned her to you before? What a fucktard," says Angie), about throwing the beer at Eric (they both shout with joy at that) and, finally, my absinthe-driven self-annihilation at Potstill.

"How come you don't like Joe?" says Pia. "I love that dude."

"Joe is great," I say. "But he's a total womanizer, you know?"

"He is? Are you sure?" asks Angie. "You know, when you're with him, you can't stop smiling."

"Really? Well, that's just because he makes me laugh. Anyway, it doesn't matter, because Joe is not into me like that. He said we're just friends. It's better that I like Topher."

Angie and Pia exchange a look.

"Just what," says Pia carefully, "is so great about Topher?"

"He is . . ." I pause, thinking. "He's *Topher Amies*. You know, he went to my high school and everyone worshipped him. Ask Julia."

"No one worships people once you're out of high school," says Angie. "That shit doesn't mean anything. Is he really a good guy?"

"He made me a sandwich once."

"Has he responded to your drunk texts?" asks Pia.

I close my eyes, reliving the horror. "No. But he was going away today, you know, with his girlfriend. She was nice . . . she said that I helped him pass his class—"

"Why?" says Pia. "What did you do? Write his paper for him or something?"

"No. I only edited it," I say.

"What?" explodes Pia. "I was kidding. You really did his homework for him like some kind of helicopter mom?"

"Dude, Topher is using you," says Angie. "I'm sorry, but he is."

Before I can reply, Madeleine comes in from her evening jog. Oh, shit.

"Hey," she says, opening the cupboard and taking out her little mason jar of homemade trail mix.

I need to apologize to Maddy for texting Pia and outing her without her permission. For being a nightmare when I was drunk and trying to play drums on stage. For everything.

"Um . . . Maddy?—"

Maddy turns around and meets my gaze. My stomach drops.

At that exact moment, Julia marches in, pink-faced with the heat and the walk from the subway, rigid with tension, still with her little backpack from work, her ponytail slightly askew. Is she still angry at me? Or about something else?

She walks straight up to Maddy.

"Why didn't you tell me you're gay?"

Oh.

Shit.

There's a long pause, as everyone in the kitchen holds her breath and waits for a response.

I guess Pia told Julia about my text. Why didn't I just shut up and wait for Madeleine to tell us when—or if—she was ready?

Madeleine turns back to the trail mix. "Because it's none of your fucking business?"

Angie looks up. "It's kind of is, if you've come out to the entire world except us."

I clear my throat. "Um, Angie, I thought you said it's no one's business except mine what I do with my vagina?"

Pia chokes slightly on her wine.

"This isn't just a vagina thing," says Angie. "This is a life choice thing."

"It's *my* life choice vagina thing," says Madeleine. "Not yours."

"But I thought I was your closest friend!" Julia's voice breaks. "We used to talk about guys. You had a boyfriend at college. You—"

Madeleine still hasn't turned around. "Why do you have a problem with this?"

"I don't have a problem with it. That's not the point!"

"Then what the fuck is the point? It's my life." Madeleine is trying hard to sound under control, but I can see her hands shaking.

I feel sick. Julia and Madeleine never fight; it's not the way it works. Madeleine and Pia might fight, and Julia and Angie, but never Julia and Madeleine.

"I think Julia just means that we wish you were a little more open," says Pia, surprisingly gently. "We're all so close but we didn't even know this about you—it's like—it's like—"

"It's like we don't know you at all," says Angie.

Madeleine is grinding her teeth with tension. "Of course you know me."

"Bullshit," says Pia. "Show us your arms. Show us what's under those long sleeves you always wear."

The entire room goes quiet.

Madeleine doesn't turn around.

Julia and Pia and Angie exchange looks. I don't get it . . . Why do we need to see Madeleine's arms?

And by the way, Julia hasn't even looked at me yet. In this really pointed way. She just keeps arguing with Madeleine, with her body positioned so Angie and Pia can see most of her face, and I only see her back. You can read the exact relationships in a group of girls just by studying body language, who looks at who, who looks back, and who laughs at whose jokes . . . Every little nuance is rich with meaning. And Julia is letting me know she's still angry with me.

"Show me your arms, Madeleine," repeats Pia. "I want to see the scars."

Scars?

Suddenly, Madeleine throws the glass jar, hard, at the kitchen floor. It shatters, and bits of trail mix fly up, hitting us all like shrapnel. Then she strides to the doorway, pauses briefly, and turns to face us one last time.

"If you were really my friends, you wouldn't treat me this way. You'd just let me live my life." Madeleine is fighting for control, trying not to cry. I've never seen her so close to losing it. "Everything is hard enough for me right now."

"We're here! Talk to us!"

"I don't want to talk to you!" screams Madeleine, then calms herself down, visibly shaking with the effort. "You can't force me to confide in you, Julia. You are not the boss of everyone in the damn world. You've been controlling poor fucking Coco for years, and look how that's turned out."

"What?" I say.

"I don't need to take this shit from you," says Madeleine. "I'm moving out."

Madeleine walks out of the kitchen, slamming the door after her.

No one says anything.

"Fuck!" Julia is incensed. "Why does everyone always want to move out? It's the same fucking thing over and over again. Now it's just me and the party twins and my goddamn sister."

"Party twins?" repeats Angie in a bored voice. "Fuck off, Julia."

"Actually, your goddamn sister is moving out too," I say quietly.

A silence follows my words.

Then Julia speaks. "*What?*"

I stand up.

"I don't want to be around you anymore. Our whole relationship is full of lies. You're taking drugs to handle your life in New York. Fine, that's your business. Want to hear my business? Last year, I slept with Eric, and I got pregnant. And I had an abortion."

Julia gasps. Pia and Angie are suddenly frozen still, hardly breathing.

I keep talking. "I didn't tell you, because I knew you'd never understand. What does that say about us? What does that say about our relationship?"

Julia is so stunned she can hardly speak. "You did? But—"

"I don't want to hear your judgment right now, Julia," I snap. "At the end of the summer, I'm moving back to Rochester to live with Daddy. I don't want to live with you anymore."

A long silence follows my words.

And I think I shocked myself as much as everyone else when I said it.

But I don't want this anymore.

I want my old life back. From before any of this happened. Before everything got so complicated. Before I started trying to be wild and made my life such a mess. When I didn't have a love life or sex life or personal life, when I didn't get drunk and text dumb shit and try to kiss guys who are way out of my league. When all I did was read and bake and eat and everyone looked after me because I was too young and too stupid to look after myself.

I'll move back to Rochester, back into our family home, and get a job in a preschool. Any job. I don't care. I'll do it after the Potstill Prom next week, so I can make sure that everything works out for Joe. Nothing is keeping me here. No one is begging me to stay.

I stare at the table, unable to meet anyone's eyes, waiting for someone to say something. But there's just silence. Total silence.

Then Julia walks out.

She doesn't even slam the kitchen door behind her, which is weird, since that's the kind of thing she'd usually do. Just leaves quietly, without a word. I can't hear her feet on the stairs either, which must mean she walked out the front door.

I look up at Pia and Angie, who are staring at their cards.

Suddenly, I feel like the kitchen walls are closing in on me. I can't bear to sleep in this house tonight. I can't hang out here tomorrow. I need space.

So then I do something that is probably the worst idea ever.

I text Joe.

CHAPTER 29

So I kind of moved in with Joe for the past few weeks.

But it's not like that.

I just don't want to be at Rookhaven right now. Anyway, this is only temporary.

Tonight's the Potstill Prom. And tomorrow I go home to Rochester.

I haven't told Joe yet. He'll be cool with it, of course. But I don't want to distract him from the prom. He's been working obsessively on the audio system in the bar. Every moment that I haven't been working this week, I've been making decorations. This is Joe's big chance to impress Gary with how huge the bar could be as a live music venue. I really want it to work out for him.

Joe's apartment is a tiny walk-up studio, way down at the bottom of Red Hook, a world away from Rookhaven. There's a galley kitchen and a small bathroom. He goes in to Potstill around noon every day to open the bar. Most days I head back to Rookhaven mid-afternoon to shower and change for my evening shift at the bar, safe in the knowledge that my sister and everyone else is already at work so I won't have to see them, It's like a totally different, totally new life. And I love it. That's our average day.

I haven't seen any of the girls in weeks. I haven't spoken to them. It's like we're all just trying to pretend the big fight didn't happen. And that we don't actually know each other. It's weird, and I hate it, and I know I'm cowardly for not doing anything about it, but . . . I'm scared. What if I asked them if we could all make up and be friends, and they told me to get lost? I haven't heard anything from Topher either. I guess he just got my drunk texts and rolled his eyes. I wonder if he showed them to his perfect girlfriend. I wonder if she laughed.

Urgh.

This morning I woke early because of the hot sun coming through Joe's bedroom window. So I snuggled up to his back like a little bear, matched my breathing to his, slow and steady, and drifted back to sleep.

When I woke up again a few minutes ago, Joe was already gone. No note, nothing.

That's okay. I am not living with him, not really, even though the past few weeks of co-habitation might make it feel that way. He's not my boyfriend. We're just friends with benefits. Including a place to crash when you need it.

I hear the front door slam, and moments later Joe walks in, carrying coffees and bags from the bakery down on Van Brunt.

"Okay, you have a choice of whoopie pie, cinnamon bun, or pumpkin chocolate chip loaf," says Joe. "A special breakfast because today is prom, and you need to keep your energy up."

"Um . . . a cinnamon bun, please." I smile lazily and reach for my coffee.

"I'm having the pumpkin chocolate chip loaf, because—"

"It's the manliest, butchest choice?"

"That's correct." Joe grins at me.

I take a bite of cinnamon bun. "Wow, that's good."

"I love watching you eat," says Joe. "You take little nibbles and then pause, really intensely, like you're *really* tasting it."

"Joe! Don't ever tell a girl you love watching her eat!" I throw a piece of cinnamon bun at him.

"Now you're in trouble . . ." Joe throws himself on the bed next to me and pins me down, and then grabs the whoopie pie from the bag and tries to force it into my mouth.

I try to push him away, but I am laughing too hard, and before I know it, there's whoopie pie frosting smeared all around my mouth.

"Oh, you have a little something on your lip. Let me get it."

Joe kisses me, big sloppy kisses that are as much about slurping up the frosting on my lip as kissing me.

A little fire lights up inside me, just like always when we kiss, and suddenly I can't help but pull him closer, and then . . . well, you know.

"Are you excited about the Potstill Prom tonight?" Joe says, a while later.

"I'm like, totes psyched," I roll over on the pillow and sigh happily. "It's going to be the best nonofficial prom ever. And I have a surprise for you."

"What?"

I pause, eking out the enjoyment. "I wasn't sure whether to tell you, or just surprise you, but then I read this thing that surprises are really overrated because what we enjoy most about a thing is the *anticipation* of a thing, and—"

"Tell me!"

"I tracked down Ian James."

"Ian *James*?"

"Remember? The music guy we met at the Ace Hotel. I found him on Twitter and invited him to Potstill Prom tonight, to see the band. And to meet you."

Joe stares at me. "Seriously?"

"Yup," I grin. "I mean, he may not come, you know, it was via Twitter, not a gilded invitation, but . . . . this could be your big chance."

"Wow. Oh, wow. Coco!" Joe grabs me and kisses me so hard that I yelp. "Thank you. Thank you! Jesus, do you think he'll come? I mean, he probably won't, right, he's way too busy, but if he does . . . I swear, Mads has the talent. She could make it. All the way."

"You think?" I smile. "I love her voice."

"So do I. So does everyone, really. That's why we've renamed the band MADS. Spector is fine for messing around with covers, but for the new stuff, we need—"

"New stuff? You mean new songs?"

"Yeah. Madeleine and Amy have been writing songs together for a while," says Joe. "You didn't know?"

I shake my head.

"You don't talk to your friends a whole lot," he says.

I haven't told him about how I've been avoiding the girls. But now that I think about it, even before the big fight, I've been kind of self-involved this summer. Between Joe and Topher and the bar and NYU . . . I was all about me. I can't think the last time I really asked any of my friends how they were doing. Not that it matters anymore, I guess. I'm leaving.

Why does that thought make me feel so sick?

I glance back at Joe. "I guess we don't talk as much as we used to."

"Millennials are always talking," says Joe. "We're in constant contact with each other, sharing via seventeen social media applications at once, or some shit, right? Personally, I think people just like saying 'millennial.'"

"Millennial?" That reminds me of something . . .

Oh, right. That interview with Vic's neice Samantha. It's today. I haven't thought about it since that time Topher and I saw her in Washington Square Park.

I should do it, right? It'll probably be boring, but it's money. Money I really, really need. It might take weeks to find another preschool job once I'm back in Rochester . . . Urgh. The future. I hate thinking about it.

Joe starts kissing and biting my neck again, and I make an involuntary, slightly embarrassing moaning sound.

Joe pulls back. "You okay?"

I nod.

Joe resumes kissing me, and I shiver and wrap my arms tight around him, drawing his body as tight against mine as possible. I can't help it: I want him. My body just reacts to him, it's practically separate from my brain.

And then it happens.

Joe pulls back, practically midkiss, and looks at me.

"No one else would have gone out of their way to track down Ian James for me, Coco, I just . . . oh, God, I love you."

I push Joe off me so fast that he nearly falls off the bed.

"What?"

Joe starts to laugh. "I said I—"

"You do not!"

"Uh, I think I'd know—" Joe laughs at my reaction. "I do. I love you."

"Don't say that!" I grab a pillow and hug it tightly, to make a physical barrier between us.

"Why?"

"Joe, I can't— I don't—" I feel sick. "I'm so sorry, Joe, I'm so sorry—"

"What for?"

"No, no, I just, I'm sorry, I—" I cover my face with my hands. "I thought we were just friends, that was the deal, that was . . . that was the deal."

Joe's face has turned to stone. "Friends. We're practically living together, and you think we're just *friends*?"

"You told me we were friends. Just casual, we said *casual*." I am filled with panic, clutching the pillow to my chest. "And anyway, um, it's probably for the best, I'm leaving tomorrow, I'm just staying until the Potstill Prom is over, and then I'm going back to Rochester."

"You're *leaving*? When were you going to tell me? On your way to Grand fucking Central?"

"I thought . . . I'm . . . sorry . . ."

"Stop saying you're sorry." Joe stands up and walks over to the window.

"But I *am*—"

"Sorry for what? For being an asshole?"

I flinch. "We agreed to be just friends, Joe. You can't just change the rules."

Joe turns around, his face white with anger. "Friends? You treat your friends like this? You used me for my apartment, right? You've been fighting with the girls? Didn't want to be at Rookhaven?"

I am speechless. How did he guess?

"I'm not stupid, Coco," says Joe. "Actually, maybe I am. I must be, right? Why else would you treat me like a fucking idiot?"

"I did— I did not," I stammer. "We were meant to be just casual, you agreed, we *agreed*." I pause, my brain racing. "You're the one who said breaking up was never a bad decision! Remember? You should be happy."

Joe can't even look at me. "Get out."

I dress as quickly as I can, my hands shaking. I'm so stupid. How could I not have seen this coming? I don't know what I feel. Guilt? Sadness? Shock? Resentment?

Resentment wins.

And as I'm going out the door, I'm determined to have the last word.

"Joe?"

He's sitting on the bed now, leaning on his knees, hiding his face in his hands. He doesn't respond.

"You came on to Angie the night I met you," I say. "You made it clear you liked her, not me, remember? You kept asking about her. I was just your consolation prize. I was your second choice. Hell, I was probably your fifth choice, but everyone else was either taken or gay. You never acted like I was anything special."

Joe looks up at me.

I take a deep breath. "I'm sorry I didn't tell you about leaving Brooklyn, but don't pretend I'm breaking your heart."

"That's the thing, Coco," says Joe, finally looking at me. "You *are* breaking my heart."

I stare at him.

I don't know what to say.

Joe stands up and walks over to the window again, trying to calm down. Then he turns around, his eyes cold and hard.

"Don't come to the Potstill Prom tonight. You're fired."

CHAPTER 30

Guilt.

Nothing is as bad as guilt. It's like being knifed from the inside out.

This is what Pia was talking about when she cheated on Aidan.

And I didn't even cheat on Joe. In fact, I thought I was doing the right thing, I thought I was just telling the truth. But the moment I slam the door to Joe's apartment, one new, awful thought is circling my brain.

I hurt the kindest person I've met since I've been in New York City.

With tears blurring my vision and a lump in my throat so big it genuinely hurts to swallow, I somehow get back to Rookhaven, shower and dress on autopilot, and catch the subway to Manhattan for that millennial interview set up by Vic's niece Samantha. With difficulty, I push Joe out of my head. I'll just answer some questions and collect my $100. Then I'll go home, pack up all my stuff, and get ready to leave.

The interview is in an office in the depths of NoLIta, and when I turn up, I see that I'm not the only twenty-something Samantha recruited. There are dozens of us, all waiting on the cobbled streets, leaning against the storefronts and in between parked cars, trying to get some shade.

It's so hot. New York is an armpit in the summer . . . I'll be back in Rochester all winter, I suddenly realize. I'll spend every night alone in the house I grew up in. The house is on a huge lot, so it's practically snowbound for months on end. It'll be just like every long, lonely winter after Mom died . . . like I never moved to New York City at all.

A harried-looking guy—one of the grad student researchers, I guess—comes out of the building and hands out sheets of paper. We all take one and pass them on.

It's some kind of a disclosure agreement, so they can use anything I say in their work or whatever. I sign it and hand it back.

Then we wait for another twenty minutes, everyone killing time on their phones. How did people handle waiting before you could get Facebook and Instagram on your phone? And how did people manage to ever meet each other before cell phones if one of them was running late, or if there was bad traffic, or they forgot the meeting place? It must have been a nightmare.

Joe hasn't texted me.

Joe will never text me again.

Stop it, Coco. There's nothing you can do.

Then Samantha appears, holding a chart. She doesn't notice me.

"Okay! Thank you all for coming today," she says. "If I call your name, come forward. If I don't call your name, try again next year. Abbott!" I look around, and a young guy wearing huge headphones around his neck, like the world's clunkiest scarf, steps forward. "Amies!"

What?

Topher steps out from behind the construction awning of a building across the street. He walks to the front, and I see a few girls turn to look at him automatically, the way you do when anyone gorgeous crosses your path. But actually . . . today, for some reason, I don't think he's gorgeous. He just looks sort of . . . empty.

Eventually Samantha gets to the *R*'s and sure enough, she calls, "Russotti."

I slowly make my way to the front and see that the only space for me is right next to Topher.

How am I supposed to treat him? I mean, we went from seeing each other practically every day, and being constantly in touch, to being strangers again. He never responded to my embarrassing drunk texts, or got in touch after that party. He just disappeared. It's been weeks.

"Coco! Buddy!" Topher gives me a huge hug. "How are you?"

I'm momentarily stunned, then hug him back. "Great! How are you?"

"So great." Topher flashes an easy smile, his teeth blindingly white compared to his newly tan face. "I aced my assignment. Thanks again for your help."

"Right." My help. I wrote the damn thing. And he promised to buy me dinner to say thanks and never did. The asshat.

"I've been up in Amagansett with Maggie. Man, I love the Hamptons, don't you? But I couldn't pass up the chance to earn an easy hundred dollars. Plus, Maggie's boss has a chopper, and she was taking it into the city this morning to go to Russ & Daughters, so I was like, why not?"

Topher starts talking about his journey into the city via helicopter, and I tune out, a practice, I think suddenly, that I used to do a lot back when we were friends. He talked a lot and I liked thinking about how much I liked him more than I liked listening to him.

Or maybe we weren't friends.

We couldn't have been. Because Topher doesn't care about me. I mean, he's polite and he smiles and says please and thank you. But he doesn't really care about anyone except himself.

And that's probably the quality that made him so popular in high school.

I can see that now. He only invited me to class because he knew I'd take notes for him when he had better things to do. Or even . . . write his assignment for him.

How could I ever have thought I liked him?

And then I realize: I didn't.

I liked *the idea* of him. The idea that Mr. Popular could see something in me that everyone back in high school missed, that his friendship could undo all those teenage years of being loveless and lonely and lost. If a guy as cool and popular as Topher could like me, it wouldn't matter that Eric treated me like shit and I didn't like myself.

But nothing and no one can change the past.

And it doesn't matter.

I smile for the first time since leaving Joe's apartment today.

"Coco Russotti!"

A tall girl with long red hair calls my name. I turn quickly.

"Follow me."

I glance back at Topher for the last time. "I'll see you around."

CHAPTER 31

I'm somewhere deep in one of those old downtown NYU buildings where they divided up an original long room into offices with weird temporary-for-twenty-years walls. It feels old, dusty, forgotten. The walls are so thin that I can hear the murmur of the interviews on either side of me.

The redheaded girl, Jessie, spends a few minutes arranging a video camera so it's pointed right at my face.

"Okeydokey!" Jessie says. "We're going to start with a straight-forward Myers-Briggs, it's a simple psychometric questionnaire. You've probably heard of it."

"Totally." Briggs what?

"We're trying to figure out how millennials break down into the classic personality types, if it's the same as older generations, specifically Generation X and baby boomers," she says. "After this study, we're choosing ten participants to interview more intensely. But for now, I'll make statements, and you answer yes if you agree with them and no if you don't. Got it?"

"I think I can grasp the concept," I say.

She doesn't smile. "Okay. Let's begin. You are almost never late for your appointments."

"Um . . . True. I mean, yes," I say. "Sorry."

"I guess you didn't grasp the concept quite as well as you thought," says Jessie. My eyes narrow. Bitch. "You like to be engaged in an active and fast-paced job."

"Um . . ." I think for a moment.

Do I like a fast-paced job? I don't know. My favorite moments working in the preschool were probably reading time, when everything was quiet and cozy, but that might have been because Miss Audrey couldn't bully me at those times.

I liked working at Potstill most when it was fairly empty, but that might be because Joe and I could just talk and mess around and laugh all night. Oh, God, Joe . . .

I suddenly get a huge, painful lump in my throat.

Why would I cry about Joe? *I'm* the one who ended it.

Pushing thoughts of Joe aside, I don't think that preschool teaching was ever the right career for me, so of course I didn't enjoy the busy times. And maybe bar work wasn't either. But how do I know if I'd like to be active once I *find* that mythical perfect career?

How do I *know*?

Jessie stares at me, waiting. "Just a simple yes or no will do."

"No," I say finally.

"You enjoy having a wide circle of acquaintances."

"No," I say. "I like just a small group of friends."

Even when we're not talking to each other, like right now. I miss my friends. I wonder if they're all okay. I hope Julia isn't working too hard, no matter how angry she is at me, I just want her to be safe and happy. And I hope Maddy forgives me for outing her without her permission.

"Coco!" snaps Jessie.

"Sorry! What? I mean, excuse me?"

"You feel involved watching TV soaps."

"Like, emotionally involved? Yes," I say. "Totally. Very involved. And reality TV shows."

Jessie ignores my extra comments and asks more questions. And more. And more.

And then finally, we're finished.

I am exhausted from thinking about myself so much.

"Well, you're what we call an ISFJ," Jessie says, without bothering to look up at me. "Pretty normal, about twelve percent of the population. You're defined by being supportive and caring, you value relationships and harmony in your relationships—"

Not recently, I think to myself.

"You retain information well, you're imaginative, reliable, patient, warm, considerate, humble, modest, helpful, traditional . . ." Jessica is listing these personality traits like I'm the most boring person in the world. ". . . and you always, always put family first. You're the caregiver. We call you the Nurturer."

"The *Nurturer*? Are you fucking kidding me?"

Jessie looks up in surprise. "What?"

I can't even answer.

I've spent all summer trying to be wild—trying to be like someone else, someone who has casual sex and gets drunk and dances on bars and steals education.

And I'm still exactly the goddamn same.

I'm the fucking *Nurturer.* I'm the good girl.

Jessie is still talking. ". . . what you're going to do with the rest of your life?"

"Um . . ." I pause. "Why are you asking me that? I don't know. I just, um, I don't know yet."

"Well," says Jessie, "I can tell you what you'd be good at. As Nurturer, your people skills—"

"Don't presume to know me," I snap. "Fucking hell, I'm sick of people telling me what I should do—"

"There's no need to use language like that."

"What does the list say, huh? For jobs for my personality type? Teacher? Librarian? Social worker?"

All the jobs my father and sister told me I was allowed to have. Literally. *Allowed.*

Because I am so stupid I couldn't *possibly* choose for myself. Who gets told what she's allowed to do with her life? Who puts limits on other people like that? It's crazy!

"Actually, yes—"

"You can go to hell!" I'm shouting now. "You don't get to determine my life! You don't know me! *I* don't even know me! Who the fuck do you think you—"

The door to the room bangs open, and Samantha is standing there. "Coco! What is going on? Everyone can hear you!"

Jessie stands up, snapping shut her laptop. "She lost it before we were past the first round of questions. I'm out of here."

She leaves, slamming the door behind her.

Samantha and I meet eyes.

"Do you want to talk about it?" says Samantha gently.

And suddenly, though it's the last thing I want to do, I burst into tears.

"I just . . . I still don't know," I keep saying, after I tell Samantha everything. "I don't know. I don't know what I want, I don't know . . ."

"That's okay," Samantha says, over and over again.

"I told everyone I was leaving, that I was moving home to Rochester, and I'd get another assistant job in a preschool. But I don't want that. At all. But I also don't know what I *do* want either . . ."

"That's okay, too," says Samantha.

"No, it's not," I say. "Everyone else knows. My sister has known she wanted to be an investment banker, like, since she was born. And my roommate, Madeleine, wants to be an accountant, and a singer, and I think maybe she wants to be a lesbian, but I'm not sure—"

"Okay—" Samantha looks confused.

"And my friend Pia? She lost her job, but she figured out what she was good at in just a couple of weeks! And even if she does quit, she'll be fine. She's just the kind of person who always figures it out. And Angie always wanted to work in fashion, and she made it happen. It's so easy for everybody else."

"Do you think they'd say that?" says Samantha. "You don't know what it's like being in their shoes."

"Yeah, but they all have . . . their *thing*. Their talent. And I don't. I have nothing. Except I know how to fucking *help people* . . . " I spit the words out. "I'm *pathetic*."

"You're not," says Samantha. "You're just figuring out what you want to do."

"What if I never figure it out?" I say. "I'm twenty-one, I should know by now."

"No, you shouldn't," says Samantha. "And your sister and friends are what, twenty-two, twenty-three? They might think they know what they want to do, but they don't yet, not really. A few years, some more adventures, and they'll discover new talents and passions. Life is full of surprises like that."

"But they're so good at their jobs—"

"Sure, but that doesn't mean that's *it* for them. Can you imagine how boring life would be if we all knew our destiny at twenty-one? It takes years to figure out what you really want. In fact, figuring it out, the process, that's the best part. You should enjoy it, Coco. This period you're in, the very start of adult life . . . it's fun."

"*Fun?*" I almost laugh, but it comes out a sort of cry. "It's hell!"

"It's not. It's a blank slate, full of opportunities. You know what hell is? Not having any choices."

I think about what she just said, and she's right. When I felt trapped in the preschool assistant job, in a life that didn't fit me, that was hell.

"You don't need to rush," Samantha says slowly. "You know, your generation of women experiences incredibly high levels of stress and anxiety. You all feel a huge pressure to succeed, without knowing what success even means for you, personally . . . And success *is* personal. There's no one-size-fits-all. And to make it worse, you've got all this information at your fingertips, you know? The Internet and social media mean you're overinformed, overfocused, and overpressured to achieve your goals. But it's not easy to achieve your goals. It's not even easy to decide what your goals are."

"Exactly," I say. "That's exactly how I feel."

"That's okay," she says softly. "It shouldn't be easy. It's too important."

"But how do I even start? How do I know? What if I get it wrong?"

"Nothing you ever do will be wrong, because it's all part of your journey. It gives you perspective, experience, knowledge . . . everything you do creates *you*. This is the only life you're ever going to get, Coco. No one else can choose what you'll do with it; no one else can make you happy. You're in control." She pauses, considering me. "Want to know what my Uncle Vic told me when I was your age and trying to figure out what I wanted to do with my life?"

"Yes," I say. "Yes, please."

Samantha smiles. "He said, 'Just think about what you truly love. What makes you smile. And after that . . . everything will be easy.'"

CHAPTER 32

I walk out of the building, Samantha's words echoing in my head.

Just think about what you truly love . . .

For a crazy, irrational second, I think about Joe. I'm hit by that same guilt and sadness and something else, something bigger and more important, something I didn't let myself feel before . . . I quickly squash those thoughts down. Joe and I are over. As friends and . . . whatever else we were. He thinks I'm an asshole. And he's probably right.

Then I think about books. About going to those summer classes with Topher, and how I felt that first day in Professor Guffey's class. About how much I enjoyed writing his assignment.

How good it felt to put my thoughts into words. To have a voice. I truly loved that.

And suddenly I realize: that was what made my stomach wriggle with excitement every day. That was what made me feel excited beyond anything I'd ever experienced before. It was never Topher. It was *college*.

And now I know what I have to do.

I walk straight over to Greenwich Village to find the one person who might understand.

Professor Guffey.

I knock tentatively on the door to her office. She answers the door, sees me, and smiles.

"Coco. I was hoping I'd see you again. Come in."

Professor Guffey looks questioningly at me, her bright eyes staring so intently that I find it hard to meet her gaze.

I take a deep breath.

"I'm not a student at NYU."

Professor Guffey doesn't say anything.

"I'm so sorry I lied. I mean, I didn't really *lie* because no one asked me, but I was coming to your class illegally, I guess, I just, you know, I loved it so much, and . . ." I trail off. Is she about to kick me out? Have me arrested?

"I know. I suspected from the start."

I'm so stunned I'm not sure what to say. Professor Guffey goes back to her desk and sits down and indicates that I should sit in the worn little chair opposite her.

"You did? How?" I finally croak out.

Professor Guffey sighs. "I don't know, Coco. Call it thirty years in the trenches. I just knew. You were too green, too eager . . . You didn't fit in."

My face falls. I wasn't as cool and as smart as her other students. That's what she means. I looked like some dumbass just stealing education.

"I mean . . . you stood out," she quickly corrects herself. "You were actively listening. Obviously thinking and responding to the literature. Taking part in the discussion. It was like there was a spotlight shining on you. Summer classes aren't usually full of students like you."

"Oh," I say.

"Then you told me your name," says Professor Guffey, "and I knew there wasn't a Coco in my class. It was my mother's name. I'd remember."

"Oh," I say again. "Um . . . I am so sorry that I misled you."

Professor Guffey smiles. "Don't worry about that. It was nice having someone care enough about my class to fake it as a student."

I grin. I guess that's true.

Her smile drops. "So why are you here now?"

"I loved your classes. I felt, for the first time in my life, that I was doing what I was meant to do. And I want . . . I want to go to NYU. I want to study literature. I don't even know if it's possible, but I was hoping that you might be able to help me figure something out . . ." As the words rush out of my mouth, I realize how stupid I must sound.

"Well, first things first, Coco. Can you afford it?"

"I have a college fund," I say. "I don't know if it's enough, but I'm sure I can get by, get a job in a bar . . . It's not the money. It's my SAT scores. They're not high enough. And is it too late? Am I wasting my time even thinking about this?"

"NYU isn't all about SATs, Coco . . . You can retake the SATs and submit those scores. You can submit your ACP scores, or get predicted result scores and submit them. But truthfully, it's more about the essays, and I don't think you'll have any problems there, right?"

I chew my lip, thinking. "Really? It's not too late?"

"It's August, so it's late to apply, but it's not too late. There are always last-minute ways around the rules if you know where to look. I can help you fill out all the necessary forms and speak to the right people."

This isn't what I was expecting. The word *no,* that's what I was expecting.

"Coco, if you really want something, you can make it happen. It's that simple."

"Why are you so nice to me?" I choke out.

"Because . . . because you remind me of me when I started college." Professor Guffey's face softens. "You're just waking up."

"I want to go back to college," I say clearly. "I want to go to NYU. And I'll do whatever it takes to make it happen."

CHAPTER **33**

On the walk from the subway to Union Street, I see a missed call from my dad. I sigh, ringing him back. I need to tell him I've changed my mind.

"Hey, Daddy, sorry I missed your call . . ."

"Fine." My dad's at work: he's using his bullish business voice. "So your flight gets in at midday tomorrow. I'll pick you up from the airport and we'll get pizza for dinner."

"Um . . ."

"Can't wait to see you, little one. I never thought you were cut out for New York City. You'll feel better as soon as you get back home."

"I, um . . ." I take a deep breath. "I changed my mind. I want to stay. And I want to apply to NYU."

I tell him all about Samantha, and Professor Guffey, and how I know, just *know*, that this is what I'm supposed to do. I reach Rookhaven and sit down on the stoop, staring at the street as I try to explain how life-changing my summer has been.

When I'm done, there's silence on the other end of the phone.

"What if you're wrong, honey?" he asks quietly. "What if it doesn't make you happy? What then?"

"Then . . . I'll deal with it," I say. There's silence on the other end of the phone.

He doesn't believe in me. But maybe that's okay. I believe in myself. "Hey, Daddy?"

"Yes?"

"What makes you happy?"

"Me?" Dad pauses, thinking. "Golf. Wine. Knowing you and your sister are safe. But especially you, I guess, you were just so young when Mom . . ." His sentence trails off, and then he clears his throat. "After everything you had to go through, knowing you don't have anything to worry about, or be scared about, is really the only thing that makes me happy."

"I'll be safe here, Daddy," I say. "I promise."

"Okay, well, I think I just have to trust that you're right," he says. "You know, Coco . . . you sound different. You sound like an adult."

I smile. "I am."

After we hang up, his words about his idea of happiness echo in my mind.

That's the reason he always told me what to do.

My dad didn't think I was stupid.

He just wanted to protect me. I was only a little girl, such a dreamy, bookish, softhearted little girl, when Mom died. He never wanted anything to hurt me ever again. That's why he's always treated me like a baby. To him, I *was* just a baby.

And the scary thing is, until recently, I liked it. It's nice to be taken care of.

But it's far, far nicer to take care of yourself.

"You okay, girlie?"

I stand up and look over to see Vic sitting on that little chair outside his door.

"You just heard my whole conversation, didn't you?" I say, grinning.

Vic smirks. "You want privacy, girlie, don't talk on the stoop." He looks up at me with a smile. "Sounds like you've figured out what you're gonna do with your life."

"No, I still don't know what I'm going to do with my entire life," I say. "And that's okay. Because I know what I'm doing next. Everything else I'll just figure out as I go along."

Vic nods. "Sounds like a plan."

"And, Vic, just so you know, I like myself now. For the first time in maybe my whole life. I like being me."

"Now you sound like me. Next you'll be talking about the loves of your life. How you can only be truly happy when they're happy."

Joe flashes into my heads again. But—

Before I can finish my thought, Angie runs out of Rookhaven, slamming the front door behind her. It's the first time I've seen her in over a week, since that awful fight with Julia. Shouldn't she be at work?

"Hi, Vic! Oh, Coco, thank God. I need you. Can you help me?"

"Of course!" I say.

"We're going to TriBeCa," she says. "I'll explain on the way."

CHAPTER 34

The memory of what happened with Joe this morning is like a bruise somewhere deep in my soul. If I press it, it hurts.

Is that just the guilt of hurting someone so important to me, someone who knew me better than anyone, someone who had become my best friend? What else could I do? I had to tell him the truth.

I just need to keep telling myself that every time I think I'm going to cry.

"Are you okay?" asks Angie, as we get on the train. She's practically buzzing with excitement, but she hasn't explained why. "Coco? Is something going on with you?"

"Yes, no, sorry," I say, shaking my head to clear the thoughts. "I'm fine. What are we doing?"

"Sam is coming home today."

Angie is so happy she almost can't get the words out.

"He's arriving this afternoon. They made really good time on the crossing and got here a few days early. I only just found out. So we're going to welcome him. But first, we're stopping at the Balloon Saloon on West Broadway. I have a plan."

Apparently, Angie's plan involves a dozen perfectly round red helium balloons, each over five feet in diameter. The balloon store guy has to take us out the back to get them, because they're too big to carry out the front door of the store. Then we walk down West Broadway, with six giant balloons each, in the scorching sunshine. Cars honk at us, kids squeal with excitement, and a small dog goes beserk, barking hysterically.

"God, I love attention," says Angie.

I laugh. "You'd think they'd never seen two grown women carrying giant red balloons before." I pause for a moment, and glance at her. "Why the hell *are* we carrying giant red balloons, by the way?"

"Well," Angie says. "Sam said that whenever he pictures himself returning to New York, he thinks about that moment when he's sailing up the Hudson, staring at the marina, looking for me, and how it almost stresses him out imagining it, because, you know, it's hard to see people well until you're pretty close, so you could be staring at the wrong person . . . I figured that with the balloons, he'd know exactly where I am."

"Wow. That's so romantic."

"Do you think it's lame?" Angie looks uncharacteristically insecure. "Be honest. I can take it."

I shake my head. "It's perfect."

When we stop, holding our giant red balloons and waiting to cross the street, Angie turns to me again. "Are you *sure* there's nothing going on with you?"

I take a deep breath. "Well, I think I'm going to stay at Rook-haven."

"Yay!" Angie hugs me, our balloons colliding in the air.

"And I'm going to NYU this year. Officially, this time. No more faking it."

"Fuck, yeah." Angie grins. "So why do you look so damn unhappy?"

"I ended things with Joe," I say. "Remember when you said it was okay to just be friends with benefits, as long as it was all he wanted too? Well, he wanted more."

"And you don't?" says Angie. "That's weird."

"Why?"

"We all thought that you and Joe just had so much chemistry. I mean, I know Julia wanted you to be with Topher, but of course she would; he's her friend. If you dated him she'd be able to feel like she was in charge of your relationship."

Wow. She's right. She's totally right. Just like my dad, Julia has always tried to protect me. How much did Julia influence my decisions even when I thought I was acting for myself?

I'm not even sure it was deliberate. I guess Julia subconsciously imitated how our father treated me: like someone who always needed to be looked after and told what to do. Maybe the dynamics of family relationships are embedded long before the kids are really aware of them. No wonder she was so upset when I started acting out: she's practically programmed to protect me. It's not conscious. It's just the way it is . . . or was.

I'm sure it comes from a good, loving place. When you think about it, it's tradition. Families have always had to protect their daughters, because if they didn't, bad things happened to us. For centuries, that's how it's been. But that meant we couldn't work, we couldn't live alone or own property, we couldn't do *anything* without someone looking after us, giving us permission to exist and excuses not to think for ourselves. We were small and vulnerable and powerless.

But those days are gone. I am strong. And I don't need someone to tell me how to live my life anymore.

By the time we get to the marina at the bottom of Battery Park, Angie is almost beside herself with nerves about seeing Sam. She keeps checking her phone, but he hasn't texted.

"Sam was supposed to be here by now," she mutters as we walk past the yachts bobbing peacefully in the water. "I can't see his boat. Can you see it?"

I look out to the Hudson. Ferries and sailboats and tourist boats zip back and forth. But no Sam.

Our balloons are tied to long ribbons, bopping gently against each other in the wind. We must look pretty hilarious, like we're about to lift right up off the ground. Tourists going past keep taking photos of us.

"Where is he?" Angie mutters. "Look for a speedboat, Coco. They're leaving the *Peripety* over in Liberty Harbor Marina in Jersey City for repairs, but he said he'd get a lift straight here. Either that or hijack a fishing boat."

"Why doesn't he just come to Rookhaven?" I say.

"This is where we said good-bye," says Angie. "Right here, right on this very spot. This is where I last saw him. So this is where we're going to say hello . . . Oh, God, where is he?"

Angie is peering so hard into the horizon, scanning every boat that comes near, that her eyes must be aching from the effort.

"Is that him?" she says as a speedboat approaches. "Shit. It's not."

"I see him," I exclaim. "Oh, no. Fisherman. Who the hell would fish in the Hudson River? Can you imagine how gross the fish must be?"

Angie doesn't respond. I suddenly realize just how much she loves Sam. How much she must have missed him the past few months, and how much it must have hurt her to say good-bye.

"How did you do it?" I ask. "How did you say good-bye to Sam, when he probably would have stayed here if you asked him? You'd just fallen in love. It must have been so hard."

Angie turns her gaze to me for a second, her face more serious than I've ever seen it.

"It was the hardest thing I've ever had to do. But I knew he'd come back to me. And I knew he had to go. When you love someone, you want him to be happy in every way, even if that means he needs to leave you to realize his dreams. That's why we thought you liked Joe, you know. You've been working so hard on that prom. It's all for him, right?"

I don't even know what to say.

She's right.

I want to make him happy. I really do. The whole Potstill Prom idea was just to make him happy. I found Ian James, just to make him happy. But does that mean—

"That's Sam," Angie chokes out the words. "There he is! I can see the shape of his head, I can see him! He's on that little speedboat!"

We both start waving madly, jumping up and down with our gigantic red balloons bobbing over our heads. Sam waves back. He's seen our balloons. He knows exactly where we are.

As the speedboat gets closer, Angie is almost in tears, she's so overwhelmed with excitement and anticipation. I slip my hand into hers, and she grips it tightly.

Sam is standing up, holding on to the boat with one hand, waving at us with the other. He's usually very clean-cut—Angie sometimes refers to him as "the Boy Scout"—but he's grown a beard while he's been away. His face is lit up with a huge smile.

The speedboat comes to a stop about fifty feet down the pier, and Angie rushes toward him, letting go of her balloons as she runs so they float up into the air. She throws her arms around Sam and they start kissing furiously.

Feeling like I'm intruding, I shift my gaze up to the blue afternoon sky, let go of my balloons, and watch them join Angie's, floating away over the city, becoming tiny dots together. It's so beautiful.

I wonder how many people across New York City can see the balloons right now. I bet they're all smiling as they look at them.

I wonder if Joe can see them. I hope so.

And suddenly I am punched in the gut by the realization everyone else seems to have known forever.

I love Joe.

CHAPTER 35

On the way to the subway, I take out my phone and call Joe. But he doesn't answer.

And unfortunately, I don't think "I love you I'm sorry please love me again" is the kind of thing you can leave on a voice mail or send in a text.

But I can't turn up to Potstill to tell him how I feel about him, and beg him to forgive me, while I'm looking like shit, all windswept and subway-sweaty. I know people do that in the movies, but this is real life. In fact, if this was a movie, I would have fallen in love with Joe the moment I met him, or the moment I kissed him, or the moment he told me he loved me.

But I didn't.

Or maybe I did fall. But I didn't realize. Whatever.

And if I'm going to really do this, I need to do it looking as good as I can.

So I need to go home to Rookhaven.

I also have some other amends to make. I need to talk to Madeleine. And my sister. They're just as important as Joe.

When I walk into the kitchen at Rookhaven, Julia is there. She's sitting at the kitchen table in her suit, staring blankly into space.

It's midafternoon on a Friday. Why isn't she at work?

"I was fired," Julia says, before I can ask.

"Oh, shitballs."

"Made redundant, officially. They got rid of my whole team, and more. Eight thousand people across the company."

"Shitballs," I say again.

Julia grins, finally swiveling her eyes up to meet mine. "It's weird hearing you swear. But kind of cute."

"I'm so sorry. Are you okay?"

"I think I'm in shock. I mean, I'm fine. They've given us an amazing severance package, and I'm sure I'll get another job. I'm just . . . unemployed." Julia's giggle is just this side of hysterical. "This was not part of my plan."

I sit down next to her at the table and grab her hand.

"It'll be okay, Ju-ju."

"I know. It's just . . . unexpected. I'm not good with unexpected."

"I'm so sorry that I didn't call you," I say. "I don't think we've ever not spoken for this long."

"I should have called you." Julia looks at me, a little smile on her face. "I hate fighting with you. I'm glad you're going home to Rochester, I think it's a smart move. I'm so sorry about Eric and everything that you went through. I wish I'd known, I would have been there for you, I wouldn't . . . I wouldn't have judged you, I swear. I love you. And I'll . . . I'll miss you."

I take a deep breath. This is going to be hard.

"Julia, you and Dad have always told me what to do with my life."

Julia opens her mouth to interrupt, and I hurriedly continue.

"No, I think I wanted you to, you know, I liked it. It felt safe. But you can't know what's best for me. Only I can figure that out. That's why I've had such a wild summer. That's why I quit working at the preschool and was messing around with Joe. I was just . . . figuring life out for myself."

Julia frowns at me. "So what are you telling me? You're now moving back to Rochester and becoming a preschool teacher again because you figured out life for yourself?"

"No. I'm not going back to Rochester. When I thought I wanted to, I was just scared. I thought maybe I could just go back to the old me. But I've changed, Julia."

"We all have," she says. "We've been living here for a year. It's a long time."

I nod. "I know what I want to do now . . . I want to go to NYU."

"Wow . . ." Julia stares at me. "That is huge. Are you sure?"

I tell her all about Professor Guffey. About how I'm sure that my future lies somewhere beyond this, that one day I'll figure out what I want to do with the rest of my life, but I need to go back to college in order to do that. I tell her how I felt when I was in class. Like a light had gone on inside me.

Julia nods. "I understand. That's how I felt at work sometimes. Like that's exactly where I'm meant to be."

"Right!" I say.

We smile at each other for a second.

"Something else. I know you think Joe is a loser. But"—I take a deep breath—"I love him, Julia. I really do. He's the best person I know. Outside of you and Maddy and Angie and Pia, obviously."

"I don't think he's a loser," Julia says slowly. "I was hard on him, but I don't really know him. And I didn't want you to get hurt, Cuckoo."

"If I'm going to get hurt, then that's just the way it is. I've been hurt, and I've survived. And if it happens again, I'll be okay. I'm in charge of my life, and if that means making mistakes, then that's my choice. You have to stop protecting me." I say it as gently as I can.

"Why would I think I could protect you? I can't even protect myself from getting fired," she says sadly.

I squeeze her hand.

"So are you and Joe, like, an official thing now?"

"No." I bite my lip to stop myself from crying. "I broke up with him this morning."

"You love him so you broke up with him?" Julia arches an eyebrow.

"I didn't realize how I felt when I . . . never mind. The point is, I want to go to the Potstill Prom tonight, and apologize, and hope that he'll forgive me."

"Do you think he will?"

"That's just it," I say. "I don't know."

Julia looks me up and down. "Well, I hate to go all Fairy Godmother on you, but you can't go to the prom looking like that."

I grin. My sister can always make me smile.

She picks up her phone.

"I'm booking you a hair appointment. And I'm calling the girls. And we're going to make you a goddamn prom queen."

CHAPTER 36

"Wow," says Pia, when I walk into her bedroom later. "Like . . . big wow."

I'm wearing a silver dress that Angie picked up for me from the design studio. She dropped it off and then went back to Sam's apartment with him, promising to meet us at Potstill later. I've never seen her so happy. She was smiling so wide, I could see her molars.

And this dress is better than I could ever have dreamed. It's one of those dresses that make you feel willowy and gorgeous, so then you act willowy and gorgeous. I paired it with some silver heels of Pia's that are high enough to make me tall but not so high that I can't walk.

I keep thinking about Joe.

About all the times he's been kind and supportive, not just to me but to my friends too. How he always made me feel better about myself. How much he made me laugh. How it made me happy to make him happy.

I was so wrong about him. I thought he was a fast-talking, flirtatious player and used to the rough-and-tumble of the friends-with-benefits game. I thought he was arrogant, just because he was confident and funny.

I am the worst judge of character in the history of the damn world.

And now that I look back . . . I can see that Joe actually cared about me.

When we very first met, sure, he flirted with Angie, but when I really think about it . . . from the time we had that moment on the stoop of Rookhaven, he only wanted me. He encouraged me, he believed in me. He was kind and sensitive and honest.

And he was right.

I am an asshole.

And now here I am, in this amazing silver dress, my hair done, Pia putting the finishing touches on my makeup, about to go to the Potstill Prom to ask him to forgive me.

Julia is giving me a pep talk, lounging on Pia's bed with her laptop, while she updates her LinkedIn profile.

"So you just need to meet his eyes. You say, 'Dude, I fucked up. My bad. I think—'"

"Christ, she loves a pep talk," Pia whispers, applying illuminator to my face as a final touch.

Thank God, Julia stops focusing on me a moment later. "I think I'm going up upgrade my LinkedIn to Premium. Do you think it's worth it?"

My God, I'm nervous.

I know it's immature of me, and I know that it's not a real prom, but in a weird way, this buzz of nerves reminds me of getting ready for my actual prom back in high school. That feeling that anything might happen. Then again, at my real prom I wore an ugly green-and-black dress that I bought because it fit, not because I liked it, and my night ended in tears and misery because Eric slept with my ex–best friend. But that won't happen tonight.

I just hope he forgives me.

Pia and Julia are coming, of course. Not just to support me, but for Madeleine. Ian James is coming tonight; this could be her big chance to be discovered.

"Personality drink?" says Pia, offering me a glass of wine.

I shake my head. "I need to stay sharp."

"I don't," says Julia, slugging the entire glass in one gulp. "I've already warned Peter the Magnificent he'll be carrying me home later. More wine, please."

I clear my throat. "So how about I say: 'Joe, I'm so sorry. I totally love you too . . .' No, that's stupid."

"How about, 'My sister is an asshat and clouded my judgment'?" suggests Julia.

"Jules, you may be an asshat, but you're *our* asshat," says Pia.

"I can't blame you, Jules," I say. "It was my fault. My life, my choices, my fault."

The front door slams. It's Madeleine. We all exchange a look, and then I quickly stand up and run out to the front hallway.

"Maddy!" I say, just as she's about to go up the stairs.

She glances at me warily and stops.

"Please hear me out, Madeleine," I say. "I'm so sorry I told everyone about your private life. And I'm sorry it took me so long to apologize. I guess I was scared that you hated me, which is so dumb I know, but hey! That's me. And . . . I'm sorry. You were my friend and I let you down."

Madeleine gives a wry half smile.

"That's okay."

We gaze at each other for a second. Should I hug her? Madeleine isn't one for hugging, historically.

"I'm really excited about your set at the Potstill Prom tonight," I say eventually. "I hear you have some great new songs. And can you believe Ian James is coming?"

Maddy's face falls. "What?"

"Ian James! You know, the big music producer . . . guy?" I falter. "Joe didn't tell you?"

Madeleine looks like I just told her I killed someone. "Ian James?"

"Joe talked to him outside the Ace Hotel that time, and I found him and—"

Madeleine's eyes glaze over, and I see the color literally draining from her face. It's like seeing someone apply an Instagram filter in real life. Suddenly, she pushes roughly past me and runs upstairs to the bathroom. I run after her, but by the time I get there it's too late: she's locked herself in.

"Maddy?" I call. "Are you okay?"

All I can hear is the choked gurgles of someone puking.

"Hello?" I say. "Maddy? Open the door. I'll hold your hair back."

There's a long pause.

"I'm going to kick open the door if you don't come out," I say.

Then I hear the rare sound of Madeleine laughing. "Really?"

"I mean it," I say. "I am surprisingly powerful. In my legs. I'm like a puma."

"A puma?" Madeleine laughs more, and my stomach unclenches. Laughing is a good sign.

"Come out, Maddy, please?"

There's another pause, then I hear the latch click open, and Maddy steps out. She's very pale, almost translucent. She leans against the hallway wall and slides down to the ground. She looks so exhausted that suddenly I feel tired too and slide right down next to her, prom dress and all.

"Fuck, Coco," she whispers. "I don't think I can do it. I feel nervous and wired and sick, my stomach hurts . . ."

"What did you eat today?"

She shrugs. "I had a green juice for lunch."

"Seriously? That's not food. You don't eat enough."

"I'm not a food freak or anything," Madeleine says, reading my mind. "It's just that sometimes . . . I am so full of, um, feelings, I guess, that I feel like I can't put anything else in myself. Like I can't even swallow."

"Is that also why you . . ." I don't know how to say it. "Can you show me your arms?"

Maddy sighs. "They're not really such a big deal. See? Just a few . . ." She rolls one sleeve up, and I see little white scars.

"You did that to yourself?" I say. "You wanted to hurt yourself?"

She nods, biting her top lip. "It made me feel better. Like I was letting the feelings out. Or something. I don't fucking know why it felt good, it just did."

"I baked when I felt bad," I say. "It was so reassuring to make something so pretty and yummy."

"I like pretty and yummy things too," she says. "I just feel bad when I let myself eat them. Like I don't deserve it. I should only eat things that I don't love."

"You should be nicer to yourself."

"So should you," says Madeleine. "You have no idea how beautiful you are."

"I never felt beautiful," I say. "Except when I was with Joe." I pause, thinking for a moment. Oh God, I hope he forgives me. "You're not going to hurt yourself again, right, Maddy?"

"I don't think so . . ." Maddy says quietly. "I don't know."

"You don't need to let feelings out that way anymore," I say. "You have music. You can sing, Madeleine. When you sing, everything stops."

She laughs, shaking her head. "I'm not *that* good."

"You are!" I say. "Ian James already loves you. He saw you singing outside the Ace Hotel that night, and he thought you were amazing. He's coming tonight to see *you*. So all you have to do tonight is be yourself. He'll be blown away. I believe in you, Madeleine."

Tears streak down her face as she turns to face me. "But what if *I* don't believe in me?"

"That's okay," I say. "I believe in you enough for the two of us."

She leans over and hugs me, the first real hug we've ever shared.

"Okay, I'll do it. I'll sing tonight. You know, Joe is lucky to have you."

"Actually, he doesn't have me," I say. "But I hope he will. With your help."

CHAPTER 37

"Potstill Prom is perfect."

Pia, Julia, Madeleine, and I pause, just after we walk in the doorway, and survey the crowded, already buzzing bar. Joe and I worked so hard for the last few weeks to get the prom decorations just right, and it paid off.

Pompom bubble garlands are strung across the ceiling. Blue fairy lights give the whole place an underwater glow. Seashells are scattered over every surface. Paper fish and coral and jellyfish stud the walls. There's a papier-mâché shark smiling happily from his vantage point above the bar. And Joe even managed to find a guy to deliver a load of perfect white sand.

The whole bar looks charmingly beachy, homemade and real, in this kind of smart-ass, funny way. It's very Brooklyn. And so as we walk in, at dusk on the night of the Potstill Prom, I just want to smile.

But I have to talk to Joe.

And I'm terrified.

The bar is already full of people—sorry, prom attendees. A few locals, people I recognize from their evenings in here over the summer. But this time, they've brought groups of friends. They've been part of the turnaround of Potstill, and they seem to have real pride in the bar.

There's a large group of girls I half remember from that night I got really drunk, and then a few couples on dates, and Julia's boyfriend—if that's what he is—Peter the Magnificent, and some of his friends.

Aidan is here too: he just flew in for the weekend and is waiting for Pia, along with Jonah, her old friend from the Italian restaurant she used to work at.

Madeleine goes straight to the stage, where the band is setting up. She kisses Amy hello quickly and then whispers to her band mates. Telling them about Ian James, I guess. They all look shocked. It's their big chance.

Then I look over to the bar, where Joe is serving drinks. My heart practically stops at the sight of him.

He's not alone. He hired someone else to help out for the night: a scruffy bearded guy that I think works at one of Gary's other bars. It's like I was never even here.

I timidly walk over and stand at one end, hoping Joe will notice me. But he doesn't look up. He's concentrating hard on making cocktails, but frowning so intensely that I can tell his mind is elsewhere. My stomach twists with nerves.

I feel like I'm seeing Joe for the first time. I had become so accustomed to looking at him, it's like I didn't even see him. And now that I can . . . he's so . . . handsome. He's perfect. And more than that—this will sound lame, so bear with me—I can see that he's just as perfect on the inside. Or, maybe he's not perfect, because none of us are. But he's perfect for me.

"Um . . . Joe?"

Joe looks up at me briefly, then turns away. "Hey."

He walks over to the other end of the bar where the cash register is. Then he turns around and serves some people there.

I wait for him to come back down to this side. But he doesn't. He just keeps serving people as far away from me as possible, refusing to look in my direction, refusing to even acknowledge that I'm still here.

"Joe, can we talk?"

He hates me. Joe really hates me. And I deserve it.

"Joe . . ." My voice is barely more than a whisper.

He's still ignoring me.

I don't know what to do. I feel like crying.

So I just stand here, at the end of the bar, waiting. Then I hear the crowd cheering and whistling, and turn to see Madeleine at the microphone. She's gazing around the bar with a sexy half smile, surveying the crowd like a pro.

"Welcome to Potstill Prom, you guys . . ."

The crowd—already well primed with Whiskey Smashes and Rob Roys—cheers rowdily.

"Okay, easy, tiger. Don't peak too soon. We're here all night."

Madeleine looks so confident standing behind a microphone now. Not like she used to be. A few months ago, she acted like she didn't want anyone to even look at her. Now no one can take their eyes off her. She glances back at Amy, who winks at her encouragingly, then turns back to the crowd.

"So, for those of you who know us, you're probably expecting us to play covers. And maybe we will, later. But for now . . ." Madeleine grins, totally in control. "It's time for something new."

Amy tears in with a guitar riff that sends a surge of excitement through the crowd. Then Madeleine starts to sing. Her voice is raspy and raw and full of emotion. Everyone in the bar falls totally silent and stares at the stage, rapt.

When the song finishes, the crowd goes wild with applause. I clap and cheer as loud as I can. The room vibrates with how much everyone in here loves her. Everyone is mesmerized, whistling and smiling and cheering with joy. I look out and see Julia, Peter the Magnificent, Pia, Aidan, Ian James . . .

Holy shit. Ian James.

He came. He's standing alone, wearing that same little hat, leaning against the wall in the darkest corner of the bar.

"Joe!" I hiss, just as the band starts their second song. "He's here. Ian James is here."

Joe's head snaps up and he looks over the crowd until he sees him.

"Go," I say. "Go talk to him. I'll cover the bar."

Joe walks to the end of the bar, where I'm standing, and pauses. He seems unable to actually leave the bar. Paralyzed by fear, nerves, something . . .

"Go talk to him!" I whisper urgently. "This is it! This is the chance you've been waiting for!"

"I . . . I can't . . ." He shakes his head. "I can't do it."

"You can," I say, impulsively squeezing his arm. "I know you can."

Joe glances at me, then takes a deep breath, and walks over.

I quickly start serving people, looking over to Ian James and Joe whenever I get the chance. They talk for a minute and then just watch the band together. After four songs, the band takes a break, and Ian James and Joe are deep in conversation.

My God, he's really doing it.

The bar is busier than I've ever seen it before. Prom is a hit. People are dancing, and drinking, and messing around. Julia is high-fiving everything with a pulse, and Pia and Aidan are making out.

"Woo! Best prom ever!" calls out a voice, and I turn around to see Angie walk in with Sam by her side. Both of them so happy, they're actually glowing. (Or maybe that's a postsex glow.)

Then, behind Angie, I see Gary walk in. Gary, the owner of Potstill, who is supposed to be in Nantucket. Who wants to sell Potstill. And who never approved this prom party.

Shit.

Gary takes in the decorations, the fairy lights, the pompom bubbles, the sand, and his face hardens. He walks straight up to the bar, shoving patrons out of the way.

"Where the fuck is Joe?"

"He's just stepped out," I say. "Can I get you a drink? Um, seltzer, right?"

"Get Joe," Gary says. "Now."

I push through the crowd to where Joe and Ian James are standing, talking to Madeleine and Amy, and overhear the last of their conversation.

"So it's set. Showcase at the studio, first thing Monday morning."

"You got it." Joe shakes his hand. "Thank you so much."

Ian James nods and drains his beer. "I've gotta go. But I'm looking forward to it. And Joe . . . good job."

He leaves, and Amy and Madeleine look at each other and grin ecstatically, trying not to scream until Ian James has left the bar.

"Um, Joe? Gary is here," I say under my breath.

Joe looks over toward the bar. "Shit."

He walks over to Gary. I follow him, leaving the band hugging and whooping behind me.

"I'm going to fucking kill you," says Gary. "What the fuck is going on?"

Joe looks him straight in the eye. "I was trying to save your bar."

"Save it? By turning it into some mermaid Disneyland?"

"It's an Under the Sea prom-themed event," I interject. "And Joe has saved this bar. We're busy *every* night now. Two months ago there were only about three customers a night. Now there are thirty, maybe more!"

Gary glances at me. "Fuck off."

"Don't talk to her that way." Joe steps closer to Gary. He's taller than him, but Gary is about fifteen years older, fifty pounds heavier, and a hell of a lot meaner.

"I'll do whatever I like. It's my bar," says Gary. "Until Monday, anyway. I sold it. They're shutting this shithole down. Opening a 7-Eleven."

Joe exhales sharply, like someone just punched him in the gut.

Gary looks briefly around the bar. "I'll be back in the morning to look over the books and get the keys."

I can't contain myself any longer. "You're an asshole!"

Gary shoots me a look of contempt, then turns and walks out, pushing his way through the crowd. Joe stares after him, and then, looks around at the crowded bar, the people drinking and whooping and partying like they really are at prom.

And he starts to laugh. Manically.

"It's okay," I say. "It's okay, Joe, we can fix this, we can—"

Joe stops laughing. "We can't. It's over, Coco. Thanks for getting Ian James here to see the band. I appreciate it."

He turns around and starts to walk away.

"Wait!" I grab Joe's arm, and he wrenches it away, but turns to face me.

"What do you want, Coco? I said thank you."

"I'm sorry, Joe, I'm so sorry—"

He nods curtly. "You said sorry this morning."

"No, no, I'm sorry because, um, because when I said I didn't love you, I . . . I was wrong."

"Right." He won't even meet my eyes.

"I didn't know—" I can hardly get the words out. "I didn't know that I was falling for you. But I know now—"

"How do you know?"

"Because you make me so happy," I say. "And because . . . because I want to make you happy."

I can't read his expression at all. The blue fairy lights are casting a weird gleam over everything, and the crowd is growing noisier and rowdier.

This wasn't how I pictured this. I never saw myself confessing love in a noisy bar surrounded by blue fairy lights and drunk strangers in prom dresses.

"I know I love you, because every time I think of you, I smile. Because you've become my best friend, and because . . . because I just *know*."

At that moment, the band starts playing again, and I hear Madeleine's voice. It's a cover that I can't quite place for a moment. She's whispering the words, making them sound urgent and sexy and serious.

"Imagine me and you . . . I do . . ."

I take a deep breath. "Joe, I read this thing in a book once that said, when you love someone, you love the whole person, just as he or she is, and not as you would like them to be. And that's how I feel about you. I know now that it's how I've always felt, but I, um, I didn't realize it until today . . . I used to have this list of things I thought I needed. I don't need any of that stuff, Joe." I take a deep breath. "But I do need you."

Joe hasn't moved. He's just staring at me. And then, just as Madeleine hits the chorus, he grabs me and kisses me so hard that I feel like I'm going to explode.

At that moment I feel it.

Perfect happiness.

That stupid Happy List was never the answer. In order to be happy, all I needed to do was choose my life for myself. I needed to be honest about my feelings, to put someone else's happiness ahead of my own. I needed to speak out about what I wanted. I'm the only one who can do those things. No one else can do them for me.

And now I have everything. I'm in love, I'm going back to college, and I'm starting adult life the way I want to. It's the best feeling in the world.

"I love you," Joe murmurs between kisses.

I smile at him, feeling my insides explode with joy. "I love you too. Kiss me again."

"Always."

Life doesn't always work out the way you think it will. But it always works out the way it should.

And I can't wait to see what happens next.

ACKNOWLEDGMENTS

Thanks.

Thank you for reading this book. I truly hope you enjoyed it.

Eternal thanks to Jill Grinberg, Laura Longrigg, Vicki Lame, Dan Weiss, Fiona Barrows, Katelyn Detweiler, Cheryl Pientka, Sarah Lambert, Niamh Mulvey, and everyone else at St. Martin's Press who helped the birth of the Brooklyn Girls book series, and particularly this little book.

Thanks to all the people who e-mail me telling me that these books make them feel better about everything, and to all young women who are starting adult life without a master plan, but who have the courage and hope to keep going anyway. You are doing a great job.

Thanks to my friends, old and new, for being endlessly hilarious, encouraging, and inspiring.

Thanks to my lovely, loving parents and sister. (And my brother-in-law. And all my Irish in-laws.)

And most of all, thanks to my perfect boys: my husband, Fox, and our little ginger army, Errol and Ned. I love you.

READ ON TO FIND OUT WHERE IT ALL BEGAN

Out **NOW!**

www.quercusbooks.co.uk

CHAPTER 1

Never screw your roommate's brother.

A simple rule, but a good one. And I broke it last night. Twice.

Oopsh.

At least the party was awesome. I'll try that excuse if Julia is pissy. And if her house is trashed. Which I'm pretty sure it is.

I'm not exactly surprised. I like parties, I'm good at them, and it was August 26 yesterday. And on that date, I always drink to forget. This year, I did it with whips, chains, and bells on.

My bare ass keeps brushing against the wall as I squish away from Mike. Don't you hate that? Doesn't random hookup etiquette demand he face the other way? I wish he would just leave without me having to, like, talk to him.

I wonder what Madeleine, his sister, would say if she found out.

She'd probably ignore me, which is what she always does these days. I wish Julia hadn't asked her to move in.

Julia, my best friend from college, inherited this house when her aunt passed away. So Julia invited me, her little sister Coco, and Madeleine to move in. And then we needed a fifth, so I asked my friend Angie. We're a motley crew: Coco's the Betty Homemaker type, Angie's all fashi-tude, Julia's super-smart and ambitious, and Madeleine's uptight as hell. And me? I'm . . . well, it's impossible to describe yourself, isn't it? Let's call me a work-in-progress.

We moved in two weeks ago. It's a brownstone named Rookhaven, on Union Street in Carroll Gardens, a neighborhood in the borough of Brooklyn in New York City. None of us has properly lived in New York before.

Carroll Gardens is a weird mix of old people who've probably lived here forever, young professionals like us who—let's face it—can't afford to live in Manhattan, and a bunch of yupster couples with young kids. There's a real neighborhood village vibe with all these old, traditional Italian bakeries and restaurants next to stylish little bars.

I like stylish little bars.

I like my bedroom, too. I've had a lot of bedrooms in my life—twenty-seven, if you count every room change at boarding school and college—but never one quite like this. High ceilings, windows looking out over the front stoop, wall-to-wall mirrored closets. Okay, the mirrors are yellowed and the wallpaper is a faded rosebud print that looks like something out of an old movie. It just *feels* right. Like this is how it's supposed to look.

That's kind of Rookhaven all over. If I were feeling nice, I'd call the décor vintage and preloved. (Old and shabby.) I'm just happy to be in New York, far away from my parents, in the most exciting city in the world, with a job at a SoHo PR agency. My life is *finally* happening.

Can I be honest with you? I shouldn't have slept with Mike. Not when things are already, shall we say, complicated with Madeleine. Casual sex only works when it's with someone you can never see again. But, as I said, it was August 26 (also known as Eddie Memorial Day, or Never Again Day). And on August 26, shit happens.

What is that damn ringing sound?

"I think that's the doorbell."

Gah! Mike! Awake! Right here next to me. I peek through my eye-lashes. Like Madeleine, he's ridiculously good-looking. I guess it's their Chinese-Irish DNA. Good combination.

"Erm . . . someone else will get it," I murmur. My breath smells like an open grave. Not that it matters. Because I don't like him like that. Even though last night I—ew. God. Bad thought. But hey! So what? So the whole sex thing was a bad idea. There is no reason to feel stupid Puritan guilt about one-night stands. I am a feminist. And all that shit.

The doorbell goes again.

"Pia . . . Come here, you crazy kitten," Mike says, pushing his arm under me.

"I better get the door. It could be someone important!" I say brightly, slithering down around him and falling onto the dark green carpet with a thump.

I wriggle into my panties, trying to look cool and unbothered as I put on the first T-shirt I see. It belonged to Smith, a guy I dated (well, slept with a few times) in college. The back says, "I brake for cheerleaders . . . HARD."

I pull on my favorite cutoff jean shorts and Elmo slippers and stuff my cell phone in my pocket.

"I'm glad you brake for cheerleaders," says Mike. "They're an endangered species."

"Um, yup, totally!" I say, and slam the door behind me, cutting him off.

Mike! God! Nightmare!

I close my eyes, trying to remember last night. It's worryingly hard. I was feeling meh after Thompson (this cockmonkey I've been dating, well, sleeping with) ignored my text (*Hola. Bodacious party. Bring smokes if you can . . .* Good text, right? Ironic use of passé slang, trailing ellipses rather than a lame smiley face, etc.). And rejection is not a good look for me. Not on August 26.

So I drank more. And more. And then more.

I remember dancing. On a table, maybe? Yeah, that rings a bell. . . . And I think I was doing some '80s-aerobics-style dance moves. The grapevine. Definitely the grapevine. I was having fun, anyway. I don't usually worry about much when I'm having fun.

And Mike was doing one-handed push-ups, really badly, and making me laugh, and then I stumbled, and next thing I knew Mike's lips were on mine. Now I *love* kissing, I really do, and he is pretty good at it, and I was trashed, so I suggested we go to my room. And then . . . oh, God.

Nothing burns like hangover shame.

The person at the door is really dying to get in. *Dingdongdingdong-dingdong.*

"Coming!" I shout, picking my way over the bottles and cigarette butts on the stairs.

I hope it's not the cops. I don't *think* there were drugs at the party, but you never know. Once time at my second boarding school I thought that my boyfriend Jack had OCD, which was why he arranged talcum powder in little lines, and as it turned out— Wait. Back to the nightmare.

I open the front door and sigh in relief.

It's just a very old man. His face is like a long raisin with pointy elf ears, on the top of a tall and skinny body.

"Young lady, where is your father?" he says in a strong Brooklyn accent. *Fadah.*

"Zurich," I say, then add, "Sir." (And they say I don't respect my elders.)

"Are you a relation of Julia's?"

"Fu— I mean, gosh, no."

"Well, that figures. I didn't think Pete remarried, and you're definitely a half-a-something."

Seriously? "I'm a whole person, not a half. My mother is Indian, my father is Swiss. Please come back later." I try to close the door, but he's blocking it.

"I need to speak with Miss Russotti."

"Which one? There are two. Russotti the elder, also known as Julia, and Russotti the younger, also known as Coco."

"Whichever is responsible for the very loud party that went on till 5:00 A.M. and caused the total cave-in of my kitchen ceiling."

I gasp. He must live in the garden-level apartment under our house. My mind starts racing. How can I fix this?

"Oh, I am so sorry, I can pay for the ceiling, sir, I—"

"I take it that there were no parents present?"

"I think my roommate Madeleine has babysitting experience, does that count?"

"Don't be smart with me."

"I've never been called smart before," I say, twisting my hair around my finger, trying to get him to laugh a little bit. No one can stay angry after they laugh, it's a fact.

His expression warms slightly, then falls as though pushing the crags and crevices into a new shape was too much effort. "Just get Julia."

"Yes, sir. Would you like to wait inside?"

"If you think I want to see what this house looks like this morning, you've got another think coming."

"Is it think or thing?"

"It's think."

"I'll go get Julia."

I run up the stairs, jumping over the leftover party mayhem, and knock on Julia's bedroom door.

"Juju?" I peer in.

No Julia, just Angie and some tall English lord guy she met in London at the Cartier Polo (yes, seriously). I saw them making out in the laundry room last night after a game of "truth or dare," which Angie renamed "dare or fuck off." Man, I hope they didn't screw on the washing machine. My laundry is in there. I keep forgetting to take it out, and it goes all funky with the heat, so then I have to wash it again and— Oh, sorry. Focus.

"*Angie!* Wake the hell up!"

I shake her, but she just gives a little snore and buries herself deeper into the bed. She looks like a fallen angel with a serious eyeliner habit. And she's *impossible* to wake after a night out.

Julia will lose her shit if she finds out about this. She and Angie haven't exactly bonded. My bad: I talked Julia into letting Angie move in before they'd even met, because Angie's folks got her a job as a PA to some food photographer woman in Chelsea and she needed a place to live, and Angie's been, like, my best friend since I was born. (Literally. Our moms met in the maternity ward.)

Then Angie walked in, said, "It's a dump, but it's retro, I can make it work," and lit a cigarette. Julia was not impressed.

"Angie! Get. The hell. Up."

"Pia?" She peers up at me through her long white-blond hair. "I had to sleep here, there was a threesome in my bed."

"Ew," I say, grimacing, as I pull Angie onto her feet. "Help me. Major crisis."

"You're such a fucking drama queen. Hugh. Dude. Get up."

Hugh climbs out behind her unsteadily. He has a very posh English accent. "Tremendous party." *Pah-teh.* He's very handsome, like a young Prince William, with more hair.

As soon as he leaves, Angie licks and smells her hand to check her morning breath. "Yep, pretty rank. What's wrong, ladybitch?"

"Everything. We have to find Julia."

"Roger that." Angie's still wearing her tiny party dress from last night and slips on a pair of snow boots from Julia's closet. "You have a hickey on your neck."

"How old school of me." I grab Julia's foundation to dab over it. "Ugh, why is she wearing this shade? It's completely wrong for her. Sorry, off topic."

We head upstairs. Angie stares at her closed bedroom door. "God, I hate threesomes."

"Totally. It's just showing off."

Angie smirks, then karate kicks her door in. "Show's over, bitches! Get the hell outta my house."

Two girls I've never seen before and a tall dark-haired guy I vaguely recognize from college saunter out of Angie's room.

"Pia, babe!" says the guy, putting on his shirt. "I tried to find you all night! Remember that party back in junior year? A little Vicodin, a little tequila . . ."

I shudder. Now I remember him.

"Leave," snaps Angie. "Now."

"Bitch," he calls, walking down the stairs.

"Blow me!" she calls back, then heads into her room. "Fuck! I'm gonna have to burn the sheets."

I hear a hinge squeak. It's Madeleine, coming out of the bathroom in a pristine white robe, her hair wrapped perfectly in a towel-turban.

"Morning!" I say, smiling as innocently as I can.

She pads to her bedroom and slams the door. Typical. Good thing I didn't add, *"By the way, your brother is naked in my bed."*

I trudge up the last flight of stairs, finally reach Coco's attic room, and knock. Julia must be in here. There's nowhere else to go.

"It's me . . ." I open the door slowly.

Julia is sitting on the bed, still wearing her clothes from last night yet sportily immaculate as ever, next to Coco, whose blond bob is bent over a plastic bucket and—oh, God. She's puking.

"Coco!" I say. "Are you sick?"

"Clap, clap, Sherlock," says Julia.

"I'm fine!" Coco's voice echoes nasally in the bucket. "So fine. Oh, God, not fine." Noisy, chokey barf sounds follow. "Wowsers! This is green! Oh, Julia, it's green, is that bad?"

"It's bile," says Julia, rubbing Coco's back and glaring at me. Furious and sisterly, all at once. "I need to talk to Pia. Try to stop vomiting, okay?" She has a deep, self-assured voice, particularly lately. It's like the moment she graduated, she decided it was time to *act adult at all costs.*

"Maybe I'll lose weight," Coco's voice echoes from the bucket.

I follow Julia to the tiny landing at the top of the stairs, closing Coco's bedroom door behind us. I feel sick. Confrontation and I really don't get along.

"I am sorry," I say immediately. "I guess you're angry about the party, and—"

"You sold it to me as a 'small housewarming,'" interrupts Julia. "This place was like Cancun on spring break, but less classy."

I hate being told off, too. It's not like I don't *know* when I've screwed up. Or like I do it on purpose. And I never know what to say, so I just gaze into space and wait for it to be over.

"I *said* no wild parties. When we all moved in, that was the rule." God, Julia is scary when she wants to be. "What the fuck were you *thinking*, Pia?"

"It just sort of, um, happened. . . ." I say, chewing my lip. "And I'm sorry about this, too, um, there's an old dude at the door? He said his ceiling caved in? I'll pay for it! I have the money and—"

"Vic?" says Julia in dismay. "I swear to God, Pia, I can't live with you if you're going to fucking act like this all the time. I mean it!"

She's going to kick me out of Rookhaven?

"I won't!" I exclaim. "I'm sorry! Don't overreact!"

"Start cleaning up!" she shouts, thundering down the stairs.

She's going to kick me out. I thought I finally had somewhere that I could call my own, somewhere that wasn't temporary, and somewhere I might actually not have to wear shower shoes. Yet again I am the master of my own demise. Mistress. Whatever.

I walk back into Coco's room. "Can I get you anything, sweetie? I've got rehydration salts somewhere."

"No," she croaks, smiling cherubically at me from the pillow. "I had fun last night. You were so funny."

"Oh, well, that's good." What the hell was I doing?

There are hundreds of books on Coco's floor. I think they're usually in the bookshelves in the living room. They're all old and tattered, with titles like *What Katy Did* by Susan Coolidge and *Are You There God? It's Me, Margaret* by Judy Blume. I loved *What Katy Did*, I remember. The sequel, *What Katy Did at School*, was one of the reasons I thought boarding school would be awesome. Stupid book.

"Why are these here?" I ask.

"I didn't want them to get, um, you know, trashed at the party," says Coco. "So I picked up all the ones that my mom loved the most and brought them up here."

"It must have taken you a while," I say.

"Every time I made a trip, I had a shot...." Coco starts puking again.

"Hey, ladybitches," says Angie, sauntering in with an unlit cigarette propped in the side of her mouth.

"For you, Miss Coco." Somehow, Angie has found an icy-cold can of Coke.

"Wow, thanks! I normally drink Diet Coke, but—"

"Trust me, Diet Coke is bullshit. Okay kids, I am officially over this post-party chaos thing. Let's clean up."

At that moment, my phone rings. Unlisted number. I answer.

"Hello?"

"Pia, it's Benny Mansi."

Benny Mansi is the director of the PR agency where I work. My parents know his family somehow and got me the interview back in June. I started working there last week. Why would he call me on a Sunday? Is that normal? Perhaps it's a PR emergency!

I try to sound professional. "Hi! What's up?"

"Are you aware that there's a photo of you on Facebook, dancing on a table topless and drinking a bottle of Captain Morgan rum?"

WHAM. I feel like I just got punched.

"Um, I—"

"Pia, we're letting you go before your trial period is over."

WHAM. Another hit.

"You're firing me . . . for having a party?"

"Captain Morgan is one of our biggest clients," Benny says. "As my employee, you represent the agency. You're also Facebook friends with all your brand-new colleagues. You were tagged, they saw it. I applaud your convivial approach to interoffice relations, but that sort of behavior is just . . . it's unprofessional, and it's completely unacceptable, Pia."

"I know." A wash of sickly cold horror trickles through me, and I stare at the yellowed glow-in-the-dark stars on the sloping ceiling in Coco's room. They lost their glow long ago. . . . Oh, God, I can't be fired. I can't be fired after *one week*. "I'm so sorry, Benny." Silence. "Did you . . . tell my, um, father?"

He sighs. "I e-mailed him this morning. I didn't tell him why." I don't say anything, and his voice softens. "Look, Pia, it's complicated. We made some redundancies a few months ago. So hiring you, as a family friend, really upset a few people, and that photo . . . my hands are tied. I'm sorry."

He hangs up.

I can feel Coco and Angie staring at me, but I can't say anything.

I've lost my job. And I'm probably about to get kicked out of my house. After one week in New York.

My phone rings again. It's my parents. I stare at the phone for a few seconds, knowing what's on the other end, what's waiting for me.

I wonder if Coco would mind if I borrowed her puke bucket.

I need to be alone for what's about to happen, so I walk back out to the stairwell and sit down. I can hear Madeleine playing some angsty music in her room on the floor below, mixed with Julia's placating tones and Vic's grumbly ones from down in the front hall.

Then I answer, trying to sound like a good daughter.

"Hi, Daddy!"

"So you've lost your job already. What do you have to say for yourself?"

My voice is gone. This happens sometimes. Just when I need it most. In its place, a tiny squeaking sound comes out.

"Speak up!" snaps my father. He has a slightly scary Swiss accent despite twenty years living in the States.

"I'm . . . sorry. I'll get another job, I will, and—"

"Pia, we are so disappointed in you!" My mother is lurking on the extension. She has a slight Indian accent that only really comes out when she's pissed. Like now.

"You wanted the summer with Angie, so we paid for it. You wanted to work, so we got you a job. You said you had the perfect place to live, so we agreed to help pay rent, though God knows Brooklyn certainly wasn't the perfect place to live last time I was there—"

"You have no work ethic! You are a spoiled party girl! Are you sniffing the drugs again?"

They've really honed their double-pronged condemnation-barrage routine over the years.

"Work ethic. Your mother is right. Your total failure to keep a job . . . well. Let me tell you a story—"

I sink my head to my knees. My parents have the confidence-killing combination of high standards and low expectations.

They also twist everything so it looks terrible. They told me if I got good grades they'd pay for my vacation, and that I'd never find a job on my own, *and* they offered me an allowance, so of course I said yes! Wouldn't you?

". . . and that is how I met your father and then we got married and had you and then lived— What do you say? Happily ever after . . ."

Yeah, right. My parents hardly talk to each other. They distract themselves with work (my dad) and socializing (my mother). They met in New York, where they had me, then moved to Singapore, London, Tokyo, Zurich . . . I went to American International Schools until I was twelve, and then they started sending me to boarding school. Well, boarding schools.

"Life starts with a job, Pia. You think we will always pay for your mistakes, that life is just a party. We know you'll never have a career, but a job is—"

"A reason to get up in the morning!"

"And the only way to learn the value of money. Do you understand?"

I nod stupidly, staring at the wall next to me, at the ancient-looking rosebud wallpaper. At the bottom the paper has started to peel, curled up like a little pencil shaving. It's comforting.

"Pia!" my mother is shouting. "Why are you not listening? Do we have to do the Skype again?"

"No, no, I can't, my Skype is broken," I say quickly. I can't handle Skyping with my parents. It's so damn intense.

"We are stopping your allowance, effective immediately. No rent money, no credit card for emergencies. You're on your own."

"What? B-but it might take me a while to get another job!" I stammer in panic.

"Well, the Bank of Mom and Dad is closed unless you come live with us in Zurich and get a job here. That's the deal."

"No way!" I know I sound hysterical, but I can't help it. "My friends are here! My life is here!"

"We want you to be safe," says my mother, in a slightly gentler tone. Suddenly tears rush to my eyes. "We worry. And it seems like you're only safe when you're with us."

"I *am* safe."

"And we want you to be happy," she adds.

"I am happy!" My voice breaks.

My father interrupts. "This is the deal. We're vacationing in Palm Beach in exactly two months, via New York. If you're not in gainful employment by then, we're taking you back to Zurich with us. That's the best thing for you."

The tears escape my eyes. I know I've made some mistakes, but God, I've tried to make it up to them. I studied hard, I got into a great college. . . . It's never good enough.

How is it that no one in the world can make me feel as bad as my parents can?

"Okay, message received," I say. "I gotta go."

I hang up and stare at the curled-up rosebud wallpaper for a few more seconds. Then, almost without thinking, I lick my index finger and try to smooth it down, so it lies flat and perfect against the wall. It bounces right back up again.

With one party, I've destroyed my life in New York City. Before it even began.

CHAPTER 2

When Julia comes back upstairs moments later, pink with fury, my stomach flips over. I hate fighting. And Jules is really good at it. She should have been a lawyer.

"You destroyed our neighbor's ceiling," she snaps. "Destroyed. A piece of plaster fell on his sister's head this morning. She's eighty-six-fucking-years old, Pia!"

"Is she okay? Oh, my God, I can't—"

"She's fine," says Julia. "It was only a tiny piece. But Vic is *pissed*."

"I'll pay for it, I promise!" I say. "I have, like, sixteen hundred dollars. He can have all of it." It's all I have in the world, and the last of the money from my parents, but I need to convince Julia not to kick me out. "I'm sorry, Julia, I didn't know it'd get so out of control."

"What were you *thinking*?"

"I just . . . I thought it would be fun, that everyone would have a good time." I can't tell her that I was drinking because it was August 26. I never talk about Eddie to anyone. Only Angie knows the story, only Angie saw me that day. "Seriously, Juju, I never meant to hurt anyone . . . or destroy the old guy's, I mean Vic's, ceiling."

"Vic and Marie have been here *forever*. Since long before I was born, or my mom," says Julia. "They're like family, okay?"

Suddenly, I understand. Her mom grew up here, and she died of breast cancer about eight years ago. Her dad has cocooned himself in silent grief ever since, and then her Aunt Jo passed away, so I guess Vic and Marie—and Rookhaven—are sort of a last link to her mom. No wonder she feels so protective.

"I'll fix the floor damage," I say, reaching out for Julia's hand. She doesn't resist, which I take as a good sign. "And I'll get them flowers to say sorry. Today. And I will not let anything bad happen to this house again. I cross my heart."

Julia takes a deep breath and leans against the wall, closing her eyes. She looks exhausted, and it's not just from the party. Her job—trainee in an investment bank—starts at 6:00 A.M. every day, and she doesn't get home until past 7:00 P.M. every night. It's step one in her plan to take over the world. She's so exhausted, she's actually kind of gray. And she's not even hungover.

"I had fun last night, by the way."

"What?" I say.

She opens one eye, a tiny grin on her lips. "It was a great party. I had fun. Right up until Coco started to do a striptease in the kitchen."

I clap my hand over my mouth. "No way."

"I carried her up here. Anyway, don't tell her. She doesn't remember. I always think it's better that way."

"Oh, I know," I say. "You never flashed an entire bar your Spanx on Spring Weekend."

"Totally. Goddamnit, I wish I'd been wearing a thong that night."

We grin at each other for a second, remembering. That's the Julia I know and love. The girl who works hard and plays hard, too. And the girl who always wants to make everything right. But I can't tell her what happened with my job and parents just yet. I need to process it (uh, pretend it didn't happen).

"Hang on a moment." Julia narrows her eyes at me. "Bed hair. Panda eyes. And stubble rash. Peepee, you got action last night!" she exclaims.

"I did not! And don't call me Peepee!"

"Have we made up?" coos Angie, peering out from Coco's room. She wraps her bare leg around the door, lifting one snow boot–clad foot up and down like a meteorology-loving stripper. "Are we all friends again?"

"Those are my boots," says Julia. "Why are you wearing them?"

"Are you planning on skiing soon? I think not." Angie sashays past us down the stairs. "It's August. I'll return them in pristine condition as soon as the house is clear of party debris, okay, Mommy?"

Julia rolls her eyes and heads downstairs. "Start cleaning."

Angie flicks the finger at Julia's retreating back.

"Real mature, Angie."

"Suck my mature."

"I'm hungry."

"You're always hungry. Let's clean."

Somehow, being hungover and giggling with Angie cheers me up and helps squash my what-the-sweet-hell-am-I-going-to-do-now thoughts. She keeps making little moans of dismay at each new inch of party filth, and pretty soon we've both got the giggles.

"When I have my own place, there will be no carpets," I say. "Carpets are just asking for trouble."

"Did anyone lose a shoe? And why did we invite someone to our party who wears moccasins?"

"Is this red wine or blood? No. Wait. It's tomato sauce. Weird."

"You wanna talk me through the hickey, ladybitch?"

I catch Angie's eye and bite my index finger sheepishly.

"You had the sex? You little minx . . ."

"With her brother," I whisper, pointing at Madeleine's door. "Bit of an oopsh."

Oopsh is our word for a drunken mistake.

"Oopsh I kissed the wrong dude, or oopsh I tripped and his dick landed in my mouth?"

I crack up. No one does crass like Angie. She looks like a tiny Christmas angel and acts like a sailor on a Viagra kick. "Or was it more like, oopsh, I'm riding his face and—"

"Too far! That's too far."

"Sorry."

"Don't tell Jules, she'd just have to tell Maddy, and it'd be a whole thing."

"Absolute-leh, dah-leng," she says, in her best imitation of her mother's British accent. "You were totally kamikaze last night."

"It was August 26. That's International Pia Goes Kamikaze Day, remember? Crash and burn."

There's a pause. "Oh, dude, I'm sorry. I totally forgot. Eddie."

I can't bring myself to look at her. Only Angie saw me that day, only Angie knows how bad it was. She always calls me a drama queen, but she knows that misery was real. You don't fake that kind of breakdown.

"I don't want to talk about it," I say.

Angie keeps cleaning. "Fuck him, Pia. Okay? Fuck him! It's been four years!"

I nod, scrubbing as hard as I can. It has been four years since we broke up. And I really should be over it. Then, thank God, Angie changes the subject.

"So I'm gonna move out to L.A. after the holidays," she says. "I don't really belong here in Brooklyn, you know?"

This news just makes me feel even sadder. There's no point arguing with Angie. She does whatever she wants. Instead I scrub harder and, stair by stair, stain by stain, we make it downstairs. Angie puts on some music, and we clean to the post-party-appropriate strains of the Ramones. I can hear Julia and Coco throwing out empty bottles in the kitchen and, every now and again, shrieking when they find something nasty. Oh please, God, no drugs or used condoms. Just spare me that.

"What time did the party finish?" I ask Angie.

"About five. Lord Hugh and I saw out the last of the party people just as the sun was coming up."

"He seems . . . Lordesque."

"He's very Lordesque." She nods. "He also knows his way around a washer-dryer."

"Did you guys do a"—I pause and grin at her—"full load?"

"Just a half load. Then we rinsed. Very thoroughly. Oh, look. Half a spliff. How nice."

We make it to the first floor, and help Julia and Coco finish up the kitchen, which primarily involves de-stickying every surface. Nothing does sticky like forty-year-old linoleum.

"That was intense," says Julia, wiping her forehead with her arm. "The laundry room flooded. That's what made Vic's ceiling collapse."

"I'll fix it," I say again.

"Oh, I know you will."

"I cleaned the bathrooms," says an icy voice. I look up, and see Madeleine, carrying a mop and bucket. "They were absolutely revolting."

"Thanks, Moomoo," says Julia. Madeleine rolls her eyes at Julia's nickname for her—she professes to hate it—and pushes past us to the sink, giving Julia's ponytail an affectionate tug. She's so nice underneath that cold-and-controlled exterior, just not to me, not anymore.

Okay, the Madeleine story, in brief: we were friends once. Really good friends. In fact, she and Julia and I were pretty much inseparable for freshman year. We're all very different, but somehow we just . . . clicked, in an opposites-attract kind of way.

Then, suddenly, at the end of freshman year, Madeleine got crazy drunk for the first time ever and, out of nowhere, told me she hated me. I was holding her hair back so she could throw up, and she just said over and over again, "I hate you. I hate you, Pia, I hate you." Then she passed out. The next day, I tried to talk to her, she shut down, and we've been in a cold war ever since. And now her brother is naked in my bed.

Hmm.

Between you and me, I wouldn't have moved in if I'd known Madeleine was going to be here, too. Jules was probably hoping we'd make up, that the five of us will become best friends and start swapping traveling ya-ya pants, or whatever. I can't see that happening. Particularly given that Julia's now busy making her own little cold war with Angie.

An hour later, the whole of Rookhaven is clear of party fallout, not including hangovers.

"Perfect," says Julia, smiling as she looks around the living room.

"C'mon, Ol' Rusty hasn't been perfect since the Eisenhower administration," says Angie.

"Don't call this house Ol' Rusty," snaps Julia. "If you hate it so much, you can always leave."

"Who said anything about hating it?" says Angie.

"I like it just how it is," I say.

"I *love* it. And I love Brooklyn. I'm a lil' Brooklynista." Angie smiles sweetly at us all.

"Can we get some food, please?" I say to distract them from their almost-argument. "I'm starving."

"I'm making French toast!" That'd be Coco. She's been trying to force-feed us comfort food since we moved in. "Everyone in the kitchen!"

"I'll just be a minute," I say.

Time to deal with you-know-who.

"Hey." Mike is groggily stretching in my bed. He looks a lot better clean-shaven and in a pressed shirt. "Where've you been? You wanna snuggle?"

I laugh. "Snuggle?"

"All the cool kids are doing it. C'mon . . ."

I put on my aviators and take a deep breath. "Mike, your sister will kill me if she finds out about last night. Let's just pretend it didn't happen, okay?"

"Okay. Fine." Wow, he's bratty when things don't go his way.

"I'm serious. She doesn't like me as it is."

"She doesn't?"

"No . . ." Suddenly I realize that talking to Mike about his sister being a bitch isn't the smartest move. "Um, you know. I'm probably misinterpreting it."

"Maddy's pretty hard to read," he says. "She never lets her guard down. Even with me, and I'm family. I think it's insecurity."

I fight the urge to roll my eyes. I am so sick of people blaming everything on being insecure. It's not a get-out-of-jail-free card, you know?

"Whatever. We're all in the kitchen. Wait ten minutes and you can leave without being seen."

"Why don't I just climb out the window and shimmy down the drainpipe?"

"That would be perfect! Do you think you could?" I say, just to see his reaction. "Kidding. See ya."

Thank hell that's over with. I have more important things to worry about. Like being unemployed, broke, and cut off from the so-called

Bank of Mom and Dad (pay interest in guilt!) with the threat of being forced to leave New York in exactly eight weeks.

If a kitchen could be grandmotherly, then this one is. It's huge, yet also 1960s-sitcom-rerun cozy. The kind of kitchen in which cakes and cookies and pies are always baking, you know? My mother *never* baked.

As we're sitting around the kitchen table, listening to Lionel Richie and eating Coco's amazing French toast with bacon on the side, I finally tell the girls everything. About the Facebook photo, work, and even my parents.

"In a nutshell, I destroyed Rookhaven, and I'm unemployed, unemployable, and broke," I say, pushing my food around my plate miserably. "I don't know what to do. Who gets fired after one week? I'm such a fuck-up. . . . If I don't get a job, my parents will make me go live with them."

"You can't do that!" Somehow, Angie manages to look cool even talking through a mouthful of bacon. "You'd never survive! Your parents can't make you do anything."

"Yes, they can!" I say. "I've never stood up to them. I just do what they say, and then avoid them."

"Sounds healthy," Julia says.

I shrug. Is anyone's relationship with their parents healthy?

"I can't believe you were fired!" says Coco. "That must have been awful." She reaches over to give me a hug. For the second time today, I have to blink away tears. I swear I want to cry more when people are nice to me than when they're mean.

"Yuh," says Madeleine. "Who would have thought dancing topless at a party would backfire like that?"

"I was wearing a bra!"

"Pia, it was a sheer bra."

"Stop it, Maddy." Julia forks another piece of French toast onto her plate. I notice she hasn't said anything about not wanting me to move out.

"Listen, I have loads of cash, you won't go hungry . . . or thirsty." Angie picks up a piece of crispy bacon with her fingers and dips it in a pool of maple syrup, and then lowers her voice. "And I think the laundry room flooding might have been our, uh, my fault. I'll help pay for it."

"I can loan you money, too," says Julia quickly, her competitive nature kicking in.

"Don't be crazy." I can't accept charity. I won't. "If I need money that badly, I'll go to a bank. Get a loan."

"Are you crazy? Take a loan? You'd have some bananas interest rate, and the loan would just get bigger and bigger and you'd never be able to pay it back! So you'd have no credit rating! It would destroy your life!" Wow, Julia is really upset about the idea of a loan.

"Okay, jeez, I won't go to a bank," I say. "Anyway, that's really not the point. The point is, I need a job. And I just have no idea what I could do."

"What was your major?" asks Coco.

"Art history."

"Art . . . historian?"

Everyone at the table giggles.

"Yes, I chose a very impractical major. No, I don't know why."

"Probably because it sounded cool," says Angie, flashing me her best I'm-so-helpful smile.

I raise an eyebrow at her. "Not helping."

"I could see you working at a fashion magazine," says Coco, hopping off her chair. "Who wants more coffee?"

"Me please!" say Julia and Angie in unison, and frown at each other.

"I'm not a writer," I say. "Anyway, it would be all *Devil Wears Prada*–y. And the models would make me feel shitty."

"Besides, it's really hard to get a job in anything related to fashion," says Angie. For a second, I wonder if she knows that from personal experience. Before I can ask, she picks up her phone to read a text.

"And I need to earn money, *now*," I say. And, I add silently, it's a fact: the cooler the job, the worse the money. My salary at the PR agency— not even that cool compared to working in, like, fashion or TV or whatever—was thirty-five thousand a year, which, if you break it down and take out money for rent and bills, works out to about twenty-five dollars a day. I mean, a decent facial in New York is at least a hundred and fifty. How could anyone ever survive on that salary and still eat, let alone have a life?

Julia is in fix-it mode now. "Let's make a list of your skills and experience. What did you do at the PR agency last week?"

I think back. "I pretended not to spend all my time e-mailing my friends, sat in on meetings about things I didn't know anything about, and watched the clock obsessively. I swear I almost fell asleep, like, twenty times, right at my desk."

Everyone (except Madeleine) laughs at this, though, honestly, it was kind of depressing. Am I really meant to do that for the rest of my life?

"If you need fast cash, get a fast-cash job, girl," says Julia. "Waitressing. Bartending."

I blink at her. "Manual labor?"

Madeleine makes a snorting sound of suppressed laughter. I ignore her. I said it to be funny. Kind of.

"With that kind of princess attitude, you're screwed," says Julia.

"I want a real job. Something that will impress my parents, which means something in an office. Something with an official business e-mail address."

"So e-mail your résumé to PR recruitment agencies in Manhattan," says Julia. "Then wow them with how bright and smart and awesome you are. Any PR agency in Manhattan would be lucky to have you!"

"Okay." I love having a bossy best friend sometimes. It makes decision-making much easier.